Praise for *Who Is*

M000222731

"This was Excellent and a [...]
development of capturing [...]
flawless. [She's] got 'it'".

— Vincent Alexandria, author of *Black Rain*

"*Who Is He To You* vividly exhibits Monique D. Mensah's ability to create and project animated images from cover to cover. The allure of her hypnotic writing style pulsates immensely within the psyche of each reader … thus addicting them eternally."

— Marc Lacy, spoken word artist and author of *Wretched Saints*

"Who is He to You is beautifully written with well shaped characters and an intriguing story line."

— Renee Daniel Flagler, author of *In Her Mind*

"Monique delivers a fast-paced, suspenseful, gutsy debut novel. Love or hate them, each character will evoke an emotion. I look forward to future works from this talented author."

— Lutishia Lovely, author of *Reverend Feelgood*

"I think Monique D. Mensah's book, *Who Is He To You*, is definitely a great read and really gave a different twist on a story about three women and how their lives are intertwined with each other."

— KC Girlfriends Book Club

"An awesome beginning for Monique D. Mensah. When I say this author is talented, you will underestimate just what I think until you actually read this book."

— Tamika Newhouse, author of *The Ultimate NO NO*
African Americans on the Move Book Club

"Monique Mensah has written a novel that is structured and put together the way you'd expect a seasoned and experienced author would do it. But in fact it's her debut novel, and what a novel it is. Wow!"

— Roland S. Jefferson, author of *White Coat Fever*

"The women created by Monique Mensah are raw and real. Mensah does an excellent job of submerging readers into each character's plight, especially Simone, as she conveys the depths of the women's emotions."

— OOSA Book Club

INSIDE
RAIN

INSIDE RAIN

Monique D. Mensah
Poetry by Nakia R. Laushaul

KISA PUBLISHING
SOUTHFIELD, MI

ISBN 13: 978-0-615-37991-3

Published by Kisa Publishing, LLC
Southfield, MI

Printed in the United States of America

First Edition August 2010

Cover Design by: Marlon E. Hines
Interior Layout by: A Reader's Perspective
Editing by: Alliance Editing & Copywriting

ACKNOWLEDGEMENTS

I have a few repeats in here, names you may have seen in the acknowledgements for WHO IS HE TO YOU. That's because these people are staples in my life and deserve thanks on every single project that I bring to fruition. They are unyielding in their love and support for me, and they have made a huge contribution to my success. So expect to see their names in the front pages of every single one of my novels.

As always, God gets the first acknowledgment. Thank you, Lord, for blessing me with the awesome talents of writing and storytelling. I've come to realize that my good fortune and forthcoming success are only because of you. You've placed everything in my life so perfectly, so purposefully, and I am reaping the rewards, living this beautiful life simply because I listened to you and decided to share my God-given talent with the world. Thank you!

My mother, Adaku Mensah. This is round two! And you've been just as supportive as you were for my first novel. I think you've sold more copies of WHO IS HE TO YOU than I have … seriously! You've been my biggest cheerleader from the time I first declared my dream to become an author, and I literally can't ask for anything more from you, although I know you'll keep on giving because you love me that much. You've been there for me from the beginning and I know you'll be there in the end. I love you.

Alana, my baaaaaaby! As you grow older, I see more of myself in you. Mommy is working hard to provide the life for you that you deserve. You are one of the sweetest, most caring people I know, and I am honored to say, "That's my baby!" You've been excited about my literary career since I've started. Thanks for promoting for me, from telling your teachers to visit my website, to helping me pass out flyers and bookmarks. You're beautiful, babe. I love you with all the love I have to give.

To my brother, Ajimu Mensah, thank you for your love, enthusiasm, and support through the journey to sell WHO IS HE TO YOU. Because of you, about half of Blue Cross knows your little sister is an author. You are a talented man, and I look forward to giving you that same support as you realize your dreams. I hope you're ready to do it again, because INSIDE RAIN is about to flood Detroit!

Nakia Laushaul, where do I begin? Hmm ... perhaps I should start with when I first met you at the 2009 Black Writer's Reunion and Conference in Las Vegas. I liked you immediately (and that says a lot). You made a huge impression on me, which is one of the reasons why we are such great friends today. You are a beautiful, talented, and intelligent woman, who has earned my respect and admiration. The poems you wrote for INSIDE RAIN ... HOT! We made the perfect collaboration and I can't thank you enough for blessing the pages of my second novel with your beautiful word art. As if that weren't enough, you gave me invaluable feedback during the writing process, and you kept me on track. Even when I didn't want to hear your feedback, you dealt with my pissy attitude and kept it real with me anyway—a true friend. I'll see you at the top!

Marlon E. Hines, my genius partner in crime, the best graphic designer in Detroit. We did it again! I was afraid that you wouldn't be able to top the WHO IS HE TO YOU cover, but guess what … You did! What did we say about this cover? Something like: crazy, stupid, sick. Yeah, that was it. You understand me artistically and you're not afraid to tell me when I'm wrong (I love that). You understand that a book cover is a work of art, when so many others just don't get it. Because of you, the covers of WHO IS HE TO YOU and INSIDE RAIN are eye-catching showstoppers—true representations of my work. Thank you!

Nikki Montgomery of Alliance Editing & Copywriting, you are amazing! You wowed me with the awesome editing job you did on this project. Just when I thought INSIDE RAIN couldn't get any better, you stepped in and made it a masterpiece. You went deep … way deep. You understood my vision and my characters, and you did an incredible job. Get ready for my upcoming projects, because I'm not letting you go!

Tia Ross, the founder of the Black Writer's Reunion and Conference. First of all, thank you for creating such a great conference that has resulted in the many invaluable and beneficial connections I've made and have maintained today. I also thank you for helping me to find an editor for this novel. You looked at sample edit after sample edit and gave me your expert advice until I finally settled on the best editor for me. Your recommendations and words of wisdom were appreciated.

To Ella Curry of EDC Creations, thank you for being an advocate for WHO IS HE TO YOU. You went above and beyond my expectations and made my internet presence a fierce one. So many people have heard of me and my book because of you. Your knowledge and diligence is immeasurable. I'll be in touch!

To all the fellow authors out there that gave me at least one word of encouragement or advice, I remember. K.L. Brady, Marc Lacy, Lutishia Lovely, Vincent Alexandria, Victor McGlothin, Tamika Newhouse, Roland S. Jefferson, and Renee Flagler. You may not remember what you said to impact me, but I certainly do and I thank you.

I can't forget the book clubs and literary organizations that gave my first novel great reviews: RAWSISTAZ and Tee C. Royal, APOOO and Leona Romich, K.C. Girlfriends Book Club and TaNisha Webb and Melody Johnson, AAMBC and Tamika Newhouse, OOSA and Toni Doe, Urban Reviews and Radiah Hubbert, and Unika Molden, "The Unique Reviewer." Thank you, ladies, for your honesty and support.

To my fellow Detroit authors: Sylvia Hubbard, Gwen Cannon, Monica Marie Jones, Renita Walker, Ber-Henda Williams, Adra Robins, Tracie Christian, Janaya Black, Push Nevahda, Cheryl Pope, and all others whose names escape my mind at this time, thank you for sharing your talent and showing Detroit that reading is still an enjoyable pastime and writing is a fulfilling art.

To my fans and supporters, you have no idea what you have done for me. At times when I felt as if this was all for nothing, you've shown me otherwise. I only hope that you continue to support me throughout this journey. It's going to be a long ride. Thank you for making my day everyday. Peace!

To Alana,
I'm striving everyday to be everything
you already believe me to be.
Superwoman.
My hard work and dedication
are for you.

Prologue

Twenty Years Ago

A cold chill invaded her bedroom. The windows were closed and the heat was on, but there was still an unjustified frost that nipped at Rain's skin as she lay snuggled in her twin-sized bed under her Sesame Street blanket. Living in Detroit, frigid nights could be expected in the dead of winter, but this was different than any other chill she'd experienced; it was eerie. That's what woke her up. It wasn't the faint sound of screaming in the near distance or the echo of heavy footsteps pounding the linoleum floors. It was the creepy, cold air that bit at her ears, fingers, and toes. Rain rubbed her eyes and lazily threw the covers off her small body. Her tiny feet dangled from the side of the bed as she sat there for a moment, yawning and wondering how long it would be before it was time to eat her usual Crunch

Berries and toast for breakfast. It was dark in her room, and the light from the hallway crept through the crack under the door. She could tell it was still nighttime. She pulled back the curtains and saw the steel moon staring back at her, confirming her initial thought; it was still the middle of the night. Heavy drops of rain drenched the window pane, running down the glass in jagged rivulets. It made the moon look like it was melting or crying. Rain allowed its blurred image to hypnotize her for a few moments, but then she heard it again: thundering footsteps followed by a shrill scream. This time she knew—it was her mother.

Rain jumped out of bed and rushed out to the hallway. The light made her squint as her eyes adjusted. She started running down the hall, but quickly slowed her pace to a measured, careful walk. At five years old, she had the senses of a grown woman. She knew her mother was in danger and that she herself might be as well. Still, her curiosity compelled her forward to find out what was going on. As she got closer to her mother's bedroom, the noise became louder and clearer. She heard her mother again, but this time she wasn't screaming. She was talking desperately. Begging.

"It wasn't me, baby. It was Rock. He forced me. He got the money. We can go get it, me and you. We can get it right now. Please, just let me get it and this whole thing will be all over."

Rain heard a smack, then a crash. The brash voice of a man bounced off the thin walls of the small bungalow. "You think I'm stupid don't you? I told you last Friday if you ain't have my money, I was comin' for you. Gimme my money now!" *Smack!*

To Rain, he sounded like a monster. Like Skeletor, his voice was deep and groggy and sent a cold shiver down her spine. Suddenly, she started to cry. Warm tears staggered down her face, but she managed to remain silent as she kept a slow and steady pace toward her mother's bedroom.

She heard her mother again. "Rock! Rock got it!"

"Rock dead. You ain't heard?" The man's cruel laughter made Rain flinch. "Yup, got himself shot in the head and set on fire."

"Oh my God! Please! Let me explain. We can straighten this out. I promise. Just let me put some things together fo' you. I got you!"

Rain finally reached the door to the master bedroom. It was open just a crack, not wide enough for them to see her, but she could see them—the whole scene. A tall, dark man stood over her mother, as tall as the tallest building Rain had ever seen. Her mother was on her knees begging for her life while he yanked her auburn-dyed hair. He was dressed in all black—black leather jacket, black shirt, and boots. Rain had seen him before. He had been near the house occasionally, but she didn't know his name. This was the first time she'd ever seen him actually *in* the house. Usually when he came around, her mother would call GiGi to tell her to come get Rain because she had to take care of some business. GiGi would get mad at her and fuss about how she was too absent from her child's life, but Rain didn't mind it at all. She loved going over her GiGi's house. It was always so much fun. Most of the time she didn't want to go back home; sometimes she didn't for a couple of days. When her mother came back to get her, Rain would ask where she had been. She would always get the same answer, "Working. Mommy had to take care of some things, baby."

But now, that man was standing in their house, in her mother's room, and he was hurting her. She was crying. Rain had never seen her mother cry before. It made her own tears come down even faster.

"You know what's 'bout to happen next, don't you? You know what happens when people fuck with my money," he growled.

Rain's mother shook her head. "Please. We got history. You know me. You know I'm good for it."

"Shut up!" He pulled a big, black gun from the back of his pants and pointed it at her forehead, right between her eyes. Rain hadn't been on this earth more than five years and a couple of months, but she had seen plenty of guns. Her mother had lots of friends who were "strapped," as they boasted. When they came over, they would pull the deadly weapons out of their pants and place them on the coffee table before plopping down on the abused couch in the living room. Her mother would always tell her to go to her room and shut the door until she was called. Most of the time, Rain followed orders, popping in a Sesame Street tape and gluing her eyes to the TV, but sometimes she didn't listen. Sometimes, she would pretend that she was going to her room, but she wouldn't really go. She would hide on the other side of the wall, so her mother and her friends couldn't see, and she'd watch them and listen to what they were saying. She learned enough to know that guns killed people and this man was about to kill her mother. She couldn't let him do it. She had to do something to stop him—to protect her. The only problem was, she didn't know what to do. Her mind went blank, and panic took control.

Pushing the door open and running into the room, Rain quickly surveyed her surroundings. The room was a mess. Clothes and shoes were strewn all over the floor. Broken glass from the dresser mirror was scattered throughout the dingy carpet and covered the unkempt bed. The dresser drawers were pulled out and the TV lay broken on the floor.

"Mommy!" she screamed. Both Rain's mother and her

tormentor jolted their heads in her direction. He dropped the gun to his side as Rain ran to her mother and wrapped her short arms tightly around her mother's neck. She had to protect her.

"Rain, baby, please go back to your room, sweetie. Everything is going to be alright. We're just playing a game right now, okay?"

Rain may have been young, but she was no fool. This was no game. It was frighteningly real. "No, Mommy. I'm not leaving you. He needs to leave you alone!" She pointed a short, stubby finger at the man.

"Baby, listen. Nothing bad is going to happen. Go to your room and count to a hundred, and I'll come in there and check on you. Everything will be fine."

"Yeah, Rain. Listen to yo' mama. Go to your room," the man snarled.

Rain shot the gunman the meanest, nastiest look she could manage with her chubby little face. She looked back at her mother. "Do you promise? You promise you'll come get me after a hundred?"

"Yes, baby. I'll be there."

She looked into her mother's eyes in search of some indication of certainty. Rain couldn't tell whether she was lying or not, but she wanted to believe her. She wanted desperately for her mother's words to be the truth, but something in her gut told her otherwise. Everything was *not* going to be okay. Rain knew that.

Rain's mother sensed her hesitation and further encouraged her. "Go ahead, baby." She begged her daughter with her eyes. "Do this for Mommy. Do this one thing for me. I promise when we wake up in the morning, it will be like none of this ever happened. Just like a bad dream."

Rain could feel her heart breaking with every word her

mother spoke through quivering lips. She didn't want to let her go, but there was nothing else for her to do. She forced herself to believe what her mother was saying. She told herself that her mommy wouldn't promise her that everything would be fine if it really wasn't going to be. She made believe that her mother had never lied to her before and that all the bad things she'd overheard GiGi saying about her mother being a good-for-nothing drug dealer didn't exist. Reluctantly, Rain released her mother's neck and slowly backed away from both of them. Her eyes were fixed on the man's cold stare as she headed backward toward the door. She was afraid of him, but somehow she thought that if she kept eye contact, he couldn't do anything bad to either one of them. She was right. For as long as she was inside the small bedroom, he remained frozen with the gun still in his hand, resting by his side. His breathing was heavy. So was her mother's, and their forceful inhales and exhales punctuated the thick silence in the room. They waited silently for Rain to exit and close the door behind her. She did.

She started to walk back to her room with teardrops pouring onto her feet beneath her. She'd only made it a third of the way down the hall when the sounds of another bump, scream, and crash made her jump. Immediately, the feeling of panic was resurrected inside her. Her heart jumped to her throat and she momentarily stopped breathing. When she heard a second scream, Rain turned quickly on her heels and sprinted back down the hall to her mother's bedroom. He was going to kill her. She knew he was going to kill her mommy.

Rain barged through the door, just as she had done before. This time the man had the gun lodged in her mother's mouth. Rain arrived just in time to see him pull the trigger. Just in time to see her mother's eyes roll backward as blood sprayed the wall behind her and her body dropped heavily, lifelessly, to the floor.

Rain heard herself screaming hysterically and felt herself dropping to her knees. She didn't know what the man was going to do next. She didn't know if he was going to kill her too, or take her with him. All she knew was that her mother was dead and that she couldn't move. She could only scream. Her eyes wouldn't stop staring at her mother's motionless body. She screamed over and over again. She knew that man was going to kill her mommy, and he had done it.

The man walked slowly toward the child. He looked like a robot, a machine with no expression or emotion. Rain's screams stopped abruptly as she held her breath in trepidation. Eyes wide and body shaking, she watched in horror as he knelt down in front of her. He was so close she could smell the sour stench of his cologne, the liquor on his breath, and the smoke in his hair.

"Now, I know that was your momma, Rain, but there's somethin' you need to understand." He paused as if he expected her to respond. When she didn't, he continued. "Your momma was a bad woman. She did very bad things, and sometimes bad people deserve to die." He stopped again and moved his face in closer to hers. "You're not a bad girl are you, Rain?"

She slowly shook her head 'no.'

"I know. That's why nothing bad is going to happen to you, as long as you don't say nothin' about what you just saw. Do you understand?"

He reached out with a large leathery hand and patted her head. She let him, too scared to move.

"As long as you stay quiet, no one is going to hurt you, okay?"

Rain nodded.

"Now when I leave, call your GiGi. You know her number, right?"

She nodded again. GiGi made sure her granddaughter knew her phone number by heart. It was drilled into Rain's memory at the age of four. She knew to call immediately if anything was wrong.

"Good. You wait 'til I leave, and you call her." He stood up and took a moment to look back at the crime he had committed. His eyes lingered for a few seconds longer than necessary before he finally turned around and walked toward the front door.

When Rain heard the front door open and close again, she jumped up and ran to the kitchen, snatching the phone from the wall and dialing her GiGi's number. When GiGi answered, Rain's mouth couldn't form any words. Her mind was flooded with confusion and horror. All she could do was hold the phone and cry an ear-piercing soprano. GiGi showed up at the house ten minutes later.

He had told her not to say a word. He had told her that if she was a good girl and didn't say anything, nothing bad would happen to her. Rain didn't want anything bad to happen to her. She didn't want to end up like her mother, murdered mercilessly after begging for her life. Rain was a good girl; she wouldn't say a word.

GiGi took Rain home to live with her, but Rain could never really feel safe. Keeping her promise to her mother's murderer, she remained silent. Rain went mute. Two years passed before anyone heard her speak another word. It wasn't until Carmen and Danny came to live with them that she finally regained her voice.

1

THE RAPTURE OF RAIN

I'm afraid to speak. I think the voices can hear me.
His lips drip with immoral anticipation.
His tongue is loose like thunder,
Parting cum drenched convective clouds,
He searches for tasty rainbows lost in a kaleidoscope of
white noise.

I am caught in the rapture.
I will the rain to be the source of life.

I'm afraid to sleep. I might not wake up this time.
Her fiery outbursts rattle society.
She stands divided by crazy people and conversations
with invisible voices
Her sorrow borrows a suffocating heartbeat.

I am caught in the rapture.
I will the rain to be the source of life.

I'm afraid of becoming her. I hate him.
Her quick temperament steals sexy minutes—fast.
She opens her walls for a longing that flips her hard onto
her back.
Her man's nasty fantasy to touch three crowds me in my
dreams.
She is lost in erratic escapades concealed from infinity by
addictive smoke.

I am caught in the rapture.
Rain is the primary source of life.
I won't let them overtake me.

* * *

THE room erupted in applause as I slowly descended the stage, taking the three small steps with graceful strides. My linen skirt gently brushed each step as I made my way down. My gold and ebony bangles click-clacked with the sway of my arms by my sides. I was gliding like a ballerina, with my head held high and my back arched; I felt like a star. I *was* a star. The deep sound of the bongos playing behind me intoxicated me, intermingling with the soft roar of the crowd's applause and praises. There were a few true poetry heads, the veterans that stuck to the tradition of snapping their fingers to show their appreciation for the art. It was all love; I'd take it however I could get it. The hazy lights and the smoke from the incense and candles cast their spell on me. I almost felt like I was floating high above the black and brown bodies packed into the small, smoky lounge. They were so enthralled by my words that they stayed glued to their seats, begging for more of my sweet words.

"Speak on, sister."

"Let's get another one."

"She da truth."

"Yeah, I know that's right."

My fans. Their words of encouragement were like rallying cries. They made me feel so powerful. Like Mother Nature, I controlled the climate of their temperament. I could make them feel love, hope, lust, then despair in just

16 stanzas. I was a queen. I looked back at the stage behind me, contemplating whether I'd give them another taste, but I decided against it. I would leave them thirsting for more, anxiously anticipating my return later that week. I loved them, and they felt the same; there was nothing but love in that room. As I walked my walk, slow and deliberate, careful to catch the praise of each and every one of my people, I saw my man in the distance. I moved through the crowd in the small room, making my way toward him. My eyes never left his. Even when I reached his table in the far right corner of the bar, our eyes were locked.

Malik, the owner of the Lyrical Lounge, introduced the next poet. His voice blared through the speakers as he spoke into the mic. "Thank you, sister Rain, for your soulful words. As always, she'll be back on Thursday to give us more of what we love. Next, we have coming to the stage, Flo!"

Some new dude, Flo, began rambling his lines, but I wasn't paying attention. I had other things on my mind. My man sat in front of me, his expression serious, his back straight. The light perspiration that covered his face made his dark chocolate skin glow. Damn, he was fine. The way he looked at me had my panties soaked within seconds. The things I wanted to do to that man! I leaned in to embrace him and release just a piece of what I had been holding in while we were apart, but I was pulled out of my fantasy as we were rudely interrupted.

"Rain, baby, you did so *good* up there! Every time I see you up on that stage, it takes all my strength not to sit here and cry like a baby. You speak with such passion, like you actually feelin' every word."

My immediate reaction, to catch a serious attitude, subsided as I realized it was my GiGi, expressing pride and adoration for her favorite granddaughter. I smiled as

I quickly averted my affection from my man to GiGi, the other love of my life.

"Aw, GiGi, you made it." Every time I spoke to my grandmother, I turned right back into the little girl she'd dedicated her life to raising. I loved my GiGi, the only mother I'd ever really known. I rushed into her waiting arms and momentarily lost myself inside her warmth.

"Of course I came. I couldn't miss my baby. Look at you, girl." She took me by the shoulders and pulled back to take a good look at me. "You are out here doing your thang. Lookin' like a beautiful African princess!"

"Aw, GiGi, stop it. You embarrassing me in front of Kyle."

"Girl, forget that boy. He know I'm proud of you. What you do to yo' hair?"

I self-consciously raked my fingers through my wild, bushy mane. The curls and frizz tangled around my fingers as I unsuccessfully tried to smooth it down.

"What? You don't like it?" I asked nervously. I wanted my grandmother's approval on all things.

"No, sweetie I love it! Don't she look just beautiful, Kyle?"

"Um hmm, she sure does. Just like an afro-centric angel."

He smiled at me and I melted. "You really think so, Kyle?" My voice grew deeper and I made certain that every word I spoke exuded pure seduction. I'd never seen a black man as dark as Kyle turn red with embarrassment, but he did as he lowered his head and smirked to himself. He didn't say anything, but I knew his answer.

"Chile, I'm gone have to come up here to see you mo' often. I didn't know you was that good. I have to show my support while you up there doing yo' thang." GiGi beamed proudly.

"Well, you make sure you make it up here every Tuesday and Thursday. Those are my nights to shine." I looked around the crowded room, squinting my eyes to focus. "Did anybody come with you?"

GiGi's round face flushed with concern and despair. I knew what she was going to say. "No, baby, nobody came with me." She knew who I was talking about and hated to disappoint me with the bad news.

"I wish they would come to see me once. Just once, they could try to support something I do."

Both GiGi and Kyle looked at each other and shook their heads, but they remained silent. It pissed me off that those two self-centered jerks couldn't find the time to come see their little sister on stage. No matter what I had going on, they had no time for Rain. Sometimes I felt like we weren't even related at all. Carmen was probably out ho-ing around with some good-for-nothing guy, and I knew Danny was all up in Maya's face. That girl couldn't breathe or take a step without Danny on her heels. I hated that my siblings and I weren't close like I thought we should be, like I wanted us to be. I always felt so isolated when I was around those two, like I was the outcast, the quiet one. Carmen would always yell at me to toughen up and get some balls. She'd command me to speak my mind and stop letting people step all over me. Carmen didn't realize that she was the main one treating me like a doormat, wiping her feet on her little sister's face every chance she got.

The only time I felt fearless and extroverted was when I was on that stage giving the crowd my gift of gab, gracing them with words of love and seduction, pain and heartache. I was free when I was up there, a different person altogether. I don't know how it happened, but one day I was up there and I became Queen Bitch, the kind of woman my siblings would admire. But the commanding persona never transferred into real life. I could never be as outspoken and boisterous as Carmen or as confident and charming as Danny. Carmen had little respect for me because of it. Danny would try to come to my defense when Carmen picked on me, but only when it wasn't an inconvenience for him. One day, though, one day, I'd put them in their places and just give them a piece of my mind. Aw, man, who was I foolin'? I've been saying the same thing to myself since I was seven years old. Nothing was going to change, no time soon anyway.

GiGi stood and put her hand on my shoulder. "Rain, you know how I feel about you talking about those two. Just leave it alone, baby. Let it go."

"How am I gonna let it go, GiGi? We livin' in the same house. I've got to see them every day. It's like I'm trapped."

Once again, she fell silent. Just then, the crowd roared as Flo exited the stage. He must have been something fierce, but I didn't hear one word. I'd have to check him out on Thursday if he came back. Kyle must have seen the clear irritation on my face and took that as a cue to end the night.

"It's time to go, Rain." He stood, grabbing my jacket from the back of his chair and swinging it over my shoulders. I quickly shrugged it off as the three of us made our way to the door. I wanted him to get a good view of the goodies, make sure his eyes were on the prize. I took a quick look behind me and smiled as I confirmed he was indeed fixated on my backside.

When we got outside, I was a little shocked by the chill of the cool spring night. The wind nipped at my navel and made me shiver as I tried unsuccessfully to pull down the half top that I wore. The little thing barely covered anything past my breasts.

GiGi laughed. "Girl, I don't know where you thought you was, but this here is Detroit. We ain't in Florida. You betta put that jacket on and stop trying to be cute."

I pouted before giving in and following her orders. Kyle handed me the jacket and I quickly slipped it on, anxious to prevent the chill from attacking my naked stomach any further. GiGi leaned over and gave me a big motherly hug before she got in her car and pulled off. Kyle and I walked to his car alone in silence. It was a comfortable silence though. That's how we were: completely comfortable with each other—a perfect match.

I hopped into the passenger seat and let him take the wheel. We had been in the car for about five minutes, about half way home, when I reached over and gently placed my hand on his inner thigh. I inched my hand up a little higher and gave him a soft squeeze to let him know where my mind was. Almost immediately, he grabbed my hand; then he gently, but sternly, placed it back in my lap.

"Lorain, we've talked about this several times."

"'Lorain?' Why you tryin' to get all serious on me? Calling me by my full name."

"We don't have that type of relationship, *Rain*. We never will."

"You trippin', baby. When are you gonna come around?"

He was beginning to piss me off. I wasn't going to be able to take much more of his rejection. Obviously, the good girl role was not paying off. So I did something I'd never done before. I did what I thought my sister, Carmen, would do. What I'd heard her talking about on so many late nights, bragging about the erotica that was her daily life. Maybe that was what he wanted.

"You are my *man*," I said with a certainty and aggression I didn't know I had. I reached back into his lap and grabbed his manhood. The car swerved sharply into the next lane. "You know you like this. You want me, don't you? I see it when you look at me."

"Rain, please! You're going to cause an accident. Now, calm down and get control of yourself."

I kept my hand in place. I knew what he wanted, and after I started to massage his package, his erection showed me just how bad he wanted it. "Ooh, I feel *that*." I squirmed in my seat. He was making me hot! He grabbed my hand again, this time with a lot more force than before, and threw my arm back over to my seat.

"I'm not going to tell you again to stop! I am *not* your man. I never *was* your man and I never *will* be. Now get yourself together and let's try to make it home in peace." His tone was laced with aggravation.

Kyle's harsh words hit me hard. I felt humiliated, rejected, and embarrassed of my own irrational behavior. Acting the way I did, I must have had one too many Long Islands at the lounge. I never acted that way, with such aggression. I had made myself look like a fool. I *knew* I was drunk when I started to cry. With my arms folded across my chest, I still tried to reason with him in between sobs.

"Well, if you don't love me then why did you come see me perform? Why do you come every night I perform? Huh?"

I heard his voice soften. "You know I can't let you come out here alone. It can be dangerous for a young woman out here by herself, especially you. I have to look out for you. You know that."

"You wouldn't do that if you didn't care."

"Rain, of course I care. That's why I do what I do. It's my job to care for you and look out for you."

Well at least he admitted that. He *did* care about me.

Maybe all wasn't lost after all. I would just have to try some different tactics to get him to see things my way.

"I care about you too. You know that, right?"

He sighed before answering me. "Yes, I know." Kyle pulled the car into the driveway of our house. At 11 o'clock at night, it was pitch black. The streetlights must have been out, and it made the whole street look like a scene right out of a horror movie. The trees that lined the sidewalk looked gloomy and sad, and the wind blew the freshly cut grass in circles on the pavement. We stayed in a good neighborhood, Sherwood Forest. GiGi would have it no other way. But this exclusive neighborhood was starting to look more and more like the inner city as the years passed—especially at night. I didn't spend much time outside, not alone anyway. What happened out here on these streets had nothing to do with me.

Kyle came around to the passenger side and opened my door. He was such a gentleman. That was one of the many reasons I loved him. We walked side-by-side up the steps to the porch. He said good night, then waited for me to grab the mail out of the mailbox and walk inside safely before he retreated to the adjoining door on the right. We stayed in a two-family flat. Carmen, Danny, and I lived on the top floor, and Kyle on the bottom floor. He looked out for us and was there whenever we needed anything. He was the perfect man—*my* man. All he needed was a little more time to get comfortable, and we'd be well on our way to happily ever after.

I walked slowly up the stairs to my flat and threw my bag and journal on the couch. The house was quiet, so I assumed that Carmen and Danny weren't home. I was grateful for that. I didn't need their loud mouths disrupting my peaceful mood. I had a minute to calm down since my little episode with Kyle in the car, and the liquor in my system was bringing me to a somber state that I welcomed wholeheartedly. I plopped down on the couch and sifted through the mail. When I came across a small manila envelope sealed tightly with clear tape, I stopped. It was so light and flexible, I partially doubted there was anything inside. It was addressed to me; Lorain Moran, and there was no return addressee. With gnawing suspension and curiosity, I tore open the top of the envelope carefully, as if it might attack me at any moment. Leaning forward slowly, I peeked inside the envelope with one eye open in order to prepare myself for the unknown. I saw that it was a photograph. For some unknown reason, I held my breath while I slid the picture out of the envelope. The coal-black eyes that stared back at me from the faded and tattered photo made me gasp and almost choke on the gulp of air I had suspended in my chest. They were my eyes—deep, black, abysmal eyes. They held me hostage for several moments, but I managed to break free. This wasn't the time. Not tonight. It had been a good day. I had killed it at the lounge and made some headway with Kyle. I couldn't allow those eyes to ruin my night. Damn her! I quickly stuffed the picture back inside the envelope and forcefully slammed it on the coffee table along with the other unopened bills and junk mail. As I stormed toward the bedroom, a single tear escaped my eye against my will. I would confront my demons some other time, right after I gave GiGi a piece of my mind. But right then, all I wanted to do was fall into a deep, coma-like sleep, and that's exactly what I did. I was out within minutes.

2 *Carmen* / *Friday, April 5th*

"WHAT do you have on right now?" I readjust myself in the oversized love seat, hanging my legs over the arm and laying my head back leisurely.

"Boxers and a wife beater."

"What color boxers?" I ask in my well-practiced voice of seduction.

"Umm … they're blue."

"Navy blue? Powder blue? Or midnight?" I roll my eyes. *Come on work with me.*

"I guess they're navy? Yeah, navy blue with white stripes."

"Mmm, sounds sexy. Do me a favor and take that wife beater off," I purr.

"Hold on." There's a muffled sound of shuffling on the

other end of the line. "Okay, it's off."

"Good, now it sounds like you're ready to have some fun with me. You wanna know what I have on?"

"Yeah, tell me what you have on."

I shift in my seat and switch the phone from my left ear to the right. "Well, nothing much, just this little white towel that I wrapped around my body after taking a hot bubble bath. I'm naked underneath. My body is dripping wet. The towel is a tiny bit too small though. My ass is showing in the back."

I hear heavy breathing on the other end of the line. It makes me roll my eyes again. "Close your eyes."

"Okay."

"Are they closed?"

"Yeah."

"Can you see me? Can you see me standing in front of you with water dripping down my legs? My hair is wet, long and curly, hanging down my back. Can you see it?"

"Oh yeah, I can see you. You look so damn good. I want to touch you. Can I touch you?"

"No, not yet. I don't want to rush. First, lie back on the bed."

"Okay."

"I'm walking toward you slowly. Now, I'm stopping right in front of you, standing in between your legs."

"Uh huh!"

"Oops, I dropped my towel!"

"Oh my God."

"That's okay, we won't be needing that. I'm bending down now, getting on my knees. Ooh, I see you're ready for me. You're standing straight up at attention."

"You like that, don't you?"

"Ooh baby, I love it. Do you feel my hand moving up

and down your shaft?"

"Oh, yeah."

"How does it feel, baby."

He moans, "Oh, shit." He moans again, "It feels good. Damn!"

"I know you like that. Now watch me as I wrap my lips around the head."

"Ooh."

"I'm taking you inside my mouth, inch by inch. I'm sliding down with my tongue."

"Carmen?"

I damn near drop the phone when I whip around in my seat to see my annoying-ass little sister staring at me like a fucking idiot. She looks so stupid, eyes bugged out with her hands on her hips. Who in the hell does she think she is?

I apologize to my client, "I'm sorry, hold on one second for me."

He's obviously confused. "Wait, what is going on here? I'm still paying for this time."

"I know; I'll make it real quick. Please just hold on for one moment." I place my hand over the mouthpiece of the phone and get up from the armchair to meet Rain eye-to-eye. "What the fuck is your problem?"

She steps back a little. As always, she's backing down. Rain is weak, always falling apart and needing to be fixed. All that mouth and no follow through—pathetic. Still, she finds an ounce of nerve to say something else to me. "I know you're doing your job and all, but do you think you can tone it down just a little?"

"Tone it down?" I snap. I step closer to her, getting in her face. Our noses are almost touching; it's a clear challenge. She takes a few more steps back and lets her hands drop from her hips.

"Yeah, I mean, don't nobody want to see you with your titties all out. You sitting here rubbing your nipples like you in a strip club or something."

"Hello? Hello!" My client is getting impatient. I can hear his voice blaring through the receiver. Who can blame him?

I quickly put the phone back up to my ear to try to calm him down. "Hey, baby. I'm sorry. I'll be back in just a couple minutes."

"This shit is making my dick soft."

I shoot my sister an evil look before responding to him. "Oh, don't let that happen. Keep stroking it for me. I'll be right back, I promise." He grunts in frustration. I genuinely feel bad. This is *so* unprofessional. I place my hand back over the mouthpiece and turn my attention back to Rain. "Look, somebody in this house has to pay the bills, and if pulling up my shirt and rubbing my titties gets me in the right mood to do my damn job, then *that's* what I'm gonna do. If you have a problem with it, don't look!"

Rain stares down at my bare chest. My shirt is pulled up to my neck. She struggles to pull her eyes back up to meet mine. I have to admit, my 34 double D's are a hell of a distraction to any woman, straight or gay.

"Don't act like that, Carmen. You know I chip in too. I have a steady gig now at the Lyrical Lounge."

"Ha!" That makes me laugh. Is this bitch serious? "You call running your mouth in that hole-in-the-wall juke joint for a couple of measly dollars a job? Please! I'm the only one up in here pulling in any real bread. Danny's lazy ass ain't doing shit but making excuses about being laid off and brown nosing that chick, and you ain't no better."

She bites down on her lip, looking like she's about to cry. I think I may have hurt her feelings. It serves her right, coming over here distracting me in the line of duty. These are unfit working conditions. I should take a strike right at her damn head, but I don't get a chance to. I guess she can't think of anything to say, because she just turns around and quickly walks away like she can't stand to look at me anymore. Good! Her goody-goody ass is making me sick to my stomach. I plop back down in the chair and reposition myself comfortably so I can get back into the mood.

"Hey, baby." I hear silence on the other end. "Hello?"

Did this nigga hang up on me?

The click and the dial tone give me my answer. That bitch! I feel like getting up and slapping Rain in her face for making me lose my client. He's a regular. Now I'll have to regain his trust. After this episode, I wouldn't be surprised if he switched over and starting calling some white beach girl or something and I never hear from him again.

I don't feel like working now. My mood has completely changed. I'm irritated and need to get me some to relieve the tension. After logging out of my phone system, I search my mental Rolodex for the perfect man to call to get me off. Rob is back in town and he's been blowing up my phone for the last three days. I'm not up to seeing his ass though. He's the type of guy I have to be in the right state of mind to see. He's all into that kinky shit, you know: whips and chains, paddles and handcuffs. I don't have enough energy to deal with him at the moment. Maybe after I watch *Mad Max of the Thunderdome* or some shit like that, but not now. Jared could be a quick fix. That man knows how to work it! But, then again, he has too many issues: baby mammas popping up and banging on the windows at four in the morning and ex-girlfriends chasing us at 120 miles an hour down the Lodge Freeway. I don't feel like dealing with the drama. I need something quick and simple.

Dave! Dave is perfect. No words, no questions, no

drama, no strings. He's the man. He comes equipped with a turbo motored tongue and a fat dick to match. I haven't hit him up in a minute. I know he'll be happy to hear from me and even happier to see me. I pick up the phone and dial his number. I know it by heart just like everybody else's. I'm good with numbers like that for some reason. Maybe I should've been an accountant instead of a phone sex operator. Oh well, too late for regrets. I do what I do, and I do it damn well. He answers the phone on the first ring.

"What up?"

"Hey, what's up, baby? Whatchu up to?"

"Shit. Who is this? Crazy-ass Carmen?"

"Crazy? What you mean crazy?"

"Come on, girl, you flipped out on me the last time I saw you. You still acting like you don't remember?"

"Acting? I don't know what the hell you talking about. You know you had me high as hell. You can't blame me if I blacked out for a minute. Shit, you was fucked up too." I can't help but laugh, remembering how his hyper ass was damn near bouncing off the walls.

"Yeah we was fucked up, but you was on some other shit. You was freakin' the fuck out!"

"Whatever, that's all in the past. I'm talking about the here and now. You not gonna let a little episode like that get in between us, are you?"

"I don't know. You crazy as hell."

"Come *on*, I'm horny. You gonna turn down some good pussy over that *old* shit? I know you remember the things I can do to you, the things nobody else can do. You *do* remember don't you?"

That seems to change his tone. I can tell I'm finally getting through to him. "Yeah, I remember."

"Good, so come get me then."

"You at home?"

"That's what you see on the caller ID, ain't it?"

"I'm on my way."

I smile as I hang up the phone. Men are so easy, so weak. The power of the pussy gets them every time. I rush into the bathroom to check out my hair. Using my fingers, I smooth the long, straight strands so they fall neatly over my shoulders. My hair is beautiful. That's one of the many things that keep these men chasing after me. It flows down my back, just beyond my bra strap, thick and black. It looks like satin from a distance. It's naturally curly, but I've spent two hours running the flat iron through it to make it straight, unlike that unsightly frizzed up, kinky mess Rain has sitting on top of her head. I'd kill myself before I would walk out of the house looking like a black Chia Pet. I smooth a thin layer of moisturizer over my caramel skin. It gives my face a healthy glow, and after a heavy application of eyeliner and mascara, my black eyes pop and sparkle. I'll never admit it aloud, but I've never really been pretty. People always talk about Rain like she's the most beautiful thing they've ever seen, but that doesn't matter. I can pull more niggas than Rain can on her *best* day. You see, it's not all about beauty; I have sex appeal. That's what's important.

I adjust my halter-top so my breasts are nearly spilling out. I turn around to take a quick peek at my ass. It looks good in my mini-skirt, which covers little more than my cheeks. Rain ain't got shit on me. So what if my mama loved her more than she loved me? These men love me every night, and I reap all the benefits. I pucker my lips at my reflection as a final stamp of approval. I'm looking good!

"Carmen, have you seen my black pick? I can't find it anywhere." Rain sneaks up behind me.

"Pick? You swear up and down you can get that curly-ass white girl hair into an afro. Looks more like a bird's nest to me," I scold my little sister's reflection in the mirror.

"Just tell me if you've seen it," Rain responds with exasperation.

"No! Danny probably got it. Using it to rake through them raggedy-ass braids."

"Where *is* Danny?"

I finally turn around to face her. "Do I look like I carry that fool around in my pocket? I told you, I don't know where the damn pick is. Get outta my face. I'm trying to get ready."

"Okay, Carmen, dang. You don't have to be so mean all the time."

I ignore her. I don't have time for the nonsense. I have a date.

"Try to remember to unplug the flat iron. You left it plugged up the other day and I almost burned myself."

I shoot her reflection a nasty look through the mirror.

She must get the hint, because she walks away. By the time I finish applying a fresh coat of lip-gloss and slipping on my shoes, I hear Dave's car horn outside. I grab my purse and trot out the door. When I get outside, Kyle's goofy looking ass is sitting on the porch reading a book—in the dark. *Weirdo.*

"Where are you off to in such a hurry, Carmen?"

This dude has some nerve getting all up in my business. "Who are you? Detroit Police? None of your damn business." I'm not about to stand here and entertain any more of his interrogation. I start to walk down the steps to my waiting ride. Kyle reaches out and grabs my arm.

"Whoa, Carmen. I don't think you should be going anywhere with any strange guys."

Is this dude serious? I'm a grown-ass woman.

I snatch my arm away from him and keep walking. "You musta lost yo' damn mind. Do I look like Rain? Stay in your lane and keep your hands off me."

His eyes harden as he locks me in a stare. "Where *is* Rain? I'd like to talk to *her.*"

This makes me stop in mid-step. I am sick and tired of this dude asking me about my sister like I'm her damn babysitter. I don't look out for anybody but Carmen. Is that not clear? "Shouldn't you know that? Isn't it your job to know where the hell she is?"

"Carmen—"

"She's in the house. Damn! You are the most annoying nigga on the planet!"

When I see Kyle reach out to grab me again, I break out into a full sprint and I don't stop until I reach Dave's old school Monte Carlo. I bang rapidly on the window for him to unlock the door and let me in.

"Carmen! Carmen, wait a minute!" I can't believe it. This dude is actually running after me!

I jump in the passenger seat of the car and tell Dave to punch it. He screeches off just as Kyle reaches the curb. I don't know what in the world is wrong with that loony bastard, but I am *not* staying to find out. I have some business to take care of in a serious way. Dave turns up the radio volume, and deafening bass sends pulsating vibrations through my chest. I lie back on the headrest and rock my head rhythmically to the beat of the song. He drives us away from the neat oak-lined streets of my neighborhood and drives to his 'hood farther east in Detroit. Ten minutes later, we're parked in a vacant, grassy lot next to an abandoned building.

Dave points to the back seat. "Let's go," he demands.

I hit him with a look of indignation and slight tinge of,

"nigga, you must be crazy as hell."

"Umm, ain't you forgettin' something?" I ask. "This ain't no free ride. You gotta pay to play, homie."

Dave replies with a dismissive chuckle, "Don't worry, baby, I gotchu." He reaches inside his pocket and retrieves a small plastic baggie. He teasingly dangles it in front of me like a bone in front of a dog. I snatch at it angrily, trying to swipe it from his grasp, but I miss. I can feel the frustration quickly turning into rage as I snap my fingers and then open my palm to let him know that I'm not playing and he'd better stop fooling around.

"Aiight, aiight. Damn, you a fiend!" He laughs while he empties the contents of the plastic baggie into my open palm.

I ignore his last remark while I examine my prize. "What the 'S' stand for?" I ask, running my finger over the engraving of the small pill.

"Where the hell you been? That's that Superman shit!"

"Superman?"

"Yeah, my man Jay-Jay got that shit that take you high in the sky like Superman."

"Huh, looks more like Skittles to me. Got me on a sugar high, tasting the rainbow and shit." We both laugh at my corny joke. I pop the Ecstasy pill in my mouth and use my tongue to flip it to the back of my throat. Dave hands me the can of beer sitting in the cup holder. I take a swig and wash the pill down with a gulp.

Soon enough, I'll be in another place, rolling. As always, the high will creep up on me with little warning, leaving me with no choice but to submit to the indescribable euphoric feeling that overcomes my body. Rain asked me once what it felt like to be high, and I had no words for her. There's simply no way to make someone understand. It's never like the first time. No, I know I'll probably never get that feeling back. But dammit, I'll spend the rest of my life trying to get it. Lucky for me, I'm sexy, and I'm not a drug addict. That means that most of the time I can get my high for little to no cost, just enough to have a good time.

I give Dave a sly look out the side of my eyes. "Let's go, Daddy." I slide down my jeans and climb into the back seat of the car. Life is nothing but one big-ass party—and I can dance all night.

3 *Danny* / *Monday, April 8th*

"OUCH! Shit, you trying to kill me or something?" I jerk my head forward.

"Sorry, baby. You so damn tender-headed, everything hurts you."

"Oh, so now it's *my* fault?" I say with a raised brow and rising anger.

"No, I'm not saying that."

"So what exactly *are* you saying?"

"Nothing, okay? I'll try to be gentler. Just relax."

I hate getting my hair braided. It always feels like this girl is trying to kill me. Sometimes I think about just cutting it off. Forget all the hassle and the headache, just wear a short cut so I don't have to worry about this mess. But every time I think I might want to cut it, Maya hooks me up and has me looking right! I've never met anybody who can throw down like my baby. Every time I look in the mirror when she gets done, I want to kiss myself, I look so damn good. Beyond an occasional trim, I've never cut my hair. It's long as hell, way past my shoulders. The bitches love it, always want to run their fingers through it. They ask me all kinds of stupid questions like, "You got Indian in yo' family?" I just smile and tell them 'yes', even though I have no idea. Maybe I do have Indian blood. When you have a father that you've never met, you don't get to know things like that. I *do* know one thing though, my father must have been one pretty nigga, because I am one of the finest creatures I've ever laid eyes on, and I'm not just saying that because it's me. I mean, I wouldn't think I was all that if these hoes wasn't out here sweating me so hard. Maya be getting all jealous when she sees how the women flock to me. Sometimes they do it right in front of her, like she's not even there, flirting and trying to pass me their numbers on the sly. That's when my girl really flips out. Then I have to let her know the deal. I don't want anything to do with any of these damn 'hood rats. All I want is my baby. It's not my fault the ladies love Danny. Can you blame me if I have high self-esteem? Some call me conceited; I say I'm confident. Whatever you want to call it, I'm fine as hell and if you don't agree with me, you can kiss my ass.

"Ouch!" This time, I scream. I turn around to face her. "I thought I told yo' ass to be careful!"

"I'm sorry, Danny. I'm trying. You got all this curly hair. It gets tangled around my fingers sometimes."

I can hear it in her voice; she's getting agitated. I have to put that in check real quick, before she gets out of hand. "I know you not getting a damn attitude are you?"

She takes a deep breath. "No, baby. I'm not getting an

attitude. I'm trying the best I can not to hurt you, but you're making me nervous."

"I'm making *you* nervous? You the one trying to snatch my hair out! Kill all the whining and the dramatics, okay? You sound like a fucking baby. Just like Rain. I get enough of that bullshit at home."

"Danny, I really don't want to argue, okay?"

"Suck yo' bottom lip in, get some balls, and man up." I shake my head, sighing deeply. "I'm sick of this shit." I look back at Maya when I don't hear a response right away, and I see her looking at the ceiling, I guess to summon some common sense from the Man above.

She finally looks back down at me. "I just wanna do your hair in peace."

"Then stop trying to pull my damn hair out." I turn back around and reposition myself comfortably between her legs.

I hear her suck her teeth and sigh before she reaches out to grab the last braid she was working on. I stop her before she can lay a finger on my head. Without turning around, I grab her wrist and squeeze. "You hurt me again and that's yo' ass. Do you understand?"

Maya struggles to break free from my hold, but she's unsuccessful. "You're hurting me!" she screeches.

I twist her wrist a little. "Do you understand?" I repeat.

Her voice starts to shake as she tries to hold back her tears. "Yes, I understand."

I let go of Maya's wrist. "Good. Now do it right this time, and check your attitude." Her only response is a sniffle as she quickly brushes a tear that's threatening to fall down her face. She knows I hate crybabies, and she doesn't want to piss me off anymore than I already am. Nothing irritates me more than a crying-ass woman—all the dramatics, the tears, the sobbing, and the quivering lips. Reminds me of my little sister, Rain—weak and pathetic. Suck it up! Take your punishment like a grown-ass woman, and if you don't want to be punished, don't fuck up. It's as simple as that.

Maya goes back to work on my head. I guess she gets the point this time because I don't have to check her again. That's the good thing about my baby. She knows how to listen and take direction. That's an important quality to have if you're going to be my woman, and Maya fits the role perfectly.

I jump a little as my cell phone vibrates against my leg. I grab it and flip it open. "Hello?"

"Hello? Danny?"

"What's up, GiGi. You need something?"

"Yes, actually. I want to speak to Carmen. Is she there? Can you get her?"

"I'm not at home. I'm over Maya's house getting my braids done. Did you call the house?"

"Yes, no one answered. That's why I'm calling you on the cell. I really need to talk to her."

"Well, like I said, GiGi, she ain't here with me. What's wrong?"

"Do you know where she went Friday night? Did she tell you who she was with?"

"You know Carmen don't tell me her business. No telling who she was with, all those guys she be messing with. Who knows?"

"Kyle told me he saw her jumping in the car with some strange man. You don't know anything about that?"

"Nope."

"Okay, if you see her or talk to her, tell her to give me a call."

"Will do."

"Thanks, and tell Maya I said hi."

"Aiight, GiGi. Bye."

"Bye, baby."

I hang up the phone. GiGi sounded upset. I don't like it when something is bothering her. I'll have to find out what my sister was into and get to the bottom of the situation. Carmen is always doing something that has GiGi worried. She's real fucked up. No self-respect, out here sleeping with every guy with a functioning dick—just nasty. But you can't tell that girl nothin'. She's as hard-headed as a cement block. It's *her* life; she can do whatever she wants to do with it. As long as she don't bring those shady-ass dudes back to the crib, I couldn't care less. Between Rain's helpless bullshit and Carmen's slutty, drugged out ass, I've had all I can take of the female drama.

I stuff the phone back into my pocket and shift my position on the floor. Maya is taking too long on my hair. My ass is starting to hurt, and I'm getting restless.

"GiGi said hello. Are you almost done?" I snap.

"A little bit more than half way."

"What? It's been an hour! What the hell have you been doing back there?"

"I've been braiding your damn hair! You have a lot of hair, you know. It's not going to be done in a couple of minutes." There she is, getting smart again. This girl must have lost her mind. "All you do is complain. I'm doing you a favor. I usually get fifty dollars for doing this, but I'm doing yours for free."

"What did you just say to me?" I jump up from the floor and look down at Maya sitting in the chair. If looks could kill, I'm sure she would drop dead right now. She looks up at me with pure fear in her eyes. She doesn't say anything, just sits there looking stupid. "Have you lost your mind?

You must have drunk a cup of courage or something. Stand your courageous ass up."

She doesn't move. She puts her head down and I see a teardrop land on the panel of the hardwood floor. "I'm sorry," she whispers.

"Oh, now you sorry. A minute ago you was Wonder Woman, but now you *sorry*?"

"Look, Danny, I didn't mean what I said. I don't know what I was thinking. I don't want any trouble."

"Stand up!" Visibly shaking, Maya finally does as she's told. She keeps her eyes glued to the floor. "Look at me." She does. The trepidation that masks her pretty little face gives me a rush, a sense of power that fuels my anger. I draw my right hand back and backhand her hard across the face. The hit is so powerful that she falls back down into the chair, whimpering like a sick puppy. I hate it when she makes me do that. I don't like hitting her. I really don't, but shit, I have no choice! You let your woman get away with the little stuff now, and before you know it, she'll be running all over your ass. I don't even know what's gotten into her. I know I've trained her better than that. She knows better than to disrespect me. Looking down at my baby sobbing and shaking in that chair, with her hands covering her face, I feel bad. I'm sorry, but I can't show any sign of weakness. It's her damn fault anyway. I wouldn't put my hands on her if she knew how to act. She brought this all on herself and always makes me look like the villain. The bitch knows exactly what she's doing.

I can feel the heat rising back through my body and the blood rushing through my veins as I reach down and grab a healthy handful of Maya's shoulder length hair. I wrap the strands around my hand and use them as a handle to pull her up out of that chair and onto her feet. The force I use makes her yelp. This time it's more like a wounded dog. I yank her head back.

Suddenly, guilt overwhelms me once again. "You see what you made me do?" Maya doesn't say anything. She bites down hard on her bottom lip. I can see the pain etched across her face from the grip I have on her hair. "You always make me do shit like this! I tell you all the damn time to watch your fucking mouth. But no, you want me to put my foot up yo' ass so somebody can feel sorry for you and I can look like the bad guy. When are you gonna learn?"

"I'm sorry," she whispers again. I believe her. I know she didn't mean it. It'll take some practice and maybe a couple of ass beatings, but she'll come around and we can possibly live happily ever after. I let go of her hair and allow her to lift her head back up to look me in the face. Her big, brown eyes make my heart melt.

I reach out to touch her beautiful mahogany face and gently wipe the tears from her cheeks. "You know I hate it when you cry."

"I know." She attempts to give me a weak smile. I appreciate the effort. I love my baby. She knows that. Everybody in this city knows that. We're meant to be together, and moments like this prove it. I pull her in close by her waist and caress her face. She's a petite woman. Standing at about five feet tall, she only comes up to my chest. She always has to stand on her tiptoes to give me a kiss; it's so cute. That always makes me smile. Maya does just that, tilting her head back and puckering her sexy lips to meet mine. I kiss her with the passion and enthusiasm of the first time our lips met. Our tongues curl around one another as I grab her ass and she melts in my arms. She grabs the crotch of my pants with eager aggression and I smack her hand away. I hate when she acts like a slut—like

Carmen. She looks at me apologetically and I forgive her instantly. She knows better. I kiss her again. We can stay like this for hours; that is, if my head wasn't a half mess. I love my baby and I get horny just like every other nigga, but I'm not gonna be left out here to look like a damn fool. Maya is gonna finish braiding my hair.

I pull back from our kiss and flash my baby a smile. "Now you know what you need to do, right?"

She licks her lips and nods. She knows just as well as I do that I need to look good at all times. I sit back down on the floor and she goes back to work on her masterpiece. Life is good. Shit, I'm like 'Pac, all I need in this life of sin is me and my girlfriend. I'll always be alright.

4 *Rain* / *Sunday, April 11th*

I awoke to the loud chime of the doorbell. I lay in the comfort of my bed for a few seconds before willing myself to move. The bell rang twice more, but I was in no rush to answer it when I saw 7:00 a.m. flashing on the clock on my nightstand. I told myself that whoever it was on the other side of the door deserved to wait. I was usually pretty attentive. I hated to be rude and offensive, but none of that applied before twelve noon, especially on the weekend. If you had the audacity to bother me this early in the morning, you deserved to get your feelings hurt. That's just how it was. I let the doorbell ring once more before I stretched my arms and legs out in a spread eagle and slowly crawled out of the bed. The cold of the hardwood floor on the bottom of my feet shocked me and sent my body into a quick shiver. After searching under the bed for my house shoes and grabbing my robe from the back of the door, I finally managed to creep toward the front door. The doorbell chimed again as if the uninvited guest knew I was taking my sweet time on purpose. I silently cursed Carmen and Danny for being too damn lazy to get the door. Then again, they probably weren't even home. Danny might have stayed the night with Maya, and who in the hell knows what Carmen had gotten into the night before; certainly nothing I cared enough to think about for more than a few seconds. The ringing stopped and the knocking began. Whoever this was had some nerve!

"I'm *coming*!" I yelled across the room toward the door. I doubt if they heard me, but I wasn't too concerned with that. They would get an earful as soon as the door swung open. When the second round of knocks came, it suddenly dawned on me who it was.

Oh my goodness! She is going to kill me!

I broke out into a fast jog, slid down the stairs to the lower level of the flat, and flung the front door open. My GiGi was standing on the porch looking just as irritated as she could be. I knew I was in trouble.

"Oh my God, GiGi, I am so sorry. I completely forgot!"

"Don't use the Lord's name in vain, and let me in this house before I freeze my butt off." I could tell she was pissed. Her lips were spread thin, and she was speaking through her teeth like she did when she was about to spank my tail for acting up back in the day.

"Sorry, GiGi." I opened the door and stepped back to let her in. She was dressed to kill, looking like she could've been on the cover of *Church Lady* magazine. She wore a cream suit, a tan silk blouse with the matching shoes and purse, and an elaborate hat that was sure to block the view of anyone within a hundred feet behind her. GiGi stepped inside the house.

"My Lord, Rain. You're not even dressed!" Funny how she was the only person on the planet allowed to use the Lord's name in vain. Of course, I didn't say anything about that at the moment.

"I know, I know. It slipped my mind. I'm so sorry. I'll run upstairs right now and get ready."

"We're going to miss the eight o'clock service, so you might as well take your time. We'll just go at eleven."

It took me thirty minutes to shower and get dressed. Wearing my hair natural shaved off about an hour of preparation time, and I was thankful for that. I stood in the mirror and stared at my reflection. For the most part, I was pleased with what I saw. I wore the burgundy suit GiGi bought me for my birthday a couple of months ago. Because we were going to church, I decided to pull my wild mane back into a ponytail. No makeup. I never got into that too much. That was Carmen's thing. Besides, who was at church that I needed to get all made up for? GiGi was always talking about meeting a good God-fearing man in church one day. I keep telling her that I don't need to find no man up in there. Kyle was all the man that I needed. I don't know if he was God-fearing, but he was a good man. He was better than any man I'd ever met. GiGi just had to come to her senses and accept that Kyle and I were going to be together despite her disapproval. I love my GiGi to death, but she worries too much. She's always preaching about love and relationships. I know she means well, but who knows better about what I need than me? She may have been right in the past, but I was younger then. I'm a different person now, and I know exactly what I want. He was tall, chocolate, and fine as all hell. Best of all, he was right downstairs. It doesn't get any better than that.

I reached down on the dresser to get my gold earrings and spotted the manila envelope with that picture inside. The immense feelings of anger and frustration immediately surged inside me as that image permeated my thoughts. I know she means well, but GiGi was taking this a bit too far. Nothing is going to change the past—nothing.

With narrowed eyes and pouted lips, I snatched my earrings up from the dresser and put them on. I had reached the bedroom door before I realized I'd left the envelope on the dresser. With a huff, I quickly turned on my heel to retrieve it before storming out the door.

As soon as I stepped into the hall, the intoxicating smell of smoked hickory bacon and buttermilk pancakes danced under my nose. GiGi knows she can throw down in the kitchen. Growing up, I never went a Sunday without a big ole' down home country breakfast. I giggled a little to myself as I thought about the time I woke up before she did and tried to surprise her with breakfast in bed. My GiGi took a couple of spoonfuls of her soupy pancakes and crunched on that shriveled up, burnt piece of sausage, all with a smile on her face. But I needed to focus on today. I had almost let the fond memory of that Sunday morning distract me from my anger. Not this time though. I had something to get off my chest.

As I approached the small kitchen, I saw GiGi standing over the stove, her back to me, flipping the bacon with a fork. I stomped my way in and slammed the picture down on the table. When GiGi didn't so much as flinch at the sound of my stormy entrance, I cleared my throat with exaggeration in a second attempt to get her attention.

With her back still turned to me she said, "I see you got my package."

With my arms crossed against my chest, I answered, "Yes, GiGi, I got it. Just what exactly do you think you're trying to do?"

GiGi looked back at me over her shoulder. "Rain, baby, it's time for you to wake up. The only way you are going to free yourself is to face the past. Face what happened."

"GiGi, I told you a million times I don't know what happened. I don't remember! Nothing is going to change that, not this picture, not some shrink, not talking about it. Nothing. Drop it!"

"You don't remember because you don't want to, Rain. Can't you see what you're doing? You've built up these defense mechanisms to shield you from the truth. You can't go on forever like this. It's not healthy."

"Go on like what, GiGi? There is nothing wrong with me. God, I am sick and tired of you trying to convince me that I'm crazy! Maybe it's a good thing that I don't remember. Who in the hell wants something like that etched into their memory? Why are you trying to take me there? Why do you want me to relive something so horrible? What are you trying to do to me?" My voice had changed quickly from a demanding declaration to a pleading whine.

GiGi finally turned to face me after taking the bacon and pancakes off the stove and placing them on a platter topped with paper towel. She must have heard the childlike quiver in my voice, so she softened her tone. "Rain, I'm not trying to do nothing but help you. Haven't I always been there for you? Haven't I always steered you in the right direction? This time is no different. I know it's hard, but you have to face the past. It's the only way you're going to get better. You hide behind Carmen and Danny as a way to mask the pain that I know you're hiding deep down inside. You have to let it go. You have to stop depending on Carmen and

Danny. It's time, Rain."

"I'm hiding behind Carmen and Danny? GiGi, I don't have any idea what you're talking about. Carmen can't stand me, and Danny is too self-absorbed to give me a second thought. Please, just let it be."

She took slow steps toward me and kept her eyes locked on mine. I felt as if she was trying to see right through me, right into my head. I dropped my head and looked at the floor before she had the chance to invade my thoughts.

GiGi placed a loving hand on my shoulder. "Baby, you have to let it go."

She reached down and picked up the envelope containing the picture she'd stuffed into my mailbox. I turned to face the kitchen entryway as she slid the photograph out of the envelope. She held the picture up to my face. Had I turned my head, those black eyes would have peered right into my own.

"Look at her, Rain. Look at your mother. She's real. She existed, Rain. I know you can remember her. I know you can remember what happened to her. It's in there somewhere. Just let it out so you can be free."

I bit my bottom lip to prevent myself from crying out in frustration. Nothing she could do would change anything. I didn't remember my mother or her murder, and I didn't want to. I whispered, "There's nothing there, GiGi."

The defeated look in my GiGi's eyes quickly hardened and was replaced with sharp slits of annoyance as Carmen made her presence painfully clear by loudly smacking her lips. I hadn't even heard her come in.

"What the hell is going on? Y'all look like somebody done died up in here." Carmen bounced into the kitchen like a cheap streetwalker.

GiGi turned her attention back to the breakfast she'd

prepared. "Carmen, now is not a good time. I'm talking to Rain about something important."

"Yeah, leave it up to my precious grandmother to make me feel unwelcome in my own home. Thanks, GiGi."

"Carmen, stop being so disrespectful." I hated when she talked to GiGi that way. You'd think we were raised in two different households.

"Shut up, Rain. I wasn't talking to you anyway. And I'm the one who should feel offended and disrespected. I live here too!"

GiGi interjected before the argument could escalate any further. "Carmen, I need to talk to Rain. Can I talk to her uninterrupted, please?" She spoke slowly in a low tone that let me know her patience was running out. I remained silent, watching and wishing Carmen would just disappear.

Carmen threw her hands in the air in exasperation. "Damn, GiGi, it's like that? I can't even get no bacon and eggs? No hash browns?"

"You know what, Carmen? You always got your hand out, expectin' somebody to give you a free ride. It don't work like that, chile."

"Oh God, GiGi, what you talking 'bout now? As a matter of fact, what are you *ever* talking about?"

"I know you on that *stuff*, little girl. Don't *think* I don't know."

"All I want is some bacon. Goddamn, Can I get some bacon?"

"Don't use God's—"

"Yeah, yeah, blah, blah, God—vain—don't do it. Yep, got it. Now, bacon *please.*"

GiGi slammed a skinny piece of bacon wrapped in a napkin down on the table. "You going to church today?"

"Oh, here *you* go. 'Are you going to church today?'"

Carmen mocked. "Damn, you know how to clear a room! I can't stand either one of y'all!" Carmen quickly whipped around and headed toward her bedroom.

"Carmen! Where are you going? Don't you turn your back on me. Come back here. I know you're gonna go get into something you have no business doing."

Carmen's only response was the sharp thuds on the floor as she continued to make her way toward the back hall.

"Carmen. *Carmen*!"

5 *Carmen* / *Sunday, April 11th*

I swear if that woman says another damn word to me about church, I can't be held responsible for what I'll do. She talks about church like it's some miracle cure. Let me be the first to tell you, if you don't know, church don't help nobody. If I want to be surrounded by a bunch of hypocritical, judgmental, brainwashed fools, maybe I'll sit through a couple of services—maybe. But when they get to all that hollering, dancing and flipping down the aisles, I'll have to get my yellow ass up outta there! I might be crazy, but those fools are on another level. Yeah, you won't catch me in *nobody's* church. The sooner GiGi accepts that fact, the happier we'll all be.

"Carmen!"

I trot toward my bedroom. I can still hear GiGi from the front of the house, yelling faintly for me to come back. That woman will never stop. Rain is always talking about her like she's a fucking saint. I guess I would think so too, if I were clearly the favorite grandchild. Too bad for me, I'm on the opposite end of that spectrum. It's bad enough that our mother chose to give me and Danny away, but had a change of heart when it came to Rain. Now I have to deal with GiGi's obvious favoritism toward her youngest grandchild. You'd think I'd be used to the mistreatment by now, but it still pisses me off from time to time. Oh well, I ain't gonna cry about it.

At the thought of Rain, I pause in the back hallway between her bedroom door and mine. My initial thought is to shut myself in my room and blast the music from the stereo to drown out Rain and GiGi until they leave, but I have a sudden change of plans. Instead, I go into Rain's room and lock the door behind me. Once inside, I quickly scan my surroundings. She's such a damn slob. Ugh! Clothes are everywhere, the bed is unmade, and a bunch of notepads and pens are scattered about on the floor. She has empty glasses sitting on the windowsill beside a sorry looking plant that's just about to keel over and die. I cringe when I step on a pair of dirty panties as I make my way to the dresser on the opposite side of the room. Standing in front of the dresser, I catch sight of myself. I almost gag at my image. I don't remember what in the hell happened last night, but it must have been wild as hell because my hair is a mess. I can't let anybody see me like this. I reach behind me to try to smooth the puffball of a ponytail, but it's no use. I give up without giving it a decent effort. Besides, I don't have time to fool with my hair right now. That nagging old woman has me fiending for a pill something fierce. I have to hurry up.

I yank off the jacket I'm wearing and snatch the canvas bag hanging from the corner of the dresser, quickly rummaging through it. Rain's bag is just as junky as her nasty-ass room. I feel some papers in between my fingers. I pull them out and throw them on the floor because they're in my way. Finally, after fumbling over some pens, a wallet, a pack of gum, and some loose change, I feel the wrinkled and weathered texture of a few dollar bills. As soon as I pull the money out and began counting, I hear banging at the door.

"Carmen?" GiGi asks as if she's unsure that it's me in the room.

I don't answer. After quickly stuffing the money into my pocket, I charge toward the door. I startle my grandmother when I yank the door back. I see her jump a little just as I rush past her. I feel her try to grab me, but I'm too quick for her. There's no stopping me when I need to get that fix. I have to get out of here. The combination of Rain's stupidity and GiGi's worrying is suffocating me fast.

"Carmen, where are you going?" GiGi demands.

She gets no response from me. I keep a steady pace toward the front door. I peek in the kitchen on my way out and see that Rain is no longer sitting there. I don't know where she went—don't care. As long as she's out of my way, I'm happy. I'm almost to the door when something suddenly occurs to me. I stop at the coat closet, open the door, and rummage through the hats and gloves before I find a red shoebox hidden in the corner shadows. I look behind me to see if GiGi is trying to sneak up on me, but I see that she's sitting on the couch in the living room with her back to me. She probably realizes she's never going to be able to control me. I do what I want to do and go wherever I want to go. She'll just have to deal with it. I rip off the top of the box and grab Danny's 9mm pistol that lies inside. I'm planning on leaving the safety of Sherwood Forest and venturing off into another 'hood. The streets are crazy nowadays, and I need some protection. I know Danny will probably be pissed at me for taking it, but I have to do what I have to do. The day some young nigga tries to rob me will be the day he dies. The thought of killing someone makes me smirk unexpectedly.

After placing the gun securely under my shirt at the small of my back, I close the lid on the shoebox and shove it back in the closet, careful to set it as close to its original placement as I can remember. I make a mental note to have the gun back before Danny notices.

As I swing the front door open, I hear my GiGi call after me from the couch again. "Carmen?"

I decide to answer this time. I'm leaving anyway. It's not like anything she can say will stop me. "Yeah, GiGi."

"I love you. Please come back here safely."

Her endearing words put a momentary pause in my steps. I *do* love my GiGi. I *do*. I just can't live up to her impossible standards. I'm nothing like Rain, and I won't pretend to be—ever. "I will, GiGi," I promise as I walk out of the flat, closing the door behind me.

I breathe in the spring air with an audible inhale. It feels good to be outside and feel the fresh air on my skin. I'll feel even better once I finally get a pill. I hop down the steps of the porch and make my way down the sidewalk, moving briskly as if I'm being chased. I travel two blocks down, then turn to make my way onto the adjacent street. I hate walking. Ever since Danny's cocky ass got the car taken from us for acting stupid, I've been reduced to footing it. Most of the time I don' t care, 'cause I usually have no problem getting to where I need to go, but on days like this, it's a serious inconvenience. Damn, I don't remember the walk being this long before. My breathing is getting heavy, warning me that I need to slow down, but I'm not dropping my speed. When I finally cross Livernois, I turn down one of the side streets. Pit bulls and Rottweilers, chained to trees in the backyards of the homes I pass, bark at me as I walk by. Charisse's two daughters and some of their friends wave to me as they dance on the front lawn. Bad-ass Rodney and his thugged out crew shout out obscenities and x-rated remarks from the porch about my ass and titties as they bounce along under my clothes. I hold up my middle finger to one of the boys when I hear him call me a bitch. They laugh at my gesture.

"Crazy bitch," I hear one of them say.

I'm tempted to pull the pistol out from the small of my back to show how crazy I really am, but I don't have time to waste on kids. They'll get what they have coming to them one day. It may not be me, but somebody will get in their asses. I'm not no damn crazy! That's Rain. That chick is loony tunes. I swear she scares me sometimes. Anyway, that's enough brain power wasted on that pain in the ass. I wipe her image out of my mind as I continue my journey.

When Rain, Danny, and I first moved to Sherwood Forest, the neatly arranged houses, manicured lawns, and huge English style tudor homes had me mesmerized. It was more than a far cry from the dilapidated houses that sat in front of patches of brown grass and trash-ridden streets we'd known in Southwest Detroit. GiGi claims she had to keep us safe under the "circumstances." Hey, it's a free home, so I ain't complaining. I loved it at first, but now as I trudge along the tattered streets of what some consider one of the worst neighborhoods on Detroit's Westside, I feel more at home. What the mayor calls "urban blight," I consider to be the city's unique spark of charisma and charm. Where else can you go and see a bum selling a picture of Baby Jesus and Mary in one hand and a half-eaten chicken dinner in the other, while hookers strut half-naked in the dead of winter?

I round the corner and feel a streak of relief and excitement travel through my body like a sudden chill. As I approach the Candy Shop, the neighborhood's nickname for the trap house on the corner of Stoepel and Chalfonte, I become increasingly anxious and somewhat aroused. I've been waiting on this all day. Granted, it's still only about nine in the morning, but that's all day so far, right? Well, it feels like all day. As I start my way toward the back of the house to the customer's entrance, I'm suddenly halted in mid-step.

"Hold up. Where the fuck you think you goin'?"

I feel a hard, calloused hand gripping the fleshy part of my forearm as a boy who looks no older than sixteen grabs me and pulls me toward him. I snatch my arm violently back from his grasp and stare at him hard in the face. He stands with two other boys on the sidewalk in front of the Candy Shop. They all look about the same age, too young to think they can manhandle me.

I speak to the one that grabbed me. "Who the fuck are you? And why you care where I'm going?"

The boy laughs and shows his remarkably white teeth. He looks at his friends with a smirk. "These fiends getting bolder every day."

"I'm going to the Candy Shop. What's the problem?" My level of annoyance is increasing by the second. I cross my arms over my chest and tap my foot impatiently as I wait on his reply.

"The Candy Shop is under new management, and we don't know yo' ass so you ain't going nowhere," he answers as he brushes an imaginary piece of lint off his red, designer t-shirt.

"What? Where Donte? He know me. I come up in here all the time and chill."

All three of the boys burst into laughter at once. One of the smaller ones says, "Donte dead. This Jay-Jay spot now."

"Jay-Jay? Who is that?"

"Bitch, you don't know Jay? You get high too fucking much. Everybody in this 'hood know who Jay-Jay is. If you don't know, you'll find out soon. Bottom line though, you ain't going in that house until we get the okay from him," Red Shirt says.

Suddenly, my right leg begins to shake involuntarily, and a chill surges through my body. I wrap my arms around myself to try to calm the anxiety that's beginning to come down on me. There is no more time for cute conversation.

"Aiight, aiight. Look, I don't care who running this spot. I need something real quick. Hook me up with a coupla pills. I got ten dollars."

Red Shirt cocks his head to the side and looks at me with a raised eyebrow. "Like I said, we don't know you. How I know you ain't the police or something?"

I know where this is going. I can see he wants to play games. He knows damn well I ain't no cop. The drug is calling to me, and I know it has to be right there in his pocket. Right there! I think about the gun in my pants, but I know better than to try to pull that stunt. There's three against one, and I know all of them are strapped. I don't have a chance. I have no choice but to play along.

"Come on, baby. You know I ain't no police. Look at me." I smooth my hands down my chest, past my waist, and over my hips. "I got the money. Come on."

Red Shirt's shorter, younger friend fixates his eyes on my thighs and taps Red Shirt on his shoulder. "Yeah, she nice," he says in response to the boy's implied gesture about my shapely figure.

"How much you got again?"

"Ten."

"You not the police, you gone hafta prove it," he declares.

I'm about to lose my nerve. I shift my weight unevenly from one foot to the other. "What you want me to do? Come on, tell me what you want. You know what *I* want."

Red Shirt moves closer to me, then he reaches out and runs a bony hand up the inner part of my thigh, stopping just short of my vagina. "You almost good enough to fuck. Almost. I don't do fiends though."

I cringe at the label he imposes on me, but I keep quiet. It sounds like he's close to giving in.

"I'll know you legit if you gimme some head."

The little boys snicker at Red Shirt's proposal, but it doesn't affect me at all. He might as well be telling me that he wants me to shake his hand or give him a hug. I knew it was coming anyway, and I don't have the time or the option to be picky or act uppity. He knows that too.

"Then what? You gonna gimme something? I ain't out here just selling ass. You gotta gimme what I need."

"Shit, I'll give it to you for five if you make me cum. You just can't go in that house until Jay-Jay say you cool."

I make a mental note to find out who this Jay-Jay dude is soon, then my thoughts quickly switch over to the matter at hand. "Aiight, whatever. Let's do it."

Our feet crunch on the rotted grass that covers the vacant lot next to the house as we walk toward the backyard to handle our business away from the prying eyes on the open street. Just as we're about to reach the iron gate that lines the perimeter of the Candy Shop's backyard, a familiar voice stops me in my tracks.

"Carmen!"

I whip my head around to see Danny standing right behind us in a wide-legged stance with his head cocked to the side. "What the hell are you doing here, Danny?" I demand.

"No, the question is what are *you* doing, and who are you about to do it with?"

Red Shirt looks at us like we've morphed into aliens. I try to calm him so Danny won't ruin my chances of getting the pills. "Hold on, baby," I say to Red Shirt. "This ain't nothing."

I turn my attention back to Danny. "Look, I have some business to take care of. Get out of my face," I say in a hushed tone.

"I ain't going nowhere. What are you about to do? Sell ass for some drugs? What the hell is wrong with you?"

"No! Ain't nobody selling no ass. You always tryin' to jump to conclusions. Me and Red Shirt, here, we have an agreement. That's all. Now get out my face!"

Red Shirt takes a few steps back from us. "What the fuck is going on?"

His boys, just a few yards away from us on the sidewalk, look confused as Danny interrupts our transaction. I see one whisper to the other, and they both laugh. Danny is embarrassing me. I'm a grown-ass woman. I don't need anybody walking up on me, checking me about doing grown woman things. This has to end now.

I hold up a finger to Red Shirt to indicate that I just need a moment to get this situation under control. He doesn't gesture or say anything in response; he just continues to stare at us. I'm beginning to think he's a little slow or something.

"Go home, Danny! I have this under control."

"Yeah, I'll go home, but you coming with me. I can't believe you out here like this. This *is not* a good look. Do you know how messed up this is? Do you know how bad this makes me look? My sister is a damn drug addict! What the *hell*! Come on, we're leaving now." Danny grabs my arm and snatches me toward the sidewalk.

Red Shirt interjects, "I don't know what the fuck you trying to do, but this crazy shit ain't gonna get you nothing for free."

"I know, I know. We still gotta deal. Just gimme a minute."

"Hell naw. I don't want no minute. I'm *straight* on you."

I try unsuccessfully to pull my arm away from Danny's grip. "What? Wait a minute! We had a deal. Five dollars, remember?" I wave the wrinkled bills in the air as proof that I'm ready to do business. "This ain't shit to worry about. Lemme handle it, and everything will be cool."

"No she won't be buying anything from you today." Danny snatches the bills out of my hand.

"Which one is it?" Red Shirt says.

Danny answers, "You just heard what I said didn't you? She ain't copping from you today."

I give Danny a look of pure hatred. Tears well up in my eyes as I watch Red Shirt walk back toward the edge of the sidewalk to join his boys, taking my high along with him.

"Jay don't pay me enough for this shit," I hear him mutter under his breath.

Keeping a tight clutch on my arm, Danny ushers me down the sidewalk in the opposite direction of the young dealers. I'm embarrassed and ashamed. What is this world coming to when a grown woman can't purchase her own shit and get high without family coming in and messing it up?

"What you doing over here anyway?" I ask, agitated and depressed over my lost high.

"I was on my way to Maya's when I saw your dumb ass about to do something stupid."

As we walk down the cracked and litter-strewn sidewalk, I look over my shoulder longingly at Red Shirt and his boys, but they don't pay me any attention. They're already busy serving someone else; *that* someone is doing a lot better than I am at the moment. Pretty soon she'll be lifted into the world of euphoria that was so violently snatched from my grasp. Danny, seeing me lagging behind and dragging my feet, reaches an authoritative arm behind my back and pushes me to make me walk ahead. I quickly swat the air behind me, trying to prevent him from detecting the gun that's hidden under my shirt at the small of my back, but I'm too late.

"What's this?" It's technically a question, but the words ring out like a thundering accusation. I try to quicken my pace to put some space between us and attempt to avoid answering the question, but apparently I'm not swift enough. Danny grabs my arm, the same way Red Shirt had done moments earlier, clutching me and bringing us to a halt.

Even though I know I'm close as hell to getting my ass beat for taking the gun, I still play it off like I'm clueless and have no idea why I'm the object of Danny's anger. "What? What's the damn problem now? You always trying to go off about something. Damn!"

"You know what I'm talking about. I *know* you don't have my pistol."

My blank stare and slumped posture must have an effect on Danny, because the next thing I know, this fool has me in a half-nelson, or maybe it's a full-nelson. Shit, I don't know the difference. The point is, I can't move, dammit, and my arm is hurting. Danny bends me over, yanks up my shirt, and snatches the gun away from the small of my back.

"Ow, nigga, you hurting me!" I say a little too loud, hoping that the fear of an appalled witness will make Danny let me go. That, just like all of my other ploys, doesn't work either. My arms remain in a twisted and awkward position.

"You stupid bitch," Danny says after snatching the pistol and tucking it away in a spot I can't see. "You always in some shit. What'd you think you were gonna do with a pistol anyway? You gonna shoot somebody now? Huh? You a thug now? Get the fuck outta here." Danny pushes me.

"But—"

"But nothing! It's bad enough you an addict—"

"I'm not a damn drug addict!"

"Really? I must have missed something, little sister, because the last time I checked, anybody that's prepared to give her last five dollars and some head for a pill is a damn fiend. Oh my bad, I guess giving head would actually make you a drug *whore*! I should tell GiGi. She'll light yo' ass up."

"Ain't nobody scared of GiGi. I'm a grown-ass woman."

"Funny how little girls trying to act all grown up are the only ones that say that juvenile shit."

I finally feel my arms slam down hard at my sides as Danny releases them. I grab my shoulder and begin to massage it to stop the pain that's searing through my muscles. "Look, you making a damn scene!" I squint to focus on the kids across the street that are staring at us.

"Take yo' ass home, Carmen, before I beat yo' ass myself," Danny says with a snarl.

"You ain't gonna do shit. I'm not Maya!"

"You damn right, you ain't Maya. You nothing like my baby. I'd kill that girl if I ever saw her acting like you. You disgust me."

I make a face at him in response. Just then, I notice that I'm still holding the crumpled five-dollar bill in my hand. I look down at it with a glimmer of hope and anticipation in my eyes. I still have a chance to get high.

"Aiight," I say. "I'll go."

Before I can hop, skip, and jump my happy ass back to the spot, Danny reaches over and grabs the money from my hand. "Yeah, I know exactly what yo' ass is thinking. Go home!"

"Aiight, shit," I say with audible disappointment. When Danny is on some righteous shit, there's no talking about it. It is what it is, and I have to suck it up and deal with it. I'm not winning this fight, so I decide to retreat. I turn and start heading in the opposite direction toward home.

I don't look behind me as I trudge along the sidewalk. I don't want to see Danny looking back at me to make sure I'm doing as I was told and heading home.

Damn, I have to get to know this Jay-Jay dude quick, I think to myself. If I had been able to go into the house, none of this dramatic shit would have happened in the first place. Jay-Jay is on my immediate "to do" list. Well, him and however I'm going to get a couple of dollars so I can get high. Everything will work out in my favor. It always does, and today is no different.

6 *Danny* / *Sunday, April 11th*

I march down the street without looking back to see whether Carmen is following orders or not. Knowing her, she'll probably take a detour somewhere between here and home, but I've done the best I can to at least make things harder for her. I look down at the dollar bills crumpled up in my hand and shake my head. That girl is a hot-ass mess. Out of all the things I thought I would ever have to deal with, having a drugged out sister was never on the list. Do you know what it's like to have to hide your stuff in your own house for fear that your little sister will take it and trade it for some dope? Do you know what it feels like to talk to someone you love and the only response you get is a blank stare or maybe a little scratching at an imaginary itch? Sometimes I find myself wondering just what it feels like to be high. I wonder what it is that makes these people act like maniacs just to get away from reality. If I wasn't so afraid that I would either die or turn into an ashy-lipped, wild-haired, yellow-toothed fool, I would try it one time just so I could know what the hell my sister was selling ass for. It has to be something good. It *has* to be. But that's just not me. I'll never have any of that poison running through my veins. My body is a temple, and it will remain sacred. I have the kind of body most dudes would kill for without even working out—all natural, and I intend to keep it that way.

I continue to walk up the street toward the end of the block. Damn, I have to come up on a car quick. I'm too damn fine to be walking around here like a lame. I fucked around and got in an accident a while back and GiGi completely overreacted, talking about it's not safe for me to drive. Really, it wasn't that serious, but the car was in her name, so here I am. She took the car from me and I've been walking ever since. I would just get another one, but I have to get a damn job first. Got laid off from the plant four months ago and Detroit's economy is not forecasting another job any time soon. Talk about hard times! But seriously, not having a car in my life is hindering my game. Good thing I already have my baby locked up. Maya doesn't care about that material shit; all she needs is me. My baby takes care of me, so I want for nothing. But, this whole Maya thing is getting kind of old; it'll be time to get me something new in a minute. Don't get me wrong: I'm not letting my girl go. I just need something on the side here and there to keep me fresh, you know what I mean? Yeah, a nigga like me *stay* fresh. But these chicks out here ain't trying to holla at nobody without a car. I know that for a fact. I have to come up on a ride within the next month or so, or it may be a wrap for getting into some new pussy.

I'm on my way to Maya's house to chill, but I have to stop at the store first to get the bare necessities: a few beers, a Pepsi, and some hot chips. I'm thankful for the few extra dollars I lifted off Carmen; that's less of my own money I'll have to spend. When I push through the glass double doors of the liquor store at the end of the block, the smell of incense and mildew invade my nostrils. This is the closest liquor store in the neighborhood, and I'm all about convenience. The next nearest one is about four blocks down. If I had more options or a car, I'd gladly pass up this hole-in-the-wall piece of shit and head to another one. These Arabs are a trip, following me around the entire store like I'm gonna take something. I've been up here a million times, and I never stole anything. They see a nigga walk up in here and they go on the defensive. Shit, niggas ain't the ones that knocked down the damn World Trade Center or went on crazy-ass suicide missions. So who should be afraid of who? Yeah, I know I sound racist, but that shit is true. Some things just need to be said, and I don't have any problem being the one to say it. I just won't say it to their faces; those fools are psycho! Anyway, I'm tired of getting the stares. On top of that, the beer is always lukewarm and they never have any hot chips! I shake my head, disappointed, as I sift through the bags of chips lined on the rack in front of me. I don't know why I even bother looking when I know they're not going to be there. I guess I'm just a creature of habit or something like that.

Just as I'm about to give up and settle for some barbeque pork rinds, I feel a large, cold hand grip my ass. Whoever this is either wants to get fucked or get fucked up. My back stiffens and I take a deep breath before turning around to face the owner of that hand. My black eyes meet the eyes of some yellow dude with a fresh Mohawk. Without thinking,

I clutch my fists in a tight ball and swing on his gay ass with all the strength and power I can muster. Homeboy is quick, though. He dodges the blow swiftly by sidestepping to the left. I swing again, this time with my left, and the slick mutha fucka ducks. Dammit!

"Hold on a minute, damn! I'm sorry alright? Calm down!" He holds his hands in front of his face to protect himself from my flying fists. I take a few deep breaths, trying to calm the storm raging through my body. I feel my face contort in disgust and anger. I can feel my heart racing inside my chest and my eyes narrowing in a hard brazened glare as I quickly try to dissect the situation. Here I am minding my business, on my way to my girl's house, and some raggedy-ass dude wants to disrespect me on some gay shit? Oh, hell naw! That shit is strictly forbidden in Danny's world. I clench and unclench my fists by my sides before taking another deep breath, finally deciding to address the sick dude standing before me.

Despite the fire raging through my body like a lingering eruption, I give my best attempt to keep my tone calm. Through clenched teeth, I say, "Ay, man, this ain't that kinda party. I don't swing that way, so keep your fucking hands off me."

With my point being made, I push him backward and storm out of the store, forgetting about the chips and the beer. My whole mood is shot. Then, I hear the door open and shut again as the dude follows me out of the store.

"Oh, you don't swing that way? Shit, you just ain't neva had no good dick in yo' life. I can fix that real quick for you," he yells. I turn around to see him grab the slight bulge in his jogging pants. He trots behind me to catch up with my hurried strides. I can feel him getting closer, closing the gap between us.

I take another deep breath, stop, then turn around. "Maybe you don't understand. I just told you I'm not into dudes. Now stay the fuck away from me before something real unfortunate happens." My teeth are clenched and my words are barely comprehensible, but I know he gets my drift. Still he won't back down.

I can tell by the way he smirks, showing his crooked teeth, that he isn't done yet and this is about to be a problem. The dude widens his eyes in mock astonishment when I walk away, rounding the corner and stomping down the residential street of the surrounding neighborhood.

From behind, I hear him whistle loudly. "Ay yo!"

Out of nowhere, four more young guys walk up to him, looking like the poster boys for what *not* to do if you ever want to be anything in life. I hear Mohawk guy greet his boys as I move on down the street.

"What up, Tone," the four of them say one-by-one as they crowd around their friend.

"What up, lil' nigga."

I can see them through my peripheral. Their acknowledgments are accompanied by fist bumps and half-hugs. I turn in a full 360-degree circle, careful to keep all of them in my line of sight. From the looks on their faces, I can decipher that the rest of the guys are quickly catching wind to the trouble in the air. I feel the oxygen leave my lungs as they all begin to slowly circle and close in on me.

"Look man, I don't want any trouble, aiight. I'm not like that. I don't do dudes. Just respect that shit and move on. I don't want things to get ugly."

"Get ugly? There ain't nothing ugly about you, baby. Why would things get ugly?" one of the other guys ask, moving in and reaching for my hand. I quickly snatch my arm up in the air to make it clear that I don't want to be touched.

"Guess what, y'all," Tone says, addressing his boys a little more loudly than necessary for them to hear, "we got us a little situation here."

"What's that?" another one calls out.

"Look, I'm the wrong one to be fuckin' with. I might look pretty, but I guarantee you don't want to test me," I warn them.

Tone releases a menacing chuckle that causes a ripple effect of laughter throughout the group of guys. "This bitch don't like dick, but I think the right dick just ain't come along yet." I size them all up and anticipate my next move. I'm no bitch, but I don't know if I can take all of them.

"What y'all niggas think?" Tone asks. The guys reply with a mixture of laughter and crass remarks to express their sexual expertise. Tone inches a little closer and I get into a defensive stance. "What you like? You like top or bottom?"

His boys giggle like they're witnessing something that they aren't old enough to see. I cringe at each word that he speaks, and I feel involuntary spasms surging through my body.

I grind my teeth in an attempt to censor the explicit words that are just dying to burst through my mouth and attack this homo. It doesn't work. "I will cut yo' balls off and stuff 'em in your mouth if you don't back the fuck up off me."

"Ooh, baby, I like it when you talk dirty," Tone replies with a look of lust and violence in his eyes.

"This bitch wanna be hard," one of his boys said to no one in particular.

"Not as hard as this dick," Tone answers him with his eyes still locked on mine. Before I have time to think of a witty comeback and try to predict his next move, he rushes toward me, grabbing for me, but I don't scare easily. These niggas bleed just like I do, and they're about to find out just how much. In one swift move, I push Tone about three steps backward and retrieve the pistol from the small of my back. I whip it out in front of me and watch in amusement as the pack of affectionate thugs back away in fear. Yeah, that's how you handle these fools. If you don't respect me, you *will* respect the open-ended barrel of my pistol, baby. I feel a sinister smirk creep across my face in a slow and deliberate movement as I wave the gun through the crowd at a steady pace, making sure her pretty mouth has the chance to pucker up at every one of the fools who had the balls to step to me. I finally rest my aim on Tone. He's the one who deserves to feel the heat of a hollow point bullet playing pinball with his internal organs.

A blanket of silence covers us all, and I revel in the feeling of absolute power.

"I told you not to fuck with me. Now you see why. You put yo' hands on the wrong one, *Tone*." I say his name clearly and forcefully.

Tone looks back at his boys in a nervous attempt to gain strength through numbers, but when he turns to face me, his expression shows his disappointment and fear because his boys had all run off to safety and left him to fend for himself. Helpless, he raises his hands into the air to surrender.

Tone speaks slowly, as if to soothe me or coax me into shifting my precise aim from the smooth area between his eyebrows. "Look, shorty, the shit ain't that deep. We was just fuckin' wit you aiight?" His quivering lips and shaking hands almost make me feel sorry for him. Almost.

I take a slow five steps toward him, until the pistol is no more than an inch from his pimply face. No more words are needed. No clever one-liners or rhetorical questions are suitable for this moment. Without speaking, I can tell he knows exactly what I'm saying and what language I'm speaking. Never taking my black eyes off his, I swiftly cock the slide back on the gun to illustrate the seriousness of this situation. He's about to lose his life.

The "che-che" sound the slide makes sharply punctuates the thick silence surrounding my opponent and me. He makes his move. I watch Tone's eyes roll to the back of his head and his body sway lazily before dropping to the ground with a loud thump. Damn, all I did was cock back! I didn't even get a chance to put my finger on the trigger and his weak ass faints. I almost break my grim face to laugh. I wasn't going to actually kill him. I mean, I won't hesitate to put a dude in his place, but murder is a little drastic. That's not to say that I never *would*. That depends on the circumstance and the offense. But little Tone here doesn't deserve to die today.

I step carefully over his crumpled body and stare down at him in disgust like he's a dirty bum begging for change to buy some liquor. In my eyes, he's on that same level—disgusting. In one last act of revenge, I kick him in his back, hard, just to see his body jerk. He lets out a soft moan in response. After securing the gun under my shirt at the small of my back, I bend low to pat down and scavenge his pockets. I find two twenties and a ten dollar bill folded neatly in his left pocket. Smiling at the small fortune, I pocket it and walk casually back to the store. This little episode isn't going to throw me off my game. Plus, my small victory is a cause for celebration. As I re-enter the store, I decide against the beer and opt for a fifth of Hennessy instead. Tone's stash is more than enough to cover the indulgence. I know Maya will appreciate that.

After paying, I walk back outside and through the side

streets and notice that Tone is no longer there. I laugh to myself and shake my head at the image of his pathetic ass lying on the concrete. I pull my cell phone from my pocket and dial Maya's number. She answers on the second ring. She knows not to keep me waiting too long.

"Hey baby," she says in that sexy voice I love to hear on the other end of the line.

"Yeah, what's up? I'm on my way. I had to handle some shit real quick."

"What happened? Are you alright?"

"Yeah, I'm good. You know I'm always good. Just be ready for me when I get there."

"Alright, baby. I'll be waiting."

I hit the "End" button and put the phone back in my pocket, releasing a sly smile. Danny Moran is fine and fearless, and I have pussy on my mind. Nobody, not even these dirty niggas, can keep me from getting to my baby.

7 Rain / Wednesday, April 14th

I flinched as a tree branch clawed at the window in my bedroom. The frigid rain pounded relentlessly against the glass, threatening to break into the room and assault me. I sat straight up in my bed to ensure that the violent thunderstorm stayed just where it belonged, outside in the cold. I thought it was supposed to be spring. Wasn't it spring just last week when GiGi came to see me at the Lyrical Lounge? I'm pretty sure it was, but now it's freezing like late fall. I wondered how the seasons flipped like that. I've never witnessed anything like it. A flash of lightning blazed through the darkness, harshly interrupting my thoughts. Forget about the season, I had to make sure my window was secure so I wouldn't be swept away into the uncertain night.

I tiptoed cautiously toward the window, trying not to disturb or further anger the thunderstorm; that thing sounded like it wanted to take me out. I had to shuffle through some loose clothes spread across the floor, a couple of shoes, and some unidentifiable hard object that made me trip and almost fall to the floor. Once I reached the window, the thunder roared again. I jumped as the sound of the crashing, clapping, and bumping startled me once more. I stood still for a few moments, waiting for my heartbeat to resume its normal pace.

Once I reached the window, I felt stifled by the darkness of the sky. Aside from the occasional streak of lightning, the sky was unusually dark. I know it had to be around three in the morning, but the sky held a different kind of darkness tonight, the kind that might engulf the house, and even the entire neighborhood, into an abyss of a never-ending shadow. I leaned into the window and narrowed my eyes to see if I could make out anything in the sea of black beyond the pouring rain, but there was nothing. Not even an outline or silhouette of anything other than more black. I got so close that my nose was touching the window. The icy glass, warmed by my breath, created a small cloud of condensation that impaired my view.

I leaned back a little, moving my hand in slow, counter-clockwise circles to clear an opening, wiping away the cloud. "What the *hell?*" I gasped in disbelief. As the lightning flashed and the thunder shook the room, I stumbled backward, but this time it was not because of my shock at the threatening storm. Out of the darkness, a feminine hand suddenly appeared and met mine on the opposite side of the window. I steadied myself and held my breath as I stared at its manicured nails and ringed middle finger, so clearly visible through the glass, even without the help of the lightning's illumination. It stayed there, stationary.

I steadied myself and slowly gained enough nerve to move back toward the window and the inexplicable hand, but I regretted my decision as the hand began to pound fiercely on the window. I jumped again, but the pounding continued. It finally dawned on me that someone may be in trouble. In full heroine mode, I raced back to the window and scurried to unlatch the lock that held it closed. As my fingers slipped and fumbled over the lock, the hand continued to pound, now at a more rapid pace.

"Okay, okay, I'm trying. Please, just hold on a minute," I reasoned with the increasingly impatient palm.

I pulled and jiggled the stubborn lock, but it wouldn't budge. That's when the screams began, paralyzing me as I started to second-guess my decision to come to the rescue. I didn't know what was going on, who was out there. What were they doing to this poor woman? Whatever it was, I didn't want it to happen to me too. The woman's hand continued to pound as I stood there, watching in bewilderment and fear. What was I supposed to do? Was this a sick joke? Was someone in trouble? If I tried to help, would I, too, be in danger? My racing thoughts locked my feet in their place. I couldn't move; I couldn't even think straight.

Then, as if this woman could sense my hesitation, her hand gave one last powerful blow to the window. The glass shattered into thousands of pieces, giving way to the unforgiving pressure of the rain. My eyes widened with fear as the hand reached into the broken window, grabbing at me. Somehow my voice found its way to my throat and I screamed as loud as I could, hoping that Carmen or Danny would hear and come to my rescue. I doubted Carmen would, but Danny might have if he was home. It was a nice thought, but no one was bursting into my bedroom to rescue me from this ... this ... what the hell *was* this? What was happening?

I continued to scream as the hand forcefully pulled me out of the window headfirst. I flinched and groaned as the jagged edges of the broken glass sliced into my flesh. When the hand finally let me go, I was lying facing down on the second floor balcony with the cold rain drenching my hair, skin, and clothes. I swiped the water droplets from my face and hopped to my feet, slipping slightly before catching my balance on the rain-slicked wood. I didn't know what was about to go down, but I wanted to be alert and prepared. Terrified, I could feel the fear rush through my body like an electric shock.

I stared straight ahead but couldn't make out a thing in the dark night. The hand was gone, and no woman was there. Confused and frozen with apprehension, I stood panting, trying to make sense of what seemed to be nothing. Just then, a quick flash of lightning sliced through the darkness, revealing the silhouette of a woman I didn't recognize. A light pink nightgown clung to her medium frame, and her shoulder-length hair was plastered against her face and neck. She was covered in rain, just as I was. I squinted, but I was unable to make out the details of her face. She stood still, staring back at me, emotionless, but I didn't move. I'm no fool; I knew this was some crazy shit I didn't want to encourage any more unexpected occurrences. The lightning flashed again and again, illuminating the strange woman; with each flash of lightning, she was a few steps closer to me. I inched backward to keep my distance, but she continued to move closer. When I felt my heels hit the bricks that bordered the balcony, I grabbed at the large pillar behind me and squeezed my eyes shut to brace myself for whatever horror this mysterious woman was bringing. She was just a few inches from me, and I could feel her breath wafting softly across my face. She didn't touch me, didn't say a word, just stood there breathing slowly. I finally gathered the courage to open one eye. I saw a black pupil set in a perfectly symmetrical cocoa-colored face. When I sensed that the woman wasn't going to make a move, I opened the other eye and my breath stopped abruptly. I was staring into the face from the picture GiGi had slipped into my mailbox. It was her—my mother.

Her mouth and chin were just like mine. Her nose was like Carmen's, and her high cheekbones were identical to Danny's. But we all had those same coal-black eyes, an undeniable inherited trait of the woman we barely remembered. I knew that her presence before me was an impossibility, but I didn't feel even a tiny bit of the terror I would have expected, witnessing her apparition for the first time. Despite the unforgiving chill of the rain, I felt a blanket of warmth as she smiled at me.

I smiled back, suddenly realizing I was looking at a stranger. Yes, she was my mother, but she was still a stranger.

"I don't remember you," I said, just louder than a whisper. Sadness overcame me as I watched her smile disappear. I felt guilty for not knowing her, not remembering her smile, her smell, her touch, or the sound of her voice. This was my mother, but I only knew of her what GiGi had told me. She reached out a cautious hand toward the left side of my face, but then she stopped as if something held her back. I watched helplessly as her beautiful face twisted in pain.

"What's wrong?" I asked in a panic, not sure of what to do to relieve her.

A powerful bolt of lightning struck her violently and surged through her body. She jerked backward and stretched out her arms like a crucifix, letting out an agonizing shriek.

I watched in horror as dark red blood poured from her eyes and mouth. I tried to say something, to run to her, but my feet wouldn't move, and for some unexplained reason I had lost my voice. I swallowed between short breaths, trying to gather enough saliva to moisten my dry mouth. She moaned and gagged, twisting her body into awkward positions. I looked down at my hands and saw that they were covered in blood; so were my feet, legs, and arms. I didn't feel any pain, but remembering my fall from the window, I patted my torso, my head, and then my thighs, searching for the source of the bleeding. I found nothing. I looked up and shook my head in disbelief when I saw that the pouring rain had turned to cold, dark red blood. In front of me, my mother continued to screech and moan. I wanted to cry for her, to go to her, but my body defied my will. I still couldn't move. I opened my mouth to scream, but nothing came out. I was mute, just like when I was five years old. I stood helpless as my mother coughed and gurgled, spitting out blood, while the blood-rain poured down steadily. Then she collapsed, her body dropping into a heap on the balcony, and the bloody rain suddenly stopped. I wanted to go to her, but I knew I couldn't. I still felt the weight of resistance holding my legs in place.

That's when I heard a deep, throaty laughter piercing the darkness. It started off as a low chuckle, then graduated into full-blown wails, sinister and punishing. I turned to survey my surroundings, but I saw no one. Whoever he was, he was laughing because he got pleasure out of watching my mother lose her life—again.

I tried once more to move my feet and go to my mother; I was shocked that it worked this time. Whatever was holding me in place had released me. I ran to the other side of the balcony to tend to her, but I found only her bloody pink nightgown lying in a heap. The horrible, haunting laughter continued. I ran to the edge of the balcony to see the shadow of a man walking away from the house and disappearing into the darkness.

"Hey! Stop!" I yelled, suddenly regaining my voice. "What did you do to her? What did you do to my mother?" The man responded with more malevolent laughter. I screamed and screamed until the laughter stopped and the bloody nightgown on the balcony vanished like the two apparitions.

"Rain? Rain?"

The darkness slid away, as the light from the overpowering sun pushed it aside. I was standing in my bedroom, peering out the window. The drooping, leafless trees of the rainy night had transformed into proud cherry blossoms and plump green leaves. The tarnished, weather-beaten grass morphed into manicured green, lush lawns.

"Rain!"

A flock of birds soared in a perfectly symmetrical "V" formation. The cold night was gone, replaced by the beauty of an early April morning. I stood there wondering what the hell had just happened. Just minutes before, I had been in the middle of a nightmare, but I knew I wasn't going to figure this out easily. The shattered glass from the broken window had miraculously disappeared, and my open bedroom window was still intact. I looked down, checking my legs for the jagged lacerations from the glass, but found no evidence of the trauma.

"Rain! Can you hear me?"

I pulled my eyes and thoughts away from the mystery that had just transpired before me and turned my attention to the voice that was frantically screaming my name from below. Wide- eyed with my mouth agape, I saw Kyle staring at me from the front lawn, waving his arms like he was trying to flag down a plane on a deserted island.

"I'm coming up!" he yelled.

I frowned as I realized my headscarf was still wrapped around my head. Despite the urgency of the situation, I still wanted to look my best for my man at all times. Before I could tell him to give me a minute to freshen up, I heard the front door open and shut with a swoosh and a bang. GiGi had given Kyle a key to the upstairs flat in case one of us needed him in an emergency. My GiGi could be overprotective at times. I mean we *were* grown. Sometimes she treated us like we were toddlers living up here on our own. But I was happy Kyle had a key, even though he never used it the way I wanted him to.

Kyle burst through my bedroom door like he was leading a S.W.A.T operation. "Are you okay? You need to sit down."

I turned to face him hastily, still breathing heavily from the shock of what I'd just observed.

"Oh, Kyle, baby, I'm so happy you're here." I rushed toward him, placing my hand daintily on his broad chest.

"Rain, sit." He guided me back to the bed, holding me by my arms. He sat beside me, giving little room between us.

"Kyle, oh my God … I mean, oh my goodness." GiGi's constant reprimands about using the Lord's name in vain made me correct myself. "Did you see that? Did you see what just happened?"

"Rain," he started slowly, "I heard you from outside while you were out on the balcony. I didn't see anything. You wanna tell me what happened?" He had a serious, but sincere expression.

"I saw her! I saw my mother. She was just outside. It was raining … and then it wasn't … and then the blood and the lightning, but … then there was a man, but not really—"

"Rain, you had an episode," Kyle said, cutting short my babbling.

I made a feeble attempt to gather my thoughts well enough to articulate them so he could understand, but it came out like senseless chatter instead. "No, no. It was real. I'm telling you. But … but, it was cold outside and the window, she broke it. Then, she died. I mean … I know she's already dead, but she died *again*."

Kyle sat silently, waiting for me to finish. He kept a straight face, occasionally raising his brow slightly. When I saw that he wasn't responding with the same sense of shock and excitement I felt, I reached out and grabbed his shoulders to shake him. "Did you hear what I just said?" I was almost yelling. "I just saw my mother. And she looked like me and Carmen and Danny. Did you hear me? I just watched my mother die again!"

"Rain," Kyle began as he gently removed my hands from his shoulders and placed them in my lap, "You have to calm down."

Butterflies filled my stomach as he wrapped his arms around me in a passionate, comforting embrace. He held me tightly and pulled my body further into his. Almost immediately, I felt my heart rate return to its normal pace. I exhaled a breath I didn't know I was holding and allowed myself to fall into him. In that moment, the horror of what had just occurred was forgotten. I rested in Kyle's arms, breathing in his scent, inhaling his masculinity and sensuality, wanting more of him. I felt his body tense up slightly. He was probably nervous, but I understood; I was too. We both knew this was coming, but now that the moment was here, it was almost overwhelming. The realization of what we were about to do sent a surge through my body. My breathing became heavy as I gripped his back tighter and began to softly kiss his neck.

Kyle rubbed the back of my arms gently as I breathed heavily, making love circles on his skin with my tongue. Suddenly, I felt a sharp pinch in my left triceps.

"Ow." I tried to loosen Kyle's hold on me, but he tightened his grip forcibly and held me close. When I tried to struggle and break free, he clutched me tighter, so tight it hurt.

"What are you doing?" I struggled against him. "Let me go. You're hurting me now!" My forearm began to sting as a warm sensation pooled and quickly spread through my arm.

"Be still, Rain. It's almost over."

I felt my body go limp in Kyle's arms, and I relaxed. My breathing became a shallow exchange of ins and outs. Kyle loosened his hold on me and laid me gently back on the bed. He rubbed my arm where he had pinched me and then told me to rest. He said something else too, but it wasn't so clear. My only response was an unintelligible grunt to let him know that I heard him, even though I didn't comprehend. As Kyle rose from the bed, he mumbled something else. I don't know what this man was talking about, but I started not to care as a feeling of tranquility washed over my body. I watched him walk out of the room, looking back a couple of times before he closed the door to make sure I was still in place on the bed. I didn't move, didn't want to. Kyle was right; I needed to get some rest. So I did, falling asleep within a few minutes.

8

Carmen / *Friday, April 16th*

M̲Y̲ eyes are barely open beyond slits, and all I can see is darkness. I have no idea what time of day it is, but it has to be late in the evening because I can't make out anything in the room and there are no sun rays beaming from outside to assist me. My night vision is horrible. I'm supposed to wear glasses, but you won't catch me dead with that shit on my face. I can't see a thing, but that doesn't stop me from squinting in an attempt to see something. It doesn't work. I try to sit up, but the piercing pain in my lower back commands that I lie back down immediately. I have a heavy feeling in my limbs. It's hard to describe; it's that feeling you get when you've been asleep for too long. Man, I feel exhausted and sluggish.

Have I been drugged? Ha! I almost made myself laugh with that damn question. Of course I've been drugged. I try to be drugged on a regular basis! But now for some reason, I can't remember when or with whom I had my last hit. I quickly shrug it off as no big deal. I've had blackouts before, where I've literally lost days of my life after a night full of sex, drugs, and alcohol. Sometimes it's hard to piece together what happened the night before. Shit, just the other day, I woke up in Rain's nasty room, surrounded by mounds of clothes and random mess scattered all about. I must have made the wrong turn in the hall when I came home. When I'm awake (and sober) I can hardly stand to be in that landfill for more than a couple of seconds. I must have been wasted off my ass to even sit down long enough to fall asleep in that cesspool.

Trying my best not to jolt my aching back, I reach to my left to feel for the lamp that sits on my nightstand. After fumbling around for a few seconds, I fail to feel anything remotely close to a lamp. I don't even feel the nightstand. That's when my suspicions start to kick in. Where in the hell am I? It feels like I'm lying on a bare mattress with no sheets. I manage to prop myself up on my elbows and try again to gain focus through the darkness, turning my head from left to right. Nothing. Then, as if to answer my question, a pungent odor slithers up to my nose, lingering long enough to tell me that I'm not at home. I'm somewhere I'm not supposed to be. I stick a slender finger under my nose to shield my nostrils from the offensive smell.

"Ay. Get yo' ass up." I jump at the sudden sound of the baritone voice that fills the room.

Frantically turning my head in all directions to see where the voice is coming from, I forget about my sore back as I shoot straight up at attention. I wince in response to the sharp pain that travels through my spine.

"Who's there?" I ask, shocked at the sound of my raspy voice quivering slightly with fear.

A bright light shines on my face. I raise my right arm to cover my eyes and say a quick prayer that this isn't a cop. I don't know where I am or what I'm doing here, but chances are it's some illegal shit.

"I said get up," the man states firmly, ignoring my request to reveal his identity.

Whether he's a cop or not, I figure I better do what he says. His authoritative tone tells me that he's somebody important, or at least powerful. Still shielding my face from the light, I rise slowly from the mattress, ignoring the pain in my back and the newly discovered ache in my legs. When I am finally on my feet, he drops the flashlight from my eyes, now holding its beam near my neck. It takes a few moments for my eyes to readjust, but when they do, I take advantage of the opportunity to check out this man who is calling the shots in this midnight black room. His chocolate skin, chestnut eyes, wide nose, and full lips do not draw a spark of recognition. But one thing is for sure: he ain't no damn cop. He's fly as hell. Daddy has it going on with his butter soft leather jacket and his black t-shirt, adorned with a diamond-encrusted chain. I even peep his designer jeans and clean-ass boots. I'm sure I shouldn't be having these thoughts in the middle of a potentially dangerous situation, but the hoe in me is wide awake as I take all of him in. I involuntarily lick my lips and shift my weight onto my left hip in a seductive stance.

Blessed with the dim glow of the flashlight, I look around the room to evaluate my surroundings. The place is a dump. I flinch at the sight of the dirty, grimy hardwood floor decorated with trash, needles, and random garbage.

I grimace at the fiends curled up on the floor, lying on the tattered orange sofa, and rocking silently in a chair to some internal tune. I look behind me to see the mattress I was lying on just moments prior and visibly shudder and brush imaginary debris from my chest and arms as I realize that is where I was actually sleeping.

"Come on with me. You don't belong here." The man turns and walks swiftly toward the door. The trash on the floor crunches under the pressure of his expensive shoes as he makes his way to the exit.

I don't know where we are or who this fine-ass man is, but it doesn't take much to convince me that I don't belong in this place. I decide that he's right and worthy of being followed to the door. We both remain silent as we walk to the SUV parked near the curb in front of the house we just left. I look behind me to see an unfamiliar two-story brick home. The boarded windows and front door give the illusion of abandonment, but having seen the spaced out occupants just minutes ago, I know that's just an illusion. I shiver a little, wrapping my arms around myself to try to create some warmth.

Hesitantly, I watch as the man walks around to the driver side of the truck and opens the door. He pauses to motion for me to open the passenger side door and get in with him. Now I know what you're probably thinking: why in the *hell* would I get into a car with a perfect stranger? I mean he could kidnap, rape or kill me. Shit, he might do all three, but for some reason, I'm not worried about all that at the moment. I'm one of those people that operates off the vibes that people give me, and he isn't giving me the crazed, murderous, rapist vibe. Okay, maybe I'm rationalizing my irrational actions, but so what? I want to go wherever he is going, so I do. This wouldn't be the first time I went against logic and did what I wanted.

I climb into the passenger side and place my hands in my lap, sitting straight up with my leather seat set at a ninety-degree angle. I keep my focus on the view in front of me. It's not much, just the back of some raggedy-ass car parked in front of us sitting on bricks, but it serves as an appropriate distraction and keeps me from thinking of the possible negatives of my decision to trust this man and leave with him. I don't even turn to look at him when he slams his door closed, starts the ignition, and turns on the radio. We drive in silence for several minutes before he hands me a joint and a lighter and tells me to fire it up.

I probably don't have to tell you that I gladly comply. I'm relieved to have some form of drug to indulge in. Weed isn't my preference, but it will certainly do for the moment. After I light the joint and take the first hit, he finally speaks.

"You one crazy bitch," he says with a certainty that tells me that he must have some sort of proof. I'm in no position to oppose him. Shit, I can't remember anything from the last several hours. As a matter of fact, I don't think I can remember anything since about two days ago. So maybe some crazy shit did go down. I don't say anything; I just wait for him to continue, hoping he'll give me some insight on my forgotten actions.

He continues, "My niggas wanted to whoop yo' ass and leave you for dead, but I couldn't let 'em do it." He smirks like he's remembering something funny.

"What happened?" I ask, still refusing to look his way.

"'What happened?' You don't remember? Damn, you crazier than I thought!" He laughs loudly, then reaches toward me to indicate that he is ready to hit the joint I'm holding. I hand it to him.

"No, I don't remember. I don't even know where the

hell I was, who you are, or where we're going. What the hell kind of pills did I take?"

"Don't worry about where we're going. You safe, and I ain't gonna do nothing to you. If I wanted to hurt you, it woulda already been done." He speaks with such assurance, I believe him.

"Okay, well will you at least tell me what happened?"

He turns to look at me with a strange expression on his face. I guess he thinks I'm bullshitting when I say I don't remember anything. I turn to him for the first time since we entered the SUV and match his stare to let him know that I'm serious.

He chuckles and hits the joint before responding. "I guess I can fill you in. You seem a little confused." That is an extreme understatement.

"You came walking up the block on your way to the Candy Shop at about nine o'clock last night. My soldiers said they recognized you from a coupla days ago. So they knew yo' ass was about to be trouble. My lil' nigga Dee said you started trippin' as soon as you stepped up to 'em, talking 'bout you *demand* to speak to management, like yo' ass was at Target or something."

I frown as I try to grasp a sliver of memory from last night. Nope, nothing. But so far, I can see how he might find some humor in the situation.

"When they told you to get the fuck on, that's when you really went wild. When I pulled up, I saw you jumping on Dee like you really thought you was doin' something. Good thing I pulled up when I did, 'cause if it wasn't for me, they mighta killed yo' ass. By the time I got out the car, they had you on the ground, kickin' the shit outta you." He laughs, before hitting the joint again.

I look at him with pure shock and horror. This man is

talking about me getting jumped by two guys and laughing about the shit like it's actually funny! Just who in the hell am I in the car with?

"Don't worry, lil' mama. They didn't do that much damage. You probably gotta coupla bruises or something." I rub my lower back as a confirmation. It hurts like hell. "Anyway, I got 'em to stop. They told me you was looking for me, so I had to see what was up with you. But you was so damn high and drunk, I don't think you even knew what the hell you wanted. No wonder you can't remember shit."

"I was looking for *you*? I don't even know who you are." He passes the joint back to me and I hit it like the pro I am.

"Well, you did last night. You kept screaming, 'Jay-Jay. Where the fuck is Jay-Jay?' You was making a scene, so we had to throw you in the back of the truck and relocate yo' ass before you brought too much attention to the spot. You ain't calm down 'til my other lil' nigga, Meeko, shot you up."

"Shot me up? With what?" I'm almost afraid to hear the answer. Now I may dabble a bit with pills here and there, but I damn sure don't shoot anything into my body. Only drug addicts slam, and I ain't no damn drug addict. I wait for his answer, hoping my worst fear will not become a reality.

"We gave you a dose of that smack. Knocked you out too. We dumped you off at one of my eastside spots to give you some time to sleep it off."

"Heroine! What the fuck? You let them niggas shoot me up with heroine? Oh my God! What if I get addicted? What if I become a damn drug addict?" I'm almost screaming as I frantically check my arms for track marks.

"Calm yo' ass down! You betta be more conscious of who the fuck you talking to. Now, I like you, but I *will* still fuck you up." He warns me with a grim look. I shut my mouth quickly. He says he likes me. That caught me off guard. I kinda like him too. I love a man that can handle his business in the street and don't take no shit. I can tell by his walk, his demeanor, and his mannerisms that he's the man, and he's definitely running things. He already likes me, so it's my job to stay in his good graces. If I can pull that off, that means free dope and new dick. That's a winning combination.

Jay-Jay slows the SUV and pulls to a stop in front of a medium-sized brick house. It looks nice, a sharp contrast to the dilapidated shack we just left.

"Get out the car," he barks before opening his door and hopping out. I do as I'm told and follow him up the winding walkway, past the manicured lawn, to the front door of the house. I wait patiently as he inserts the key into the lock and swings the door open.

Three young guys sit on a chenille couch in the living room. They're watching a Pistons game on a huge flat-screen mounted on the wall. When we walk in, they give their attention to Jay-Jay. I smile, noticing the combination of fear, respect, and admiration in their eyes as they greet their leader one-by-one. I recognize one of them as Red Shirt from a few days before. He glowers at me behind tinted Cartier glasses, but I ignore him, feeling a sense of superiority as Jay-Jay's new girl.

"Come on," Jay-Jay instructs me to follow him toward the back of the house, down a narrow hall, and into the master bedroom. Once inside the room, he locks the door behind him and tells me to have a seat. I plop down on the bed.

"What you call yo'self? Carmen?"

"Yeah, that's right."

"Aiight, Carmen," he says, tossing me a small baggie containing three pills, "You know who I am, right?"

"Well, I've only heard," I reply, quickly snatching open

the plastic baggie to retrieve my prize.

Jay-Jay smirks. "Well you gonna get to know me real good. I run the Candy Shop and six other spots around the city. Chances are, if you getting high, it's off my supply. So in short, I run this shit. You need to recognize that."

"Oh, I peeped you, Daddy. Believe me, I know," I say, right before popping the first E pill in my mouth.

He reaches into my mouth and grabs the pill before I can swallow it. "Hold up a minute. I need you to be alert for this shit I'm about to say." He removes his leather jacket slowly and kicks off his boots. "I saved yo' life last night. That was some shit I didn't have to do. It was some shit I wouldn't normally do, especially since you deserved to get yo' ass beat, or worse. But I see something in you. Something special I couldn't let go to waste. Stand up," he commands.

I stand up. He walks over to me with a sexy swagger. He stands in front of me so close that I can almost taste his scent, and dammit, I like it.

"You work for me now. As long as you wit' me, you ain't gotta worry about shit. Ain't nobody gonna fuck with you. I got you."

That sounds good to me. I just nod in response. This man could tell me he wants me to eat shit, and I would gladly obey. Okay, maybe not *shit*, but you get my point.

"I heard about you. Out here popping pills and giving away yo' pussy. You better than that, baby," he speaks in a low tone that sends chills down my spine. "The first thing you need to do, check that crazy-ass attitude. That shit ain't good for you. You can't make no money being a bitch. Niggas don't like that shit."

"That's part of my charm." I giggle.

"Shut the fuck up while I'm talking to you. You might miss something important." I clamp my lips together. "Now, like I said, you don't make no fucking money acting like you did last night. I'm not usually violent with women, but I'll have my lil' niggas get in yo' ass if I catch you getting out of line, and they don't mind beating a woman down. Do you understand?" Still complying with the "shut the fuck up" order, I nod to show my understanding. "You my bitch now, and you need to play the role."

He pauses, so I take it as my cue to finally speak, "Why me, Jay-Jay? Why you save me instead of letting them kill me?" I ask meekly and somewhat in awe of what this man is telling me.

"I told you, I like you. I've seen you around. I know what you about, where you coming from. You don't take no shit and you street smart. I like that." He places his right hand between my thighs and slowly slides it upward. "You sexy as hell too. I *really* like that."

I squirm at the touch of his warm hands. It feels damn good, and I don't want him to stop. I reposition my stance to give him more access to my body.

He steps back, handing me the pill. "Pop this and take off yo' clothes."

Shit, he doesn't have to tell me twice. I swallow the small blue pill, then snatch off my shirt and drop my pants, almost in one movement. My breasts bounce as I release them from my black lace bra. When I begin to pull down the matching panties, he stops me.

"Leave 'em on," he commands, unbuckling his belt and unzipping his pants. I'm sure I feel salivation in the corners of my mouth. I'm staring at one of the most beautiful, chocolaty brown dicks I've ever seen. He has to be packing at least nine inches. Like I said before, he's my kind of man.

"Suck my dick," Jay-Jay orders.

I drop to my knees so fast, you'd think somebody literally

pulled the rug from under my feet. The E is starting to kick in, and I feel my world become a little more colorful, warm, and pleasant. I gently, firmly take hold of his stiff dick with my left hand, then cup his balls with my right hand. I take a moment to saturate my mouth with saliva, and then I slide my warm, wet tongue up and down the sides of his long, thick shaft. I hear him release a soft moan as I circle the head with the tip of my tongue right before sucking him in with my lips. I feel his body spasm slightly as I graze the slit at the tip. When I have his dick nice and wet, I ease my hand up and down the shaft with rhythmic precision. I continue to use my right hand to massage his balls while I match the stroke of my left hand with the slow and steady slide of my mouth over his erection. I try the best I can, but I can't manage to fit the whole length of his dick into my mouth, so I rely on my hand to make up the difference. I take in as much as I can, pulling back far enough to tickle the tip with my tongue on each stroke. My tongue does twists and turns over his shaft as I move back and forth, sucking so hard my cheeks cave in.

"Aw shit," he moans.

I pick up speed when I feel him grip my head, wrapping the strands of my hair around his hand; that shit turns me on. I begin to moan, sending vibrations through his dick that cause him to lean his back against the wall in order to keep his balance. I start to taste the tangy, bittersweet juice seeping from his dick and I suck even harder with the increased pace of my stroke.

He moans, grunts, and whispers obscenities as his climax nears. I can feel his dick pulsating inside of my mouth, forewarning a massive eruption. I pull him out of my mouth, but keep stroking his shaft with one hand and kneading his balls with the other. I may be a freaky chick, but I don't swallow without throwing it back up. That shit is disgusting. I aim his dick at my upper torso and watch as his cum splatters and oozes down my chest. I lock my eyes on his as I smear the white cream over my titties seductively, like lotion, until my double D's are glistening. When I'm done, I lick and suck my index finger to show him how sweet he tastes.

"I like that nasty shit, baby," Jay-Jay says as he licks his lips.

I smile in response. I know what niggas like. Shit, I make a living off knowing what niggas like. The nastier, the better, and nobody is gonna beat me at that game. I'm pleasantly surprised to see that he's still standing at full mast after shooting that load. I know what's coming next and the anticipation makes my pussy go from moist to saturated. Still on my knees, I frown as I watch him retrieve a condom from his jeans that lay on the floor.

Catching my expression, he says, "If you gave me some shit, I'd have to kill you."

I don't utter one word of opposition. I don't care too much for condoms, but I know not to express too much resistance with this man.

"Stand up," he commands. I do.

He points a stern finger at the mahogany dresser sitting opposite the king-sized bed. I know exactly what he wants. I walk over to the dresser, slowly remove my panties and bend over so my elbows and arms are resting on the top. I stare at my image in the dresser mirror. I have hardly any traces of makeup on my face, my hair is a wild mess, and my eyes are a tad bit red from what I guess to be dehydration. I'm ugly. I look a mess and I pray Jay-Jay doesn't see what I see. I wish I would have had time to freshen up before fucking this man in front of the damn mirror. I close my eyes tightly and push my disheveled reflection out of my head.

I arch my back deeply and spread my legs to let him know that I'm ready for him. He takes his cue, clutching my ass cheeks and squeezing them right before he grabs my hips and jerks my lower body backward toward his. I moan softly as his dick eases inside my slippery pussy. He's only halfway in before he pulls out, teasing me by slipping it in just a little and pulling out again. He wants me to beg for it. I clench my teeth in anticipation and look back at him with a combination of pleading and desperation. I'm like a dude when it comes to sex. Give it to me hard and fast; fuck the games. He smirks at me, knowing he has full control and visibly enjoying it. I slam my palm on the dresser in frustration and push my ass toward him. I watch in the mirror as he licks his lips and grabs my hips once again. This time, he pushes inside me with force and determination. I almost scream as I feel the full length of his manhood invade my walls. He grabs the back of my neck with his left hand and uses it as leverage to push and pull my body back and forth. I dip my back in even deeper and start to throw my ass back so my cheeks smack loudly against his lower stomach with each thrust.

I don't care that we're in a house full of guys, I scream, moan, and grunt like I'm auditioning for a porno. Oh, it feels so good; I think I may die from over-stimulation. He doesn't make a sound as he pounds me from behind. With every stroke, I can hear the slurping sound of my soaking wet pussy. I pulse my pussy, gripping his dick again and again. That induces an audible reaction from Jay-Jay. I smile mischievously in the mirror, ignoring my less than perfect reflection, as I see his straight face scrunch in agonizing pleasure. I lick my lips in the mirror and revel in the faces of ecstasy we both make. I start to go wild when he tightens his grip on my neck and reaches around to fondle my clit with his free hand. That does it! I can feel my orgasm threatening to emerge. We haven't been fucking for more than a few minutes, so I don't want to stop, but the way this man is working me, I know I won't be able to hold it in much longer. When he starts hitting it harder and faster, I know he's near his climax as well. I decide to ride the wave and let nature take its course. My moans and wails do a quick crescendo into screams and blasphemous obscenities. The orgasm surges through my body like an electrical tidal wave. My clit pulsates and my body seizes before I fall limp. I pray that he got his too, because I have nothing left. My prayer is answered when he grabs both my ass cheeks and slams my body back hard and fast until I can feel his hard dick pulsing inside of me. His grunt and moan confirms his finale.

I'm panting and sweating when he slides out of me.

"Damn! You got some good pussy, baby," he exclaims between heavy breaths.

I can't form any words; I'm too busy trying to catch my breath. I straighten up and turn around to face him. He's seated on the bed, still naked with his dick lying limp between his thighs. I watch as he punches in a text message on his cell phone.

"Get dressed," he orders. Everything he says to me seems to be a command. I like it. The bossier, the better.

I scramble to find all the articles of my clothing on the floor. By the time I buckle my pants and slip on my shoes, I hear a car horn honking outside. Jay-Jay grabs his jeans from the floor and puts them on. He leaves his shirt off and his feet bare.

What now? I check to make sure the other two E pills are secure in my pocket. I can tell by the way he sexes me that we have a connection. He picked me out of every girl in the 'hood, and I know he can get anyone he wants. He says he *likes* me. My own mother and grandmother don't even like me, so that *has* to mean something special. Visions of him running the city with me close by his side dance in my head. I can see him trusting me with his deepest secrets, along with his stash, taking me on exotic vacations, and throwing me stacks of money to go on shopping sprees. He'll move me into his house so I can finally get away from Rain and Danny, making me wifey and queen of the streets. I'm his bitch now, and I need to play the role.

"Come on," he says.

With a smile spread across my face, I follow him out the bedroom door and into the front room. The young guys that were sitting on the couch earlier are gone. He heads to the front door and swings it open.

"Where we going?" I ask.

"I ain't going nowhere, baby. You are."

I frown in confusion. Where in the hell am I supposed to go with no damn car?

"What the fuck you waitin' on. Yo' customer waiting outside in the Cadillac."

"What? I thought I was gonna be your *girl*, Jay-Jay. What's this about?" I hear my tone approaching a serious attitude, but I decide to check it before I get into trouble.

"I said you my bitch, and you are, but you have to prove your loyalty. Now bring me back my money." He opens the screen door and pushes me outside.

I let the reality of his words sink in as I do a slow walk toward the waiting car. I mean, I have to be real with myself. Like Jay-Jay said, I've been running around with different guys, giving away the pussy for pills or for free. If I want to prove myself, I have to show him that I'm a hustler just like he is, and more importantly, that he can trust me. It's a small price to pay to claim my spot as his woman, so as

I look back at Jay-Jay standing in the doorway, I smile and wave. I'm still soaring from my E high, so I know I can rock this nigga's world with some of the best sex he's ever had. This is the beginning of a beautiful future, starting with Mr. Cadillac.

9 *Danny* / *Thursday, April 22nd*

I stretch and yawn as I leave the kitchen with a grilled cheese sandwich and a cup of grape Kool-Aid in hand. There's a better selection of food in the house, but after the day I had, the last thing I feel like doing is cooking. Besides, that's not my thing. I'd rather wait around for Carmen or Rain to hook something up in the kitchen. Well, Rain, not Carmen. Come to think of it, I don't think Carmen even knows how to boil water, let alone prepare a meal.

It's already pushing six o'clock in the evening and I still haven't heard from Maya's ass. I'm starting to get agitated as I begin to mentally calculate the hours since we've last spoke—about sixteen. This chick must've lost her mind. I plop down on the couch and grab my cell phone from the cocktail table after setting my sandwich and drink down. I push the "Talk" button on the phone to activate the last call I've made. Of course it's Maya's number. I've been calling her all damn day with nothing but the voicemail as an answer. I swear to God if she's fucking around, I'll kill her! When her phone goes straight to voicemail for about the twentieth time, I start to visualize wrapping my hands around her throat and squeezing the life out of her tiny body. Damn, that woman makes me so mad sometimes. After this shit, I might just drop her, but I have to put my foot up her ass first. I mean I don't need this kind of stress in my life. I do everything I can to treat her right. I spend all my time with her, I'd give her my last dollar, I protect her, eat her pussy like a pro, and this is how she repays me? Do I look like somebody who needs to be chasing after a bitch? Let me answer that for you: Hell no! I got hoes just sitting around waiting for Maya to do something stupid so they can slide right on in. I'd love to see the look on her face the day I decide to let them slide.

I slam the phone back down on the table with a huff and take a bite of my grilled cheese. When I reach up to scratch my itching scalp, I almost spit the food right out of my mouth. My braids are a frizzy mess on top of my head. Maya has me out here looking like a raggedy fool! Ooh, I can't *wait* to get in her ass.

"What's up, Danny?" Rain sits down beside me on the couch. I swear that girl must be part ghost the way she eases up on me all the time without warning.

"What up, lil' sis." I'm grateful for the company. I need something to take my mind off Maya and the beat down I'm going to have to give her. I take a swig of my Kool-Aid and turn to face my youngest sister. She's really coming into her own, getting comfortable with herself. I'm happy about that because when we were growing up, she was always so damn shy and scared about everything. She just lacked confidence, and I always had a hard time relating to that. But now, as I look her over, she seems to hold her head just a little bit higher. She isn't afraid to sport her own style. That Afro-centric, neo-soul shit isn't my thing, and she looks a little like a weirdo to me, but hey, if it works for her and keeps her spirits up, I'm all for it.

"Nothing much. About to head down to the Lyrical Lounge in a little while. I know GiGi must have told you how I tore it up last week." She smiles and sticks out her chest to illustrate her pride and self-assurance. Her smile is contagious, and I catch myself showing my pearly whites too.

"Yeah, you know she did. She's always bragging on you. You know GiGi loves her some Rain. I'm proud of you though. Keep it up, Apple Head." Rain blushes and giggles at the childhood nickname she earned when she was seven. Her head was big and round just like an apple. I couldn't resist branding her with the name; it was so fitting.

Rain's smile fades almost as suddenly as it appeared. "Danny, why don't you come down and see me some time? I mean, I'm always looking for you and Carmen to check me out, but you never come. I figure Carmen probably won't because she hates me and there's nothing in it for her, but I thought it would be nice to at least get your support."

The gloomy expression she bears, along with the twinge of pain that is apparent in her words, pulls at my heart. It's never my intention to hurt either one of my sisters. I just get caught up doing my own thing sometimes, well, all the time. I don't mean to be neglectful; I guess I'm just careless. I quickly find myself making a promise I'm not sure I'll be able to keep, but my intentions are good. "I tell you what, let me know the next time you're performing and I'll have my ass in the front row," I say, with the best look of sincerity I can invoke. I really mean it too. I will try my best.

That perks Rain right up. "Thanks, Danny! Well, like I said, I'll be heading down there tonight. Kyle's gonna take me. I'm scheduled to perform at eight o'clock."

Damn, she did say tonight, didn't she? I make up my mind now that I'm not gonna disappoint my little sister. I'm the eldest, so it's my job to look after her. Right after I deal with Maya, I'm heading straight down to—

"What is that place called again?"

"The Lyrical Lounge. You know, it's right there on Grand River and Lahser."

"Yeah, yeah, I know the place. I'll see you there at eight, babe."

"Cool," she beams.

"Hey, and I don't want to hear anything else about Carmen hating you. That's our sister. You have your differences, but she doesn't hate you."

"Whatever. I can't tell," she says with a huff.

I take a generous bite of my sandwich. It's starting to get cold. Dammit, I hate that. I take advantage of the break in the conversation and try to call Maya one last time, no answer.

"Y'all look bored as hell!" Carmen prances her overly made-up, tight-clothes-wearing ass into the living room and plops down on the couch on the other side of me.

Rain sighs and rolls her eyes. I respond, "I ain't bored. My mind is going a million miles a minute, sweetheart. Don't underestimate me."

"Ha. Yo' mind ain't doing nothing but thinking about Maya's ass." She smirks, reaching over me to grab at my grilled cheese sandwich. I smack her hand away before she can touch my food. "Ow!" Carmen whines and rubs the back of her hand. I chuckle and take another bite.

"You damn right, I've got that chick on my mind. She has no idea. When I see her ..."

"I hope y'all not gonna be up in here fighting," Rain interjects.

"Oh, it ain't gonna be no fight, little one. It's gonna be a straight TKO up in here."

Rain shakes her head silently as if to scold me in her mind. Carmen laughs loudly. She loves drama, especially if it isn't her own. I have plenty of that to pass around. My girl and I keep the real life soap opera going twenty-four seven. I guess some people would call us dysfunctional, but it's not like that at all. Whenever there is as much passion and intensity in a relationship as we have, some drama is bound to pop off every now and then. I pick up the phone to check the caller ID as if Maya might have called without my knowing. She didn't.

"I'm so glad me and my man don't have to go through that shit," Carmen boasts as she lies back on the couch, kicking her feet up on the coffee table.

"Your *man?*" Rain and I both exclaim in unison. I sit straight up in my seat and turn my attention to Carmen. With all the guys she goes through, she's never once claimed any one of them to be her man. This was a serious news flash, and we want all the details.

"Yes, my *man,*" she repeats without turning her head to meet my gaze, "I know you know Jay-Jay, right?" She gives a sly grin and cuts her eyes at me.

"Never heard of him." Rain hunches her shoulders with a look of disinterest.

"That's because you don't know shit," Carmen snaps. "Everybody knows my man. He's *the* man. Act like you know."

Rain rolls her eyes.

"Wait, you mean that nigga, Jay, that be up there on Stoepel and Chalfonte? The dope boy?" I ask, feeling the level of disgust rising inside me. This chick is always into some bullshit. Now she's the dope man's girlfriend? This is way too much. It's bad enough she's on drugs; now she has a free supply? I can see the downward spiral my sister is quickly slipping toward.

"Yeah, that's him. That's my baby. He takes real good care of me."

"You call feeding your addiction 'real good care'?" I'm almost yelling, "You better hope I don't catch that nigga in the streets. I got something for his ass!"

"You ain't gonna do shit, Danny. I swear, sometimes you really do think you're invincible. You ain't bulletproof, nigga."

I scowl at Carmen with a look that tells her I'm dead serious. I meant what I said, if I catch that dude anywhere around my sister, it's on.

Carmen smacks her teeth. "Whatever."

Rain sits silent, looking straight ahead, seeming not to focus on anything in particular. It's apparent that something is on her mind. Carmen turns away from me and flings a small throw pillow across the couch. It hits Rain in the face. "Why you so damn quiet all of a sudden? You usually running your mouth about something nobody cares about."

Rain scowls in aggravation, but I'm the one that speaks up first. "Carmen, lay off. You can be such a bitch sometimes." Carmen sticks out her tongue. I ignore her and turn to Rain. "What's on your mind, baby sis?"

"It's nothing. Like Carmen said, it's probably something nobody cares about anyway," she says meekly, still staring into nothing.

"Fuck what Carmen's talking about; I care. What is it?"

Carmen sighs loudly and leans up in her seat. She pushes her ear forward in an exaggerated "I'm listening" gesture. I roll my eyes—brat.

"Well …" Rain hesitates.

"Well?" I urge.

"I had another vision about … about Mom."

"Aww shit, here we go!" Carmen rolls her eyes and throws her hands up in the air in exasperation. She mocks, "I had a vision 'cause I'm crazy as hell."

"Shut up, Carmen," both Rain and I scold.

"This one was different. But … it was kind of the same. You know, like all the other ones she was there, but this time I could see her face. She was right there in front of me. I looked her right in the eyes." Rain shakes her head slowly like she's reliving the vision.

"Maybe it's because of the picture GiGi gave you," I offer.

Carmen leans back on the couch and tries the best she can to look as disinterested as possible. I turn up my cup and gulp down the last of my grape Kool-Aid. I decide against the last few bites of the grilled cheese. It's too cold by now.

"Maybe so. I don't know, but she was right there. It was so real. I wanted to touch her. I wanted to hug her, but then …"

"What, Rain? Huh? Then what? She died? Like she always does? Whoop dee fucking doo. How about you do us a favor and come up with some new material. I'm getting bored with this same old story."

"Carmen, if you don't chill, I'm gonna have to send you to your room like GiGi used to do to yo' bad ass back in the day. Shut up!"

Carmen makes an ugly face at me. I flip her the bird.

"No, this one was different y'all," Rain continues, "This time, he was there."

"Her killer?" I ask. This revelation makes both Carmen and me sit up at attention. Even Carmen is taken aback by the news of the possible identity of our mother's murderer, despite her resistance to be anything close to genial to our younger sister.

"Yeah. I mean, I didn't see his face but …"

"Aww! You got me all into this stupid as 'vision' and you leave us with a fucking cliffhanger? You suck. I have more important things to do."

"Like what?" I ask with obvious sarcasm.

"Like make some money. I'm out." With that, Carmen jumps up from the couch and heads toward the door. Neither of us cares enough to ask where she's going or even look behind us to see her out. I can only take that chick in small doses, and her time expired about fifteen minutes ago.

I keep my focus on Rain. "But what, Rain? Now that she's gone, you can get it out."

"Well, I could I hear him. He was laughing. I could see his shadow. It was like he was right there! Right there! But I wasn't close enough to see."

"Does this bring back any memories?"

"No. When I'm in the here-and-now, it's still like it never happened. It's still like Mom never existed. I don't remember a thing." Her voice begins to quiver, forewarning tears. I slide closer to her, placing a comforting hand on her shoulder. "If I could remember, everything would be alright. Everything would be normal."

"Aw, sis, don't let that shit GiGi be talkin' get to you. There's nothing wrong with you. I mean, anybody who witnessed something as horrible as you did is bound to have some problems. Shit, to me, that *is* normal."

She nods, accepting my explanation for her sometimes-strange behaviors. Just then, I hear a commotion outside. The sound of muffled angry voices floats from the front lawn, up to the balcony, and through the cracked window in Rain's bedroom. I jump up almost immediately as I recognize Maya's squeaky voice, raised in agitation. Yes, my little sister is in tears and yes, she is reliving a traumatic childhood incident, but damn all that; I have to take care of something real quick.

As I rush toward the back of the house to Rain's bedroom, I feel a twinge of guilt. To comfort my little sister, and to make myself feel better about abandoning her in her moment of need, I do a half turn in between quick steps and say, "I'll see ya at the lounge." I add a weak smile for extra good measure.

Rain responds with a limp wave and a bowed head. She'll be alright; she needs to toughen up anyway. I push the bedroom door open so hard that the doorknob bangs against the wall. When I reach the window, I have a perfect view of the whole scene taking place on the lawn. It's Maya and GiGi arguing.

"Look GiGi, I know you mean well and all, but Danny and I make our own decisions. We're not perfect, but we do okay just as we are." She's holding up her hands in a defensive gesture.

"Listen to yourself, chile. Listen to what you're saying." GiGi grabs Maya's arm with a motherly authority. "This relationship isn't healthy. Why would you want to be wrapped up in something like this?"

"I admit, Danny is far from perfect, but we love each other. That's all we need to make it. The rest will work itself out." Maya tries unsuccessfully to snatch her arm away from GiGi's grasp.

GiGi lowers her voice to try to calm the both of them. She places both hands on Maya's narrow shoulders and reasons, "Get out while you can. It's not going to get better. Danny doesn't want to get better, and as long as that's the case, you'll always be in danger. Think about it, chile. The only thing you'll get from this relationship is pain."

I grind my teeth and clench my fist at each syllable GiGi speaks against me. What in the hell is she doing? She's bad-mouthing me like I'm some stranger on the street. Me, her own grandchild! What goes on between my woman and me is my business. Who in the hell is she to interfere?

"GiGi, I appreciate your concern. I really do, and I understand why you worry as much as you do, but I've made my decision. I knew what I was getting into very early on in our relationship and I chose to stick it out. This is my choice. Love is worth the sacrifice." Maya matches GiGi's low tone as she eases her way out of GiGi's embrace. I smile at Maya's loyalty as I watch her walk away from my grandmother and start up the porch steps leading to the front door. I tell you, there's nothing like a loyal, devoted woman on your team.

GiGi slowly follows Maya up the steps. I make my way to the front door just as I hear the doorbell chime. I descend the steps to the lower level of the flat and open the door to let my guests in. As I move to the side to let Maya and GiGi into the house, my proud smile quickly changes into a hardened grimace. No matter how well Maya's little front lawn performance was, it doesn't negate the crime she committed. She knows damn well not to go that long without answering my calls, not to mention the added offense of my raggedy head. Let's not get started on that. GiGi enters the foyer just behind Maya, wearing a mask of frustration and annoyance. Catching wind of my state of displeasure, Maya eases past me cautiously. Keeping as far a distance from me as she can, her back brushes against the stairwell wall as she slides up the steps to the upper level of the flat. I catch her ass right before she reaches the third step. Ignoring my grandmother's presence, I reach behind me and pop Maya in the back of the head. I giggle a little as I watch her stumble and try to balance herself with the banister. She doesn't make a sound. As soon as she's able to steady herself, she continues up the stairs in silence until I hear the door of the upper level open and close.

My GiGi doesn't like that at all. "Danny! I didn't raise you like that!" she exclaims with a mixture of shame and horror. "I swear I don't know where the hell you came from. This mess you put me through …" She trails off into an inaudible mumble that ends in her just shaking her bowed head.

"GiGi, I can't believe—"

"Shut up! Just shut up. I don't wanna hear it. I can barely stand to look at you right now. Nothing I do or say right now is gonna change anything. Same goes for you, so just save it."

I close my mouth, huffy like a child who had just been chastised. I know when to try GiGi and when to just let it go. This is one of those times to keep my mouth shut and let it ride.

"Anyway," GiGi continues sharply, "I only came to drop something off for Rain. She said she was going to that lounge today so I wanted to make sure she had this before she left." She narrows her eyes and looks deep into mine. "Is she here?"

"Yeah, GiGi, she's right upstairs. She told me she'd be heading out in a little while."

"Well, I won't be able to see her perform tonight, and I

have to run, so give her this for me, will you?" She hands me a colorful, silk scarf doused in a floral scented perfume. "I want her to wear this tonight, so I'll still be there with her."

"I'll give it to her, GiGi." I take the scarf and throw it over my shoulder. GiGi turns slowly and walks out of the house without another word. For a moment, I feel ashamed of myself. The way I acted up in front of my grandmother defied my upbringing, but it was only for a moment. After locking the front door, I rush up the stairs, taking two steps at a time. I hear Maya gasp as the front door slams shut with a loud bang. I'm fuming; the look of fear on her face puts a momentary pause in my step and sends a light flutter to my heart. But this is no time to back down and show weakness. She needs to be taught a lesson, and her tactics to evoke my sympathy are pointless. I remove the scarf GiGi gave me for Rain and place it on the dinette as I pass the kitchen entryway. I steal a quick peek into the living room to see if Rain is still sitting there. She isn't. She must be in her room getting ready for her gig. I begin to walk angrily toward Maya.

"My phone … I couldn't find it all day. I left the house without it and I didn't even know. As soon as I found it, I came right over. I swear, that's the truth." Maya is rambling and stumbling at the pace of an auctioneer.

I take slow, steady strides toward her, intimidating her with every step. She seems to be sinking and shrinking into herself as I draw nearer. I'm not in the mood for lame excuses. The more she talks, the more she pisses me off.

"I know you're mad, okay. I know, but just listen to me. Hear me out …"

I ball my fists tightly by my sides and begin grinding my teeth; it's a bad habit I've had since childhood.

"I spent the whole day looking for my phone. I promise

I did. I know how important it is to keep in touch with you!"
Maya's lips begin to quiver, and her voice is shaking. I hate
crybaby women!

I wait until I'm just inches away from her before I speak.
With my nose almost touching the middle of her forehead,
I can smell her fear. It exhilarates me and compels me to
carry out the punishment she more than deserves. "You
were with somebody else." It isn't a question; it's a statement
of conviction. My breathing becomes heavy as intense anger
floods over me. I feel myself losing control, breaking into
pieces with visions of my woman giving her love away to
another. I hate her right now. I want her to suffer.

"Baby, I promise. I wasn't with anyone else. I—"

Before her lips can form another lie, I clutch her throat
with my right hand, carefully placing my thumb and middle
finger on both sides of her trachea. As I block her air
passage, she gags and scratches at my hands, trying to free
herself from the chokehold, but she isn't getting away from
me that easily. I force Maya backward as I march forward,
leading her to my bedroom near the back of the house. She
shuffles along the floor on her toes, trying to relieve the
pressure of my vice grip.

"You think I'm stupid, don't you? You think I don't
know what the fuck you doin' when you get away from me?
Bitch, I'll kill you before I let somebody else have you," I
hiss through clenched teeth. When we reach the doorway
to my bedroom, I notice Maya's eyes beginning to roll to
the back of her head and her face losing its mahogany hue.
"Oh, no you don't! You don't get off that easy," I scream,
throwing her down on the bed. The last thing I want is for
her to pass out and miss out on this ass whooping she has
coming.

Taking advantage of the moment of freedom, she rolls

over and scrambles toward the head of the bed, curling herself into a tight ball to protect herself from the blows I'm about lay on her. Thinking quickly, I remove the wide, leather belt from my waist and wrap one end tightly around my fist, leaving the end with the oversized metal buckle dangling free. I see Maya put her arm up to shield her face just as I whip the belt up in the air and strike her exposed thigh with the buckle. She screams in pain as I raise the belt again for another blow. I allow myself to enjoy this moment with a sadistic smile.

She screams, "Please! Stop. I'm sorry! I'm so sorry, baby, *please!*"

Stopping is not an option. If you go too easy on these chicks, they'll start to think you're soft. That's when you lose control and they take advantage. I'm not having that; Maya isn't about to go Carmen on me. I hit her one more time with the belt, just to hear her yelp. Then I move to the head of the bed and yank her by her hair. When I have enough leverage and her body is in the right position, I mount the bed and straddle her legs. I let go of her hair, using one hand to hold her legs steady while I position myself. Then I grip both her wrists. Each punch I issue to her chest and stomach provokes a low groan followed by a whimper. I don't dare hit her face. I won't be caught dead running around with some bruised up and battered chick on my arm. That shit is embarrassing.

"Danny, get off her right now!"

I pause in mid-punch when I hear Rain's shrill voice screaming at me.

"Rain?" Maya pleads between sobs. The uncertainty in her voice tells me that she's relieved for the salvation and questions whether it's real.

"Mind your business, Rain. This has nothing to do with

you," I warn without even looking at her. I keep my eyes locked on Maya's in a threatening stare.

"I'm not going to sit here and listen to you beat that girl. Stop it *right now*! I don't know what the hell is wrong with you," Rain yells. Then, looking at Maya, she shouts, "Or *you*!"

A few moments of awkward calm fill the room as Maya and I try to catch our breath. Maya is the first to interrupt the silence.

"Rain," she speaks slowly. She's still captive under my weight, with her arms and legs locked in place. "Please stay. Please don't go."

I still refuse to look at my little sister. I look down at my girl and I'm immediately filled with remorse. All of a sudden, I'm drowning in shame. Rain doesn't need to see this shit. She doesn't need to witness the dysfunction that has taken over my relationship. I'm the oldest, and I'm supposed to set the example. Her mere presence makes me want to disappear.

"I won't go anywhere, Maya, but maybe you need to leave," Rain responds.

Now that's where I draw the line. She isn't going anywhere! I have to do something to get Rain out of the room. As long as she's here, Maya and I will never resolve this thing ourselves. "Rain, it's over," I say as convincingly as I can. To prove that I'm being truthful, I release Maya's wrists and ease off the bed, freeing her legs. I hear Maya breathe a sigh of relief as I transfer my weight from her body to the floor.

"You're going to be okay?" Rain asks Maya with a raised eyebrow, seemingly unconvinced.

"I think so," she answers meekly, looking to me for reassurance.

I give the confirmation she's looking for, "Yeah, she's gonna be alright. We're done."

"Okay, I have to get going down to the Lounge. If you need to stay here and work things out, I understand. Don't worry about coming to see me," Rain offers.

As Rain turns and walks out of the room, I yell behind her, "GiGi left a scarf for you to wear on the kitchen table." She doesn't reply.

Now standing, I tower over Maya as she lies on the bed. Her face reveals a host of emotions that range from fear, to love, to self-pity. I can't deal with them all at the same time. I need to make those expressions go away. They're making me feel just as battered as she looks, and I don't like feeling that way. I hate when she makes me feel guilty. To ease my pain. I bend down over my baby and gently graze her forehead with my mouth. As I travel down her face, kissing the bridge of her nose, her lips, and then her chin, I offer sweet apologies and promises never to hurt her again. She gasps lightly, as she reaches up for me and pulls me down on the bed. I lie down behind her and spoon her, wrapping my arms around her small frame. It's our favorite position.

As I nuzzle my nose into her neck gently, I whisper, "Don't ever do that shit again."

"I won't," Maya promises.

That's my girl. I kiss her on her neck and hold her tightly until we both drift off to sleep. I'm grateful for Rain's suggestion to skip her performance tonight; now I don't feel so guilty for not wanting to go. After we wake up, Maya will have to do my hair, so I would have missed the show anyway. I'll be sure to catch Rain next week.

10 Rain / *Tuesday, April 26th*

I sat in the car, waiting impatiently for Kyle and GiGi to end their conversation so we could head to the Lyrical Lounge. They asked me to wait while they took care of some business. What business, I don't know. I didn't ask either. I was ready to go, and I didn't want to delay our departure by asking a whole bunch of questions. I looked at the clock above the car radio. It read 7:50 p.m. I released a loud sigh. If I was late, I knew Malik would be tripping and threaten to give away my spot. Huffing with my arms crossed defiantly across my chest, I turned toward GiGi and Kyle, who were standing on the porch on the edge of the steps. Kyle placed a hand on GiGi's shoulder and gave her an encouraging smile. GiGi shook her head. Okay, now I really *did* want to know what the hell they were talking about. I reached over the armrest that separated me from the driver's seat and lightly tapped the car horn three times. I didn't want to be rude, but they were messing with my money. The two of them could carry on this conversation some other time. They both turned their heads toward the car. GiGi raised a finger to signal that they would only be a moment. I smacked my teeth. Luckily I was in the car and she was outside, so she didn't hear me do it. I know GiGi would've ripped into me for acting like a spoiled brat.

GiGi reached inside her purse and pulled out a wad of money. My eyes grew wide as I watched her count the bills and hand them over to Kyle. I was shocked to see Kyle take the offering with no hesitation and stuff it in his pocket. What was going on? Why would Kyle be taking money from my grandmother? I was certainly going to get to the bottom of this as soon as he got in the car—whenever that was. I leaned over and honked the horn again. This time I was less polite as I lay on it for several seconds, venting my frustration with the high-pitched noise. They both looked at me again. This time, they parted and began to walk down the steps of the porch. Finally! GiGi was the first one to approach the car. She tapped on my window. I pushed the button to roll down the window so I could hear what she had to say.

She leaned over. "Rain, be careful tonight. I wish I could be there with you, but you know I have a church meeting with the Ladies of Faith. You have the scarf?"

As soon as GiGi started speaking, my anger subsided. How could I stay mad at her when she had that soothing, nurturing voice? I loved my GiGi, and she was the only person on the planet that returned that love wholeheartedly; I was still working on Kyle.

"I understand, GiGi. You have your obligations and the

whole church would just fall apart if you weren't there to keep it going. I have the scarf. I'll be fine."

GiGi leaned further into the car and planted a warm kiss on my forehead. I smiled as I rolled the window back up. Kyle got into the driver's seat and started the car. I waved to my GiGi as we drove off. I looked at the clock again; it was already eight o'clock. I felt the anger rising inside me again.

"Just what was all that about?" I asked, glaring at Kyle with steely eyes.

"Rain, I told you GiGi and I needed to take of some business." Kyle offered no explanation.

"Well, what kind of business do you have that involves my grandmother paying you?"

"Rain, we've explained this to you before, and I'm not going to do it again right now. Like I said, we were handling some business and that's all you need to know. There's nothing going on that you don't already know about." Now he was speaking in some secret code. I hated when he did that, like I was a child who was incapable of understanding anything. Still, I could see that I wasn't going to get anywhere tonight, so I decided to drop it.

Kyle and I rode in the car in silence. I couldn't stand it. For the first time in a while, I felt slightly uncomfortable around my man, and the stillness was making it nearly unbearable. I leaned forward in my seat and pushed the knob to turn the radio on. Loraine Dubois's bluesy vocals blared through the speakers. I loved her. She was so soulful, just like me. We even had the same first name. From one artist to another, she'd earned my respect. Just as I was getting into the groove, Kyle cleared his throat loudly and turned the volume down a couple of notches.

"Rain," he said with a seriousness that seemed to foreshadow a lecture of some kind, "Before we go to the

Lounge, I want to make some things clear."

"Okay," I responded cautiously, wondering just what he was about to say.

"First, you will not be drinking tonight."

"What? Why?"

"You slipped those Long Islands past me last time. You know you shouldn't be drinking. You don't know how to handle yourself. It's hard enough keeping things under control when you're sober. Just do me that favor. No drinking."

"Okay, you are really tripping—"

He cut me off mid-sentence. "For me?"

Well that threw me all the way off. I was fully prepared to go into full-blown spoiled brat mode, bitching and moaning until I got my way, but those two little words made me change my mind. For him? Of course I would do it for him. I'd do anything for my man.

"Secondly," he continued, "We will leave right after your performance. Your episodes are starting to get more and more elaborate and they seem to last longer. I don't want to risk you having one while you're in a large crowd. It could be dangerous."

"Kyle!" I whined. He knew how much I loved to hear the other artists perform. I was in my element when I was at the Lounge. I was at home, with my family. All this over a few stupid visions?

"I'm serious, Rain. This is not up for negotiation."

I slouched in my seat, folding my arms across my chest and pouting like a child. Just because I was having dreams about my mother didn't mean I was in any danger. I wish he would stop treating me like some helpless, injured child. I guess I didn't have a choice but to go along with his demands. He was the man and he wore the pants in this relationship.

That was clear. With his point being made, Kyle turned the radio back up so Loraine Dubois could croon to us for the rest of the ride.

When we pulled up to the Lyrical Lounge, I could tell by the jammed-packed parking lot that the crowd was hot. That excited me. The more people, the better. Kyle opened my door for me and reached for my hand to assist me out of the car. I stepped out slowly, feeling like the star that I was. Kyle held onto my arm as we pushed past the poetry heads that filled the tiny smoke-filled space. When I spotted Malik near the stage, he waved me over.

"Go ahead," Kyle permitted.

I eased out of my jacket, revealing the decorative, silk scarf GiGi had left for me at the house last week. I ran my hands over the material and inhaled its floral fragrance. It was so smooth and beautiful. It went perfectly with my turquoise dress. After handing the jacket to Kyle, I slithered through the crowd that was blocking my path to the stage. When I finally reached Malik, I greeted him with a hug. "Peace."

"Peace, Rain. How are you?"

"I'm great. When am I on?"

"Well, you're kind of late. You missed the first round. I'll have to push you back to the nine o'clock spot," he said while looking down at his clipboard.

"Nine o'clock! Come on, Malik. I wasn't *that* late. At least give me the eight fifteen spot," I tried to reason.

"Rain, we talked about this. You are supposed to be one of our regulars. I agreed to make you a feature performer, but you're beginning to be unreliable. You didn't even show up last week. What happened to you?"

"Last week?" I frowned trying to remember what he was referring to.

"Yeah, last week. Thursday. Remember? The eight o'clock spot."

"I'm sorry, Malik. I had every intention of coming. I got caught up in something else," I said, still trying to remember the events of the past seven days. That was the day Danny and Maya had gotten into it.

"Yeah well, if you're gonna be a feature, you have to show up—on time," he scolded.

"I know, I know. Just give me one more shot. *Please*, I'll show you. Put me on next, and I promise I won't let you down. I've got something hot. You'll see."

Malik shook his head as he considered my request. "Alright. I'll put you on, but you better be good for it," he warned.

"Thanks, man." I smiled and threw my arms around him, giving him a small peck on the cheek. I quickly scanned my surroundings to see if Kyle had witnessed the gesture of affection. I didn't want to make him jealous. After spotting him at a small table near the door, I was able to confirm that he was busy checking out the menu and not focused on me. I waited patiently by the stage as Honey, another regular, spit the last of her lines. She was just okay. I didn't really get too much into that depressing stuff. You know, spoken word about abuse and neglect. That wasn't my thing, but the crowd seemed to eat it up as they snapped their fingers and shouted words of encouragement her way.

When she was done, Malik ascended the stage and announced my name. Prompted by my introduction, I climbed the three side steps to the stage, feeling strong. This was my time to shine. I looked behind me and cued the musician to start the rhythmic play of the bongos. He knew how I liked it. Before starting, I ran my hands over the scarf one last time and threw the hanging right side over my left shoulder so it wrapped around my neck. The scent it gave off was intoxicating and familiar. I wanted to keep it close, so I could smell it during my performance. I knew it would make my lines flow that much better.

THE ULTIMATE FANTASY

Multiply me times an intimate number of fantasies
You, the lover of my life
The hierarchy of my dreams—control me
I am your love slave—your machine
Program me into the delight of your life—command me

Blindfolded, eager for heights of indefinite measures
He worshiped my body in pleasurable places
He knows what I can't see allows me to enjoy it ever *more*
freely
The hierarchy of my dreams—he controls me

"Open your hand," he commanded.
Traced heart shaped kisses in my palm with his tongue
Wet circles surrounded tingling fingertips
Pushed digital buttons until my nerves went numb
I was his love slave—his machine

"Open your mouth," he commanded.
My King fed me succulent fruit
Greedy lips salivated sticky with desire
Cream dripped down my chin, from neck to breast
He programmed me—I let him command me

He closed my mind of apprehension
Stripped away tension with masculine precision
"Open your heart!" he roared.
He loved me so deep
He made my soul weep

* * *

I inhaled deeply between each stanza. I couldn't get enough of that smell. It filled me up and lifted me into a world of tranquil bliss. GiGi was on the mark with this one. As I recited my last line, the crowd erupted in thunderous applause and sharp finger snapping. Yeah, I definitely killed it. I looked out amongst the poetry heads. Not surprisingly, I didn't see Carmen or Danny. I'd decided to just give up on them. When my eyes traveled to the back of the room, to the table near the door, my breathing stopped.

"Thank you, Rain for giving us what we love." Malik's smoker's voice bolted through his handheld mic. I knew that I should have been making my way off the stage, but my feet wouldn't move. Frozen with apprehension and shock, I stared intently at my mother as she sat at the small table opposite Kyle. Her black eyes were unmistakable. What was she doing here? Why *then*, when I was in public? Why was she haunting me?

"Rain must be thinking about giving us an encore," Malik added when he noticed that I wasn't moving.

The crowd began to chant, "Encore" in response to the suggestion. My mother waved at me in the distance. I lifted a slow and unsteady hand in the air to return the gesture. The audience continued to urge me on for a repeat performance, but I couldn't speak. Kyle stood abruptly and waved his hands wildly in the air, signaling for me to come to him. I couldn't. My mother blew me a kiss and smiled sweetly. I wondered whether Kyle could see her. She was right there. So real. So solid. He continued to wave.

"Rain, you alright?" Malik placed his hand over the mic and whispered in my ear. He slightly nudged me on the shoulder when he got no response.

Kyle began to make his way toward the stage, pushing aggressively past each person that stood in his path. I didn't want him to come up on the stage and embarrass me. I knew I had to move.

"Uh … yeah, I'm cool," I finally managed to say to Malik, "No encore tonight though. Peace." I quickly shuffled off the stage, tripping on the last step. Kyle caught me before I toppled over. Immediately, I found some comfort in his embrace, though not enough to calm my nerves.

"Rain, what's going on?" he asked with a concerned expression.

I looked frantically between him and my mother, who was still sitting at the small table near the door. She, too, bore a look of unease at the sight of my visible anxiety.

"Rain?" Kyle asked again.

"She's here … I … you … you can't see her?" I stammered, trying desperately to formulate some comprehensible words.

"Who, Rain? Who's here? What are you talking about?" He helped me to stand upright, but he kept his hold on me.

"My mother!" I screamed at him, "My mother! She's right over there. She's sitting at your table!" Unexpected tears began to roll down my face.

Kyle sighed loudly. "It's time to go, Rain. I was afraid this was going to happen."

"No, you don't understand! She's there. I can see her

face! Why am I starting to see her face? She's coming back to me. She's coming back," I cried, doubling over in anguish.

Kyle didn't speak as he guided me gently back to the table. If anyone else in the lounge noticed my outburst, they didn't let on. Either that, or I wasn't paying attention. To me, there was no one else in that entire place except me, my mother, and Kyle. I kept my eyes locked on hers as we grew nearer. Half of me didn't want to approach her. I didn't want to get that close. This was new to me, only the second time I've encountered her presence so clearly, and I didn't know how to react. The other half of me wanted to rush into her arms and allow her to give me the motherly affection I so longed for, but didn't realize I needed until now. The fear and longing bubbled up inside me like boiling water, sending my insides into a frenzy. My heart was racing at an immeasurable pace, and my stomach fluttered with what seemed to be bird-sized butterflies. The walk to the table was a long one. At each step, I said a small prayer for some sanity—normalcy. It didn't work.

When we finally reached our destination, my mother smiled at me. She reached her arms out to me for a hug. My heart stopped.

"Here, let me get your coat," Kyle offered as he grabbed my jacket off the back of the chair.

Ignoring him, I leaned in to get closer to my mother. As I came nearer, arms outstretched, the floral scent of cherry blossoms and lilies surrounded me. It was the same fragrance I smelled in the scarf I was wearing, the scarf GiGi gave me. The closer I got to my mother, the more overpowering the scent became. It was her scent—my mother's perfume.

Kyle caught me right before I could touch her face, right before I could wrap my arms around my mother. "It's time to go, Rain," he said sternly as he hooked his arm around my waist and began to pull me toward him. I couldn't let him take that moment from me. I couldn't allow him to steal her presence, leaving me dissatisfied and incomplete. Not this time. I needed to touch her. I had to connect with her. He wasn't going to stop me.

"No!" I screamed. I clawed desperately at the arm wrapped tightly around my waist. My mother's warm smile transitioned to a look of despair. Kyle tightened his grasp and used his other arm to lift me slightly. "No!" I screamed again.

"Rain, calm down."

The people in the crowd turned to stare at us with astonishment, but I didn't care. I had to touch her. I had to. I kicked my legs wildly and began flailing my arms in hopes of catching Kyle's face with a blow. I felt him flinch and duck to avoid contact with my arms and hands as I swung them backward. My mother shook her head slowly and returned her arms to her sides. I sobbed loudly and continued to scream as I realized she was fading. She was leaving me again.

"Let me go! She's leaving me. I can't let her leave me," I shrieked.

With his free hand, Kyle struggled to grab both our jackets, which had fallen to the floor during our struggle. I felt the anxiety and rage drain slowly from my body as my mother disappeared before my eyes. I stopped resisting and grew silent. Only a periodic sniffle accompanied my tears.

"Is she okay?" Malik was standing by my side, looking to Kyle for some form of explanation for my frantic spasm.

"She's fine, man. I'm really sorry about this. I thought I would be able to get her out of here before anything happened. I left her medication in the car," Kyle explained.

"Medication? What's wrong with her?" Malik asked.

"Aw, don't worry about it, man. It's nothing. She'll be perfectly fine next week."

Malik didn't respond. He stared at me with pity in his eyes. I didn't know if he would even want me back next week, or any week after that, behind this mess. I felt defeated and tired. I just wanted to go home. I allowed Kyle to guide my steps and control my movement. He let me go only for a moment to help me put on my jacket. After I slipped my arms through the sleeves, I stole another whiff of the scarf. I held it there under my nose for a few seconds, secretly hoping it would bring her back. Kyle took my arm and walked me outside.

We rode most of the way home in silence. I closed my eyes and rested my head back on the headrest, letting the rhythm of the tires' rotation over the bumpy freeway lull me to sleep.

She barged through the door, just as she had done before. This time the man had the gun lodged in her mother's mouth. The little girl had come just in time to see him pull the trigger. She was just in time to see her mother's eyes roll to the back of her head right before her blood sprayed the wall behind her and her body dropped heavily, lifelessly to the floor.

My eyes suddenly popped opened. I was beginning to remember!

11 *Carmen* / *Wednesday, April 27th*

I sit here and hold the phone's receiver loosely in my hand. The earpiece barely makes contact with my ear, and the mouthpiece dangles below my chin. What in the hell is this dude talking about on the other end? I mean, I've been doing this phone sex thing for about a year now and I've been a good sport, but these guys are just lame. When you're reduced to calling a sex line to get your rocks off because you can't get some pussy on your own, it's just pathetic. Don't get me wrong, I've enjoyed my job up until this point, but the freaks that call 1-900-WETGIRLS are something else. It's getting harder to bear with each passing day. The fact that I'm making real money with my man makes this shit an unnecessary evil. I know I won't be doing it that much longer.

"Ooh, baby, I just wanna suck your pussy until it bleeds."

Is he serious? Suck it until it bleeds? Does that sound remotely close to something that would feel good to any woman? That one doesn't even deserve a response. I keep quiet while I sit in the love seat, leaning my elbow on the armrest.

"Then, when I get done with you, I wanna swallow your piss." He moans—I cringe. "Yeah I wanna taste that sweet, hot piss running down my throat. Uh ... oh shit ... damn, I'm about to cum ..." He makes a deep gurgling sound followed by what I think to be a growl.

I gag and quickly place a hand over my mouth, attempting to keep the bile from rising into my throat. I fight hard to keep down the vodka and E cocktail I drank just an hour before, but it starts to creep slowly up on me, coating my tongue. I slam the phone down hard on its cradle before the pervert on the other end has the chance to provoke anymore unwanted bodily reactions. I run to the bathroom with both hands cupping my mouth, reaching the toilet just in time to spit up clear liquid. I guess it was a false alarm, because I could have sworn I was about to completely empty my insides. Now I *know* that I'm done with that job.

I tear a small piece of toilet paper from the roll and use it to wipe my mouth. After standing over the sink and gargling some water to rid my tongue of the fresh taste of vomit, I take a moment to stare at my image in the mirror. I look tired. Dark circles surround my eyes, and my face seems to sag a little. I place my hands on my temples and pull the skin back tightly to give myself an instant facelift. I've been up for about two days straight now. Jay-Jay has me working around the clock, and I need to be sure I can keep up with the workload, so I stay doped up on E. I'm able to sneak in a nap here and there, but they never last longer than thirty minutes. That man has me on the grind. If we aren't making runs, picking up money or dropping off packages, I'm on a date with a customer serving him up some of this good pussy—and it *is* good. I have these dudes going crazy over this wet box. They've been talking about me so much out here on the streets that Jay-Jay had to up the prices. He says I'm his star player and I deserve a raise. Damn right! I deserve every penny I get, too. I don't mind that Jay takes most of it, leaving me with about a quarter of the small fortune I earn with each trick. He takes good care of me. How else would he be able to do that if he wasn't getting paid? He buys the sexy clothes I wear to accentuate my curvaceous body. He keeps me looking good. He pays for every meal, and the dope is plentiful. I find myself pill popping constantly, washing it down with straight vodka. I can't even remember the last time I've been sober. Jay-Jay has been watching me like a hawk, making sure I'm putting in the necessary work to maintain my spot as his girl. I do what I have to do to please my man and stay in his good graces. I'm a good girl for Daddy. I'm yearning to see him *bad* today. No work, just me and my baby.

I hear the shrill tone of my cell phone ringing in the living room, and I run out of the bathroom to get it before the call goes to voicemail. I have a feeling it's my man, and I wouldn't dare miss his call. I stumble over a pair of Rain's shoes on the way. Damn her for being alive and causing me to almost fall flat on my face. After regaining my balance, I reach the phone before the third ring finishes.

"Hello?" I answer between heavy breaths.

"Yeah, baby. Where you at? I need you." Jay sounds sexy as usual. His voice induces inappropriate thoughts and a subsequent wetness between my legs within seconds.

"Well, you know I'm here for you, Daddy. I really want

to see you. I tried calling you earlier, but you didn't answer. Where were you?"

"Don't question me. Just have yo' ass ready in fifteen minutes. I'll honk when I'm outside," he says quickly, before hanging up the phone.

I rush back to the bathroom to fix myself up before he gets here. Lord knows I can't keep him waiting because I'm primping in the mirror. I don't even have time to flat iron my hair! I throw some water on my face and pull my hair back into a neat, tight ponytail. Quickly, I smear a light coat of foundation on my face, taking a little more time to cover the circles around my eyes. I stick my finger down into my panties to do a quick swipe and check. Yep, I'm fresh. I don't want to work today, but I know Jay will probably want some ass, and I never deny him that. He's my man and I give him whatever he wants, whenever he wants it. Just as I pop the last E pill from my small stash, I hear a car horn blaring outside the house. I trot out of the bathroom and swoop my purse up off the back of the dinette chair. As I run down the stairs, I pray silently that Kyle will not hear me outside his door and I will be able to creep past him without interruption. The thought of him coming out to try to stop me again makes me slow my pace and tiptoe down the last couple of steps before unlocking and opening the front door carefully and closing it behind me softly.

When I approach Jay-Jay's SUV, parked parallel to the curb in front of the house, I can see that someone is in the back seat. As I reach for the passenger door handle, Jay rolls the window down before I start to get in.

"Get in the back," he orders.

Confused and somewhat intrigued, I open the back door instead. The backseat passenger scoots over to make room for me. I slam the door shut.

"Carmen, this here is my man, Rod. Say hi."

"Hi, Rod," I say with a smile.

"What up," he replies, biting his bottom lip and looking me up and down with unforgiving intensity.

Jay-Jay continues, "He just got out of prison last night and I told him I'd hook him up. Give him some head, baby."

"But Jay, baby, I didn't think I was gonna have to work today. Remember we were just supposed to chill," I whine, avoiding eye contact with Rod.

"We are gonna chill today and this ain't work. You ain't getting paid for this one. It's a favor for a friend. Do it for Daddy, baby, and then it's just me and you." He's talking to my reflection in the rearview mirror. I twist up my face in defiance.

"Carmen!" he barks, "Remember what the fuck we talked about. If you gonna be my girl, you need to prove your worth. Now, I'm not gonna ask you again ..."

Damn, I think I've proved myself enough already! I'd been proving myself for the last couple of weeks. I want it to be just me and him. When will it be just me and my man? In my desperation, I begin to reason with myself.

He takes care of me. If not for Jay, I wouldn't have any money. I wouldn't have shit but Danny and Rain ... and GiGi. He promised to make me his. I need that. He is the man, the biggest dope boy in the D. I have to do what I have to do to claim my spot.

"Okay," I concede, turning toward Rod. His pants are unzipped and his dick is in his hands. This bastard doesn't waste any time. Jay-Jay pulls off just as I lean my head down and go to work.

"Don't get no cum on my seats. Use that towel back there," Jay-Jay continues to give directions from the front.

When we're done, Jay-Jay pulls in front of a beat-down house on the eastside. He lets Rod out of the car.

I remain silent, looking straight ahead as they speak. The smile stretched widely across Rod's face, along with the air of cockiness in his walk, lets on that he's satisfied with the services he has received. I don't always want to do it, but I must say, I do take pride in my work. It's becoming clear that I'm unmatched in the sex game. Like I always say, I do what I do, and I do it well.

"Get in the front," Jay-Jay says.

I slide out from the back seat of the truck and re-enter from the passenger side. Jay-Jay places his hand on the back of my neck and starts to massage it. It feels good. I let the sensual movement of his fingers lull me into a state of relaxation. His touch is like magic, and he's playing tricks on my body.

"Good girl," he coos. "That's a good girl."

"You know I'll do anything for you, Daddy," I reply, leaning my head back with my eyes closed.

Suddenly he tightens his grip at the back of my neck and begins to squeeze until I squeal in pain. I try to reach behind me and force his hand away from my neck, but I'm not strong enough to pry his fingers loose. He shakes me twice and I shriek again.

"Let's get some shit straight, *Carmen*," he starts, "I don't like games and it seems like you've been playing games with me."

"What ... what are you talking about?" I ask in the softest most submissive voice I can produce under the pressure.

"You fucking disappeared on me for three days. Three fucking days! I don't like that shit, Carmen. I don't like having to look for you."

"Jay-Jay, baby, I'm sorry. Whenever you call, I'm there. Whenever you need me, you got me."

"Then where the fuck were you? Huh? I even stopped by your house and some square ass nigga answered the door and started asking me a bunch of questions. Who the fuck was that?"

"Oh, that must have been Kyle. He lives downstairs. When was *that*? He didn't even tell me."

"The day before yesterday. I didn't want to draw any attention to myself so I played it cool, but that nigga got one more time to get in my face about some bullshit."

Jay-Jay was still holding my neck with one hand while he worked the steering wheel with the other. "What did he say?" I ask.

"Asking me who I was and what I was doing with you. Who the fuck is *he*?" Jay-Jay is just an octave below yelling.

"He's nobody. He lives in the lower level of the flat. My grandmother hired him to be a caregiver for my crazy-ass sister, but he goes overboard with that shit, trying to control me and Danny too. That's all. He's harmless, really. I mean, you saw him, he can't do shit anyway. He's just nosy."

"Well, you better check that nigga, before I have somebody else do it." Jay-Jay finally releases my neck. I rub it with my hand to soothe the burning pain. "Wait, you said your sister and Danny? You ain't never tell me about anybody else living with you."

"Oh yeah, just my stupid brother and sister, Danny and Rain. We all live on the upper level."

"Rain?"

"Yeah, Rain. She's the baby. I can't stand her ass either. That bitch drives me crazy with her stuck-up, helpless ass."

"Tell me about her."

At Jay-Jay's strange request, I turn toward him to see a quizzical look on his face. The slight furrow in his brow indicates that he's thinking about something that he doesn't care to share.

"Umm … well, there's not that much to tell. She's a lame-ass poet. Not much to look at. Shy, weak, annoying. Oh, and she crazy as all hell. Panic attacks, delusions, the works. That's why Kyle is there. That about sums it up." I keep it short and sweet, not knowing where he is going with his line of questioning. "Why do you want to know?" I ask with a twinge of jealousy.

"Don't worry about all that. I just wanna know." He quickly dismisses my inquiry.

"Well, like I said, she's a lame. She wouldn't be into this shit. She's a straight-up square. Always having some kind of emotional breakdown. She couldn't hang in my line of work." I try to deter his attention away from my baby sister.

"Well, you never know what people would be into when they're presented with the opportunity. I want you to bring Rain to me. I want to meet her."

"Why, Jay-Jay? I told you she ain't into this shit. She won't do it. We don't even get along." I'm almost pleading. The thought of my man showing attention to another woman, especially Rain, is beginning to make me sick to my stomach. Why is he asking for Rain? I don't like this shit at all.

He snaps his head in my direction and glares at me. "Bitch, what the fuck I tell you about questioning me?" His sudden change in tone makes me jump in my seat. I don't say anything in response. The more time I spend with the Jay, the easier it is to decipher what to say and when not to say anything at all. "Just do what I said, and shut the fuck up."

I nod in compliance. He softens his harsh tone to just above a whisper. "That's my girl," he purrs at me. "That's why I love you."

My heart flutters at those last three words. He said he loved me. I can die right here and now, a happy woman. My world is now complete. I just know that Jay-Jay is the man I'm going to marry. I won't be turning tricks for the rest of my life. It will only be a little while longer, and we will be running these streets together. I smile to myself at those visions of a blissful future in my mind.

"I love you too, baby." I say those words with conviction. I know I mean them; I've found the man of my dreams.

"Let's hit the mall and get you some new clothes."

That makes me perk up in my seat. I clap my hands like a kid who was just told that Christmas will be coming around for a second time this year. He always knows what to do to make me feel good. He says the right words, has the right touch, and he *loves* me. I push the idea of bringing Rain to meet him out of my mind for the moment. No need to worry about that shit until it's time to do it. For the moment, it's all about my man and me. Everything else is irrelevant.

12 *Danny* / Friday, April 29th

*D*AMN, *what time is it?* I think to myself as I roll over on the couch. I stretch my arms and blink my eyes open, trying to shake the sleep-induced disorientation from my brain. I struggle to sit up on the couch, almost toppling off the side onto the floor. When I finally do get up, I immediately want to lie back down. My head feels heavy and my body feels sluggish. I sit for a few moments, silent and still, trying to regain composure and figure out what day and time it is.

"Rain!" I call out as loudly as my banging head will allow. I'm sick of these migraines. I don't receive a response. "Carmen!" I holler, half hoping she doesn't respond. Nothing but silence answers my call. I'm alone, and I'm not too sure if I'm happy about that. I reach over to the coffee table to retrieve the remote control. When I tap the "Info" button, the screen illuminates, displaying April 29th, 8 p.m. Damn! It's eight o'clock in the evening? Where in the hell did the day go? I must have been sleeping all day, so why am I so damn tired? This is one of the rare moments I'm happy I no longer have a job. Well, I'm always happy not to have to punch a clock and answer to some power-hungry idiot who micro-manages my every move.

I stretch again before standing up and easing to the bathroom. Maybe splashing some cold water on my face will wake me up. Something has to work, because I feel like a zombie rising from the dead. I turn the faucet on, letting the water run for a few seconds before submerging my cupped hands. Before I can splash the water on my face, I hear a knock at the door. Carmen or Rain must have left the lower-level front door unlocked, allowing someone to walk up the stairs to the upper flat—dumb asses. It can only be one of two people, Maya or GiGi. Maya knows better than to come without calling or an invitation, so I'm hoping it's not her. I'm in no condition to have to teach her a lesson today. Then again, I'm not in the mood to hear GiGi's nagging either. For a moment, I consider not answering the door at all. If I stay quiet, no one will know I'm here anyway. I go about my business, dousing my face with a hefty amount of cold water. As soon as I turn the faucet off, the knocks echo through the house again.

"I know you're in there." I hear Kyle's voice resounding from the other side of the door. How in the hell does he know anything, and what in the hell does he want?

"Rain's not here." I poke my head out the bathroom and yell toward the closed door, hoping he will go away. He should know that anyway. He's supposed to be keeping an eye on her, and he's doing a fucked up job, if you ask me. If he keeps his focus on his client and stays out of everyone else's business, maybe he'll be more effective. I understand Kyle taking the big brother role with all three of us, but Carmen and I are grown and, more importantly, sane. We don't need his overbearing ass clocking our every move like we're at some kind of boarding school. Sometimes I can't stand him. I mean he's cool and all, and I know he means well, but the dude is just plain annoying. I find myself sneaking out the house sometimes just so I won't have to answer his interrogation. "Where ya going, Danny? What time ya coming back? Where is Maya? Don't walk, I'll take you." I just want to smack that permanent smile clean off his face. Maybe he is the one that needs a caretaker instead of Rain.

"Open up," he yells.

He's being persistent, and I know I'll have to give in. He has a key to the place, so I would lose the front door stand-off anyway. I start to walk out of the bathroom, but trip on the long black cord of Carmen's flat iron sitting on the counter. Once again, she left them plugged-up, despite constant reminders from both Rain and me to put them up after she's done using them. "Dammit!" I curse her carelessness as I yank the cord out of the wall and throw the hot flat iron into the drawer just below the sink. I wish Carmen was standing right here so I could hit her with the damn things.

I walk slowly to the door, dragging my feet. No one is going to rush me. I still have a few ounces of power left, even when I'm being coerced into doing something I don't want to do. When I reach the door, I unlock and open it just a crack.

"What, Kyle?" I ask with a monotone pitch of disinterest.

"You okay in there? You've been knocked out all day. I came up when I heard your footsteps from downstairs."

"How do you know I was knocked out all day?" I ask suspiciously.

"Well, I hadn't seen or heard from you, Rain, or Carmen all day. I got a little worried, so I came on in at about two and saw you passed out on the couch. I came up again at about five, and you were in the same position. I checked your pulse and temperature to make sure you were alright, then I left."

I'm growing increasingly annoyed with each passing second, "Look Kyle, we appreciate you looking out for us and all, but GiGi hired you to take care of *Rain*. Carmen and I were not a part of the contract, so why don't you lay the fuck off? Coming into our home uninvited is taking it way too far. Don't be surprised if you sneak your happy ass up in here one day and find a pistol pointed at your head."

"Whoa, Danny," Kyle starts, while pushing the door open a little more so he can see my entire face and body. I push back in resistance. "You have a gun in here?"

"Uh … no. I was just speaking hypothetically. You know you just need to be more careful before you come all up in people houses … you know." I struggle to produce a believable lie. I know I'm failing miserably. I silently curse myself for slipping up and letting on about the gun. Kyle pauses for a few seconds, contemplating my words. I take advantage of the opportunity that the pause presents me with and use my full body weight to try to push the door closed in his face. But he moves too quickly, wedging his foot in the opening between the door and the wall. I lean against the door, pushing it with all of the strength I can muster, but it doesn't budge.

"Danny, I'm coming in," he says in that authoritative

tone I hate. He gives one hard push that sends me stumbling backward.

"Asshole!" I yell, trying to catch my balance.

He charges through the door, looking around frantically like he's a police dog on a drug bust. "Where is it, Danny? Where's the gun?"

I smirk at him. If he thinks it's going to be that easy for me to give it up, he must be high on something. We stand facing each other, Kyle by the door and me in front of him. I shrug my shoulders to further agitate and tease him. He begins charging through the house, opening up cabinet doors, flipping over couch cushions, and lifting the mattresses on the beds. I stay in place, laughing as I watch him lose his breath and his sanity as he rips the house apart in search of a gun that he's not sure exists.

He pauses, looking at me determinately with his chest heaving up and down. "Where's the gun, Danny?" He says it slowly as if a change of cadence will evoke a different reaction. I flip him the bird. He's standing in the living room with me, just inches away. When I see him turn his head back toward the coat closet near the front door, I hold my breath. He begins to walk, almost stomping, toward the closet. I reach out quickly to grab his arm, but I'm only able to catch the end of his sleeve.

"I told you, there ain't no gun in here. Why don't you just go!" I yell.

Kyle shakes off my grasp and continues toward the closet. I shuffle behind him, then run in front of him to reach the door before he does. I jump in front of the closet and spread my arms out over the width of the door to serve as a barrier.

"Move, Danny. I don't want to have to use excessive force with you."

"If you touch me, I'll kick yo' ass, then I'll tell GiGi, and she'll fire your ass. So go ahead," I answer, while I try and fail to catch my breath.

He laughs. "I doubt that. I'm sure she'll understand." Kyle's firm grip pries my arm away from the door as he gently, but sternly pushes me away. Defeated, I watch as he shuffles through the coats, hats, and gloves that line the closet. When he reaches up and starts to feel around on the top shelf in the back corner, I can feel the panic filling my insides. I rush to Kyle's side and try to pull his arms down. He's unaffected, continuing to dig through the rubble of umbrellas, hats, gloves, and scarves. When his hands land on the red shoebox in the upper right corner, he shoots me a look that promises trouble. I step back, knowing there is nothing else I can do now to avoid the inevitable. Kyle lifts the top off the shoebox and reveals the 9mm's hiding place. He removes the gun from the box slowly and takes a few steps back.

"Where did you get this, Danny?" he asks, unloading the bullets from the clip.

I don't answer. I wouldn't dare reveal my source. Maya hooked me up with her cousin, who gave me the gun for a good price. All it took was some haggling and convincing with Rain and Carmen, and I had the three hundred dollars to pay for it in no time. If I tell Kyle that, he'll probably tell GiGi and they'd snitch about the illegal firearm for sure. I keep my lips clamped together.

"You know, it doesn't even matter. I'm turning it in to the police station right now, and you're coming with me." He continues to inspect the gun. "Have you used this on anyone? Tell the truth. I don't want to go into this blindly."

"Are you asking me if I'm a murderer, Kyle? No, I haven't used it on anyone," I reply, slightly disappointed that

I didn't get a chance to pop off at least one dude that got out of pocket. Damn, maybe I should've shot Tone's ass in the parking lot that day. At least I would've gotten my money's worth.

"Good, let's go."

"Kyle, I need that gun to protect my little sisters. What are we supposed to do?"

"Don't give me that mess, Danny. I have a feeling this is for your recreation, and it has nothing to do with Rain and Carmen's safety."

I twist my face sarcastically. "I'm not going anywhere. If you wanna save the world by taking one gun off the street, then do it by yourself."

"That's where you're wrong. You *are* coming with me. I don't trust you. I need to keep an eye on you."

"You don't trust *me*? What the fuck are you talking about, Kyle? You already took the damn gun! Whatchu think I'm gonna do now? Huh? Damn, you treat us like we're kids. You and GiGi. I'm not Rain! I don't need your supervision. Do what the hell GiGi paid you for and worry about her ass. Leave me out of it."

"Danny—"

I step back and throw my hands in the air. "Look, Kyle. I'm not going anywhere anyway, okay. I don't have anywhere to go and I don't have any way to get there. So don't worry about me. Just leave me alone. I'll be here when you get back." He's really starting to wear on the last few nerves I have left, and I'm about to lose it.

"I'm too tired to fight with you right now, and I don't feel like trying to get you under control. Stay put! I will be right back, and I *will* check to make sure you're still here."

"Under control? Whatever," I mumble as I make my way back to the couch in the living room. I don't care about anything he's saying at the moment, and I decide not to dedicate any more of my precious time listening. I plop down on the couch and use the remote control to turn up the volume on the TV. I hear the door open and shut as Kyle finally leaves me in peace. Just because Rain's ass is crazy doesn't mean he needs to take my gun.

About ten minutes into a History Channel show about Skinheads, I feel my phone's vibration in my pants pocket. Confused, I look at Jay-Jay's name flashing across the screen. I know this dude wouldn't be calling me. Better yet, I don't have his name programmed into my phone and he doesn't have my number. At the sound of the third ring, it dawns on me that I'm looking at Carmen's phone instead of my own. I'm clueless as to how we could've gotten our phones mixed up. The way that girl guards that thing, you'd think she would have it surgically attached so she wouldn't miss his call. The ringing stops and I'm prompted to look for my own phone, realizing that I haven't had any communication with the outside world all day. That means Maya's number should be filling my call log by now. Before I can get up to start my search, Carmen's phone rings for a second time. It's Jay-Jay—*again*. I toss the idea of answering the call around in my head for several seconds before finally deciding to pick it up. I push the "Talk" button on the cell phone.

"Yo." I hope I come across as brash as I want him to perceive.

"Yeah, who is this?"

"This is Danny. What the fuck you want?"

Jay-Jay laughs a harsh chuckle. "Danny, huh? Well this is—"

"Jay, yeah I know. You didn't answer my question," I snarl.

"You something else. You a real hard-ass, huh?" He

chuckles some more.

I don't see shit funny about this low-life running my sister into the ground then talking to me like we were supposed to be the best of friends. I want to jump through the phone and whoop his ass right now.

"Listen real good. Stay the fuck away from my little sister. You ain't doing shit for her but making her more fucked up than she already is. I'll kill you before I let you ruin her."

"Your little sister, huh? Isn't that sweet. Well *Danny*, your little sister is all grown up. I can personally attest to that. She makes her own decisions, as I'm sure you know, so get used to me, baby. I'll be around for a long time." His tone makes my stomach twist into knots.

"Yeah, you'll be around until you meet me, nigga. You think I'm playing? I don't like people fucking with my family. So, you better pray you don't run into me." Yeah it's a little bit of a bluff. Since Kyle took my pistol, my confidence level in eliminating this dude has dropped drastically, but I continue to play hard, like I have a death wish with his name on it.

He laughs again. He's really starting to piss me off. What the hell is so funny? "You're really serious with this shit, huh? I mean you actually believe that you can protect your little sister from me? This shit is hilarious. Now I can say that I've seen and heard it all. Go on 'head, do what you gotta do. I'm sure we'll be seeing each other soon, and when we do, I'll be ready for yo' punk ass. Let's hope you got the balls to match that big-ass mouth of yours." Jay chuckles again before he ends the call abruptly, leaving me to yell my obscenities into dead air. I hate him. I hate everything about him, and I don't even know him. Shit, I know enough. I know that he's a low-life criminal that's using my sister for his financial gain, sucking her deeper into addiction. I don't know if I could actually bring myself to kill him, but he deserves something harsh and painful for his actions, and I will be more than happy to be the one to deliver it.

Jay-Jay's call distracts me, but not for long; I still need to find my phone. I use Carmen's phone to call my own. I hear it ringing in my bedroom. I hop up from the couch and follow the shrill ring to the dresser that sits opposite my bed. After checking the missed calls, a smile creeps across my face. Maya is a good girl; she called seven times. The thought of her loyalty makes me want to see her right now. I love my baby.

"Hello?" Maya's voice stirs something in me, and not just below the waist. She sounds sleepy, like I had just awakened her from a nap. I picture her lying on her back in her queen-sized bed, wearing a sexy black teddy. I wish I was there to take it off.

"Hey, baby. I'll be there in a minute."

"I've been waiting to see you all day. I've been calling."

"Yeah, I know. I was sleeping. I'm on my way out the door now though. I'll be there in about fifteen minutes."

"Okay, baby." She sits silently, waiting for me to end the call. She always waits for me to hang up first. It's a cute little tradition of ours, one that was created at my suggestion. I tap the "End" button on the phone and head toward the door. I know I have to be funky; lying around the house all day must have taken a toll on my hygiene. But I'm too anxious to see my woman; I'll just shower at her house. I did make a promise to Kyle to stay put until he comes back from the police station, but who cares about what he wants any damn way? Not me. Like I told him before, I'm not Rain, and until I miraculously morph into her fragile ass, he need not worry himself with my business. Still, I look cautiously through the crack in the front door to make sure he isn't pulling up as I walk out. The coast is clear. I start my fifteen-minute stroll to Maya's.

At 8:30 p.m., there are just a few minutes separating the smoky gray dusk from complete darkness. I know my 'hood, so I'm pretty comfortable walking the streets of Sherwood Forest without the fear of someone fucking with me; they all know better anyway. I'm carrying a change of clothes inside a plastic bag hanging from my right hand. Once I shower at Maya's I'll be able to peel off these dirty clothes and get into something more comfortable.

As I round the corner, the wind begins to blow fiercely as if it's warning me to turn around and make my way back home. I put my right hand over my eyebrows as a visor to shield my eyes from the gusts of wind that whip past my face. Near silence accompanies the blanket of darkness that surrounds me. Not even crickets sing out in the night as I trudge my way to Maya's. The only sound is the whispering howl of the harsh wind cutting through the air. As I approach the next block, the corner liquor store comes into view. Without the lights of the neon signs that border the windows, the store looks more like a small prison with its barred windows and doors. Those Arabs are so afraid that somebody is going to break into their precious store and take something, they'd probably rather have the box-shaped building serve as a prison so they can keep us under watch. I have to fight the urge to pick up a large rock and throw it through the front window, just to spite the arrogant mutha fuckas. It isn't worth it though. I would just be proving them right, and I won't dare give them the satisfaction.

As the wind calms down a little, I'm able to lower my hand from my brow and relax it by my side. Suddenly the boisterous sound of laughter echoes through the alley that lines the street on the right side of the store. Almost immediately, I become defensive, straightening my back and squinting to focus. I slow my pace and look around me as I pass the store and approach the entryway to the alley. As I grow closer, I can decipher the voices of a group of men, young and obnoxious.

"Did you see that nigga? Man, I thought he was gonna shit in his pants?"

"Hell yeah, Mike you an ole scary-ass nigga. I was waitin' for you to start calling fo' yo' mama or something." The group burst into laughter.

"Man, shut the fuck up. I ain't see y'all doing shit. I was the only one with the balls to step to that nigga. Everybody else was actin' like some pussies."

I stop just short of the opening to the alley as I silently curse Kyle for robbing me of my pistol, leaving me unarmed and vulnerable.

"Pussies? Nigga you wouldn't know a pussy if one was sittin' on yo face," one of the guys shouts in a high-pitched voice that suggests he's barely into his teen years.

"Y'all know this dude is a virgin right?" another one joins in on the teasing.

"Hell yeah, Tone. Why you think his right arm so big. It ain't from lifting. It's from jacking his dick every night 'cause he can't get none," another one responds. They all break out into another fit of laughter.

Tone? The sound of his name makes my face contort like I've just smelled something funky. I don't know how many of them are standing in the alley, but if my last encounter with Tone and his crew is any indicator, I know there are at least four of them.

"Ay, pass that bottle. You been babysitting that shit all night."

That's Tone, by now I can recognize his scratchy voice easily, and it puts me on edge. I ball my fists by my sides and clench my teeth.

I pivot slowly and do an about-face. Facing the opposite direction, I take my first step, careful not to make a sound. I keep my right arm stretched out in front of me to ensure that the plastic bag with my clothes won't hit anything in my path. I look behind me to make sure I'm not being followed, but with my eyes diverted, I fail to detect the tin can in front of my left foot. The can goes flying until it crashes into the brick wall of the liquor store. I freeze, hoping that the loud noise will go unnoticed by those I'm trying to evade.

The group of guys fall silent for several seconds. I hold my breath and survey my surroundings quickly for a makeshift weapon—nothing. I hear the hushed whispers of Tone and his boys as they shuffle toward the end of the alley where I stand.

"Who is that?" one of them calls out.

Instinctively, I turn my head, revealing my identity. *Shit!* Six young thugs stare back at me.

Tone exclaims, "Get that bitch!"

Not again. I can't understand why these homo-thugs wanna keep fuckin' with me.

Panicked, I drop my plastic bag and start to run full speed down the block. Within seconds, they're all close on my heels. I try to pick up the pace, but my legs are failing me. I can hear their heavy breathing and even heavier footsteps as they close in on the distance between us. Suddenly, I feel the weight of someone's hand grasping my shoulder from behind. My knees buckle beneath me as a fist pounds my back. I collapse, hitting the cold, rugged concrete with a thud. I struggle to gain enough leverage to get back on my feet. I quickly realize that I'm surrounded as the boys stand over me in a semi-circle. That doesn't stop me though. If they're going to overpower me, I'm not going down without a hell of a fight. Steadying myself on shaking hands, I begin to lift my body from the ground.

"Where the fuck you think you going?" Tone snarls at me as he reaches down and yanks me up by the back of my t-shirt. I swing my arms wildly in all directions. My eyes are open, but I can't see anything beyond the rage that blinds me. I feel the impact as I make contact with what I think to be one of the guys' faces, but I'm quickly stifled with a harsh blow to my stomach that causes me to double over in pain. I groan and cough, holding my mid-section while I try desperately to catch the breath that has been knocked out of me. Someone behind me cuffs my arms in a tight hold that leaves me no room to move anything above my waist.

Tone stands in front of me. He laughs. "You ain't so hard now are you? Where yo' heat at? Huh, bitch?" he taunts me.

Still aching from the blow to the gut, I manage to lift my head and look him in the eye. "Fuck you!" I bark right before I spit in his pock-marked face. Tone closes his eyes to keep my saliva from hitting his pupil. It lands just to the right of his wide nose and eases its way down his cheek, resting on the tip of his square chin.

"Bitch!" Tone yells while wiping the spit from his cheek. He strikes me in the face with a closed fist. If not for being held up by one of his boys, I know I would've been back on the ground. Instead, I stumble backward, my body slumping against the one behind me. I can taste my own salty blood as it trickles from my nose into my mouth.

Tone cups my chin and squeezes my face. "What was you saying? Somethin' bout fucking me? I thought you'd never ask." He licks his lips. I try to free myself from his sweaty hand.

"Ay, we need to get off the street," one of them says.

"Yeah, drag this punk back to the alley," Tone instructs them.

I feel my eyes grow wide as panic washes over me. I know what's coming, and the realization almost makes me pass out. I manage to stay alert as two of them begin dragging me backward toward the alley. I try kicking my legs in front of me and fight to break their hold on me, but I'm not strong enough to resist them all. For the first time in a long time, I feel weak. I feel helpless, like a woman. When we reach the alley, they throw me down. My head hits the corner of a metal, industrial sized dumpster. I reach up to place my hand over my head to soothe the pain and gather myself onto my hands and knees, but a quick kick in the back sends me crashing back to the ground.

"Remember all that shit you was talking last time?" Tone asks with no expectation of an answer. "Let's see if you mean it. Let's see what you got to say now."

I cough in response, unable to produce any comprehensible words. He reaches down and forcefully pushes me over so I'm lying face down.

"I don't wanna see yo' face when I'm fucking you," he hisses.

I'm no longer able to move. I look to the side and see his boys standing around us in a half-moon formation. The expression on their faces range from amusement, to lust, and excitement.

"Hold this pussy down," Tone commands.

I'm not moving, can't move, but one of his friends holds my arms firmly over my head just to be sure. I try to struggle, but my legs and arms are locked into place. I squeeze my eyes tightly closed as Tone snatches my jeans open, then tugs them violently to slide them down my legs. It seems as though my senses are heightened; I can hear everything around me. A night creature scavenges through the trash inside the dumpster. The guys snicker and whisper crude comments between sips from a shared bottle of liquor. I hear Tone unzip his pants, and his baggy jeans drop down the length of his lanky legs with a swoosh. I can smell the cognac on his tart breath as he hoists his body over me. With my eyes still closed, I can feel his face close to mine. He grabs me by the neck with one hand and rips my underwear with the other. As he leans down, his lips brush my ear. The mixture of liquor, smoke, and garbage, make my stomach turn. I hold my breath as Tone tries to balance himself while pulling his dick out of his pants.

"Be good, and I won't hurt you too bad," Tone whispers in my ear.

The sound of his voice makes me cringe. I struggle, but it's futile; my body becomes stiff as I hold my breath in preparation for what's to come. He clutches my thigh so hard I can feel his fingernails digging into my flesh. I wince in excruciating pain as he jams his penis inside me. The pressure I feel from behind resurrects me, and I scream as loud as my choked vocal chords will allow. My eyes shoot open. I fight desperately to free my hands and buck my legs, trying to push his weight from my body. My screams are stifled as I feel the sting of Tone's fist on the back of my head. He strengthens his clutch on my neck, causing me to gag. Then he places his other hand tightly across my mouth to muzzle me. He thrusts himself in and out of me hard and fast, tearing my flesh. I blank out; my body falls limp and my eyes close as he rams into me. His grunting and panting linger in my ears.

Tone hisses, "Yeah, take this shit, bitch."

I'm numb, unable to feel his forceful thrusts. My mind goes void and darkness overcomes me. I feel my spirit leave my body right here on the cold concrete. There is no more pain. No more sounds or smells to torture me. I don't cry, scream, or speak a word. I'm not here.

Suddenly, he stops. I come back into my body, thinking it's all over. With a loud moan, Tone collapses on top of me.

"Was it good for you, baby?" He removes his hand from my neck and dismounts me. I keep my head to the side, focusing on the wire fence that borders the left side of the alley.

"Who's next?" Tone turns to his anxiously waiting friends while he pulls up and buttons his pants. When I feel the second man's weight on my back, my eyes roll to the back of my head and I black out again.

I don't remember what happened next.

14 *Danny* / *Monday, May 2nd*

I stand in the mirror, staring at the tattered image of what used to be me. The glass that tops the dresser is intact, but I'm clearly shattered.

How could you let them do this to you?

I walk around this muthafucka like I'm King Kong, like I own the city and everything in it. Big—bad—strong. But, now as I look at my slumped shoulders, puffed red eyes, and pale skin, I know it was never anything more than a well-crafted façade.

They should have killed me.

Death has to be better than this. My broken spirit is evident in my every movement; it seems almost tangible. I've shut myself off from the rest of the world, weaving in and out of consciousness with sleeping spells that never seem to do anything but further exhaust me. I toss and turn in my sleep, only to wake up with tremors and a sweaty t-shirt. It wasn't enough to just batter and rape me in a filthy alley; they had to infiltrate my dreams too, making sure I live through their violation over and over again.

They should have killed me.

I place my hands over my face and hold my breath. I can't stand to look at the reflection anymore, but I'm unable to pull myself away from the mirror. I count to three in my head, then slide my hands down the sides of my face. I silently wish that somehow, miraculously, a new reflection will appear before me, resurrecting the Danny I knew and loved. The tears start to flow when I realize my wish can't come true.

"I hate weak-ass niggas! I hate him—Danny—me. I violently swipe tears from my face, but they fight back with a vengeful flow. "Stop it!" I yell. "Stop it, you weak bitch!" I slam my fists on top of the dresser with powerful frustration. What's happening to me? What did I let them do to me that night? With no answers to my lingering questions, my body slumps with defeat.

If I had only fought harder, yelled louder, run faster, it would have never happened. I have no one to blame but myself.

Maybe I deserved it.

I wasn't even strong enough to stay alert. I had blacked out after Tone finished, giving them the freedom to do with me whatever they wanted. My body begins to convulse involuntarily as I try to guess how many of them had violated me, tearing my insides, drenching me in their sweat. When I had awakened, after what seemed like days of unconsciousness, they were gone. There was no one there to claim their victory or give a remorseful helping hand. I remember feeling cold sprinkles of rain drizzling lightly across my cheeks, eventually transforming into heavy streams in the approaching thunderstorm. That's what had transported me back into my own body. I lay on my back on the cold, wet concrete, fluttering my eyelids and wiping my face. It had taken a few minutes to remember where I was and why I was there. The pungent smell of trash from the nearby dumpster brought it all back to me, and when the ugliness of it all came back to my memory, it sent me into a fit of rage. I had begun to hyperventilate as I looked down at my exposed bottom half. My jeans and underwear lay soaked and tangled around my ankles. Calming myself, I managed to stand and pull up my jeans, wincing from the immense pain in my lower body. I slowly turned and looked around, fearing that I may not have been alone, but I didn't see anyone. A scrawny gray cat was my only companion. He yawned as he clawed through the stray rubbish that had missed the dumpster and was scattered on the ground.

Sobbing, I folded my arms to warm and comfort myself. The cat jerked his head abruptly in my direction and scampered away at the sound of my crying. My moans echoed loudly through the alley. I heard glass cracking under my feet as I walked. I looked down to see the fragments of the liquor bottle one of the guys had been drinking. Blood glistened at the tip of the spout. I shivered as I wondered whether they had stuck that bottle inside my body.

I saw the plastic bag that I had carried with me in a dark corner; the clothes it had held were dispersed nearby. I didn't bother to pick them up as I dragged myself, head down, teeth chattering, toward the opening at the end of the alley to start the long walk home. I didn't know where my phone was. Didn't care. I didn't want to talk to anyone anyway. I *couldn't* talk to anyone. No one would ever find out about my shame. No one would ever find out how weak I was—how pathetic.

The fifteen-minute walk home took forty-five that cool, stormy night. I didn't see Kyle's car in the driveway when I had finally reached the house, which meant I wouldn't have had to explain my whereabouts and the horrible condition I was in. I keep reliving that night, cursing myself for not doing more to prevent my fate and condemning Kyle for robbing me of my only protection. I'll hate him for the rest of my life, and eventually he'll pay for his role in my demise. I've burrowed into the safe confines of my locked bedroom for three days. I only know the time of day or day of the week because of my occasional attempts to watch TV as a way to distract myself from the recurring nightmare. Kyle has come upstairs twice, once with GiGi, to find out what's going on and whether I'm okay. Carmen and Rain have tried a couple times too. They never get more than a few grunts of confirmation that I am still alive. I can't bring myself to let them see me like this. I don't eat—no appetite. The only reason I leave my room at all is to use the bathroom and maybe grab a drink from the kitchen on the way back to the comfort of my bed. When I do venture outside my bedroom, I only do it when I am sure no one else is in the house. I'm sure Maya has been going insane, wondering about my sudden disengagement. I haven't seen or talked to her either. For what? I'm ruined. She wouldn't want me anyway. I'm supposed to be her protector—the one that holds shit down. How can I ever look her in the eye, knowing that I'm nothing more than a weak nigga who allowed himself to be torn apart like a lamb in a lion's den? She wouldn't want me, and I don't want her to want me anymore.

Finally the tears stop, and my breathing slows to an even

rhythm. I examine my face closely, searching for any signs of the assault. The single bruise that had branded my cheek is almost healed. The cut hidden just under my nose has scabbed. Slowly, I pull away from my reflection and drag myself back to the bed. I almost don't notice the light tap at the door as I bury myself under the covers.

Tap, tap, tap. "Open the door, baby, it's me." Maya's soft voice floats toward me from outside my room. *How in the hell did she get in the house?* The mere thought of her, the pain and worry in her face, makes me squeeze my shut eyes even tighter and throw the covers over my head.

Tap, tap, tap. "Danny, please. I know what happened."

Her last statement jerks me into an upright position. I throw the covers off me and swing my legs over the edge of the bed. *How could she know?* Nobody is supposed to know.

"Please, baby. Talk to me."

Hesitantly, I rise from the bed and head toward the door. I place my hand on the doorknob, and then stop. "Who's with you?" I ask with suspicion, my voice hoarse from days of near silence.

"Nobody. GiGi asked me to come over 'cause nobody was able to get through to you. She let me in. She went back downstairs though. It's just me and you."

I open the door without looking into Maya's heart-shaped face, and I turn immediately to head right back to the bed. She follows.

"Oh, baby, I'm so sorry," she coos, placing a soft hand on my leg.

I don't look at her. I can't stand to see her face. "What do you know?" I ask in a whisper so low she has to lean in to decipher my words.

She swallows, then takes a deep breath. I can tell she's having a hard time forming any words. "I know what those sick niggas did to you. I know they—"

"Shut up!" I yell. I glare at her with a look that dares her to speak that revolting word.

"I'm sorry," she starts again, "I know this is hard for you."

I quickly turn away from her again. "Who told you?"

"Ray. He knows Tone and them."

"He was in on it?"

"Naw, you know my cousin cool with you. He wouldn't do nothing like that. Tone was over Ray's house a coupla days ago and he was braggin' about it."

"What did Ray say?" I ask, still avoiding eye contact with Maya and hoping Ray at least had the balls to come to my defense. I know he doesn't like the drama that goes on between his little cousin and me, but we're on good terms, for the most part.

"He played it cool. Didn't even let on that he knew you. You know he's still on parole, so he can't afford to get off into all that shit. He told me he wanted to help you take care of it though."

"Yeah? And how's he gonna do that?"

"I know you, Danny. I know the only way you're gonna feel better and get back to being yourself is if you take care of it. You know what I mean."

"Shit, I woulda taken care of it that night, if Kyle hadn't snatched my damn gun."

"GiGi told me about that too." Maya rummages through her oversized bag and pulls out a shiny, black, .22-caliber pistol. I look at her for the second time since she entered my room. "I love you, baby, and I just want you to be okay." She pushes the gun toward me. "You know what to do."

* * *

Tuesday, May 3rd

I fondle the gun between my palms. Its cold, smooth steel arouses me. I breathe in, imagining the moment of justice—the final moment.

Take care of it.

Maya's words resound in my mind. There is nothing else I can do. There is only one way to make it right. No more pain, no regrets, no fear. This is it.

You know what to do.

I point the barrel of the gun precisely, leaning it right against the temple. My finger trembles lightly on the trigger. I tap the fingers of my free hand nervously on my thigh. I swallow, but there is no saliva to ease the dryness of my throat.

"You ain't gonna do shit," I hear an unfamiliar voice taunting me.

"Shut the fuck up!" I say through clenched teeth.

I'm running out of time. It's either now or never. I choose now. Holding my breath and closing my eyes, I slowly pull the trigger back until the gun jerks.

Click!

My eyes pop open and I stare at my reflection in disbelief. The gun had jammed. I let out the breath I was holding and lower the pistol from my temple to my side. Suddenly, rage overwhelms me and I begin to scream uncontrollably. With the strength I thought I'd lost four days ago, I throw the .22

at the dresser mirror and watch in fury as the mirror shatters into a tangled maze. Tiny shards of glass spew out at me and I duck to avoid being cut. The gun lands on top of the dresser with a loud thud. Defeated, I dive onto my bed and cry myself to sleep—something I haven't done since I was three years old.

* * *

Thursday, May 5th

I have no idea what time it is when I hear the banging at my door. The shades on my window are closed, but the absence of natural light in my bedroom makes it hard to see anything beyond the thick darkness. It must be late evening. I've spent the whole day in the bed, drifting in and out of sleep, tossing and turning, trying to escape the horror of my dreams. This day has been no different than the last four, and I have no intentions of changing anything. I've found comfort in solitude and self-loathing; nothing else seems appropriate.

Whomever it is standing on the other side of the door knocks again. I make no effort to move toward it. I don't even turn over. I keep still in the bed, lying on my back, staring at the ceiling with the covers pulled just below my chin. I don't feel like seeing Maya again and if not her, there's definitely nobody else I want to entertain.

"I know you in there. If you not gonna open the door, I'm coming in. So, I hope you're decent." GiGi sounds as if she has the authority to do and say whatever she feels at any moment. For the most part, she's right, at least when it comes to this house.

I grunt in response and turn on my side, facing the wall away from the door. The next thing I hear is the door flying open and GiGi stomping inside. The light from the outside hall spills into the room, causing me to pull the covers over my head to shield my eyes from the imposing brightness. GiGi flicks up the light switch and I squeeze my eyes together tightly just hoping she'll go away.

"Danny?" she asks in a soft, sweet tone. The commanding voice she used to barge into my room a moment ago has faded. She doesn't wait for an invitation to come closer. Within a few seconds, I feel the weight of her body on the left side of the bed, making the springs creak beneath her as she sits down. She places an arm on my side; my body jerks involuntarily, not accustomed to the touch of another person—not since that night.

"It's okay, Danny. It's just me, your GiGi."

I remain silent as a single tear escapes my eye and darkens the fitted sheet that lines my bed.

"Baby, I don't know what's going on, but I know something ain't right." Her voice sounds heavy, like she's deeply burdened. It hurts me to know that I'm the cause of that pain. "Baby, whatever it is, you can tell me and I'll do whatever I can to make it better, I'll do whatever I can."

I sniff loudly as I try to hold back the tidal wave of tears fighting to break through. She gently pulls the covers back and reveals my head, topped with matted, disheveled hair, bloodshot eyes, and oily, dirty skin. She gasps at the sight of me. I haven't seen myself in a few days, but I know I must be looking something awful, considering the circumstances; not to mention the stench that rose and escaped from my body once the covers were lifted. GiGi seems to ignore that though, too concerned with my well-being.

"Danny, you know I love you right? You know I'll do anything for you?"

"Yes, GiGi, I know," I whisper.

"Then please tell me what's wrong."

I finally turn toward her, look into her deep brown eyes. "I can't," I say in a tone so low she has to bend down to hear me. It's true, I can't bring myself to report the torment that has dominated my life for the past week. It's much too painful. It's easier to just immerse myself in my own self-pity and wait for death to take the pain away.

GiGi reaches down and gently strokes my hair. "You know, sweetie, no one is here to judge you, but if you don't feel like talking, you certainly don't have to. I will always love you regardless of what happened, but, baby, it's more important for you to love yourself. Do you love yourself, Danny?"

I don't know how to answer that question. If she had asked a week ago, I'd shout my proclamation of self love for all to hear. I thought I was the finest, toughest, most charming man this side of the city, and nobody could tell me any different. But now … now, I just feel useless. I feel like I'm not even worthy of the effort it would take to even show myself some kindness. "I don't know, GiGi." It's all I could say to express my quickly diminishing emotional state.

"I try my best to give you everything you need. I do what I can to make sure you'll always be alright, but, baby, you have to live right in order to see the beauty of life."

I frown, not knowing where she's going with this

conversation. She leans down and kisses me tenderly on my forehead. "Come on. Sit up for me."

Slowly, body aching from lying in bed much too long, I gather myself and manage to get into an upright position.

"Now, Danny, I know you're a good person. You mean well and I'll always love you because of it. But sometimes it's necessary to evaluate how you live your life and how that affects your future."

"What do you mean, GiGi?"

"Baby, you seem so angry most times. Aggressive even. You take it out on people all the time." She stares intensely into my black eyes. "Especially Maya."

I know what she's getting at, but I'm not ready to go down that road. "What do you mean, GiGi?"

"Do you ever think that your aggression may have something to do with your mother's death?"

"I don't know. I guess I never really thought about it."

"I do. I think about it all the time. I think you've created this hard-core persona to try to hide your true feelings about her murder because you don't want to face them. You don't know how to face them. So you end up bottling it up and taking it out on those that love you. Baby, you don't deserve that, neither does Maya or anyone else that you come across."

I take a moment to process her words. I've never really given any conscious thought to how I feel about my mother's murder. I've always brushed it off as indifference, but maybe GiGi has a point, maybe my abrasive behavior is a result of my lack of coping. Maybe if I'd handled things differently in the store the day I met Tone, the tragedy of the other night would have never happened. No, it wasn't my fault, but it could have been prevented.

"I don't even know how to start coping, GiGi."

"Baby, it's never too late to change. You have to learn to accept your mother's death, and furthermore, learn to accept yourself. Self love is a powerful thing, and you are the only one that can control it.

"What do I do, GiGi?"

"We can do this together, sweetie. Starting today. We can talk about your mom and anything else that may be on your mind. If you want to tell me what happened, you can; if not that's okay too, just as long as you're getting those bottled up feelings out in the open."

"I *am* angry that somebody took my mother from me."

"I know you are, baby. We can work on that together." She softly rubs the side of my face. "Starting with a nice warm bath to make you relax. You can cry out your pain, and get cleaned up all at the same time. Lord knows you need some cleaning." She makes a funny face, wrinkling her nose and scrunching up her mouth. I chuckle at her little joke, loving her even more for making me laugh in the middle of my misery.

GiGi takes me into her arms and squeezes me with a strong, loving embrace. "I love you so much, GiGi. Thank you."

She rubs my back with the tips of her fingers. "I love you too, baby." She kisses me on the cheek before letting me go. "Now, I'm gonna go get this bath water ready for you. You just sit tight until I come back."

I nod and smile as I watch her walk out of the room. I look forward to learning more about my mother and uncovering some feelings that I never even knew I had. It has to feel better than this. Anything is better than this. It's a fresh start that I'm more than happy to embrace. At this moment, I vow to change, starting with Maya. I know right now that I will never hit her again.

15 Rain / Friday, May 6th

YOU LEFT ME

You left me. alone with your dreams and i love you
You left me. tangled in a web of deceit and i hate you
You left me. broken in a state of duress and i'm confused
You left me. i barely knew you and I couldn't care less

i'm desperate.
following the shards of your heart
maybe, just maybe
the broken pieces will guide me back home
i love you and you couldn't care less

i'm crazy
mending the seams of your dreams
maybe, just maybe
they'll lead me back to you
i hate you and you couldn't care less
i'm confused
brimming with scents of your aura
maybe, just maybe
its more than déjà vu, this euphoria
No! see what you did, you've created a fool

I blame you.
look at me, searching for you in the dead of the night
in the eyes of my enemies
in the cracks of my life
in the words that I write

* * *

I closed my journal and tossed it onto the bed beside me. Writing was starting to give me a headache; I just couldn't do it anymore. I had missed both Tuesday's and last night's performances, and Malik was getting more and more impatient with my sporadic attendance. My voicemail was loaded with his messages, ranging from concerned to downright enraged. I knew my time at the Lyrical Lounge was approaching its end, if it hadn't ended already. Honestly, since the last time I was there, when my mother appeared, I hadn't been too keen on going back. The whole episode kind of turned me off. I wasn't sure yet, but I was considering trying to find another poetry spot.

There was too much going on now to even think about performing anyway. Danny had been moping around the house for an entire week. I don't know what had happened, but Danny wasn't the same. Not talking to Carmen or me. Not even taking calls from GiGi or Maya—something was definitely wrong. I tried to get Danny to tell me what was going on, but I never got anything more than a sigh before he rolled over in bed to face the opposite direction. The sharp contrast of his usually overconfident demeanor to the Danny I had seen this week was disturbing. Carmen hardly ever set foot inside the house these days. When she did, she was always floating on a high. I knew she was spending most of her time with that Jay-Jay character, letting him turn her into more of a junkie than she already was. Every time I looked into her dilated pupils, I'd have to turn away because the mere site of her, wired and jumpy, bothered me beyond words. As if her drug addiction weren't enough, I had an inclination that she might even be prostituting herself. She always had money with no explanation of where she got it, and if Danny's description was any indication of Jay-Jay's true character, I could easily imagine him as her pimp. My sister's and brother's situations weighed heavy on my mind.

I lay back on the bed and placed my hands on either side of my pulsating head. It seemed as if my life was just *happening*, with little to no input from me. My visions, or *delusions* as Kyle called them, were more frequent and vivid. I was beginning to remember my mother's murder, and I wasn't sure how I felt about it. I didn't know if I should be excited that I was filling a twenty-year void or afraid that the full memory of her murder would haunt me for the rest of my life. Nearly the entire scene would play out in my head with colorful detail. Only it was as if I was a bystander witnessing a tragedy in someone else's life, not my own. I concluded that this distance, this displacement, was my mind's way of protecting me from what I wasn't prepared to handle. Still, choppy scenes would play out before me like a movie trailer. When I closed my eyes, I could see, smell, and hear all that surrounded me that night. The only thing that was missing was his face. I still hadn't seen the man that took my mother's life, and the missing piece of this puzzle was driving me close to insanity. If you asked Carmen, she'd tell you I was already there, but who cares what she thinks anyway?

The house was quiet. Danny was sleeping and Carmen was running the streets, as usual. Kyle came up to check on me earlier in the afternoon. He insisted on my staying in the house and getting some rest. He was so caring, overprotective even. How Kyle continued to deny the sexual tension between the two of us was beyond my comprehension. He cared for me. The love was overpowering and the attraction undeniable. It was only a matter of time before he came around and caved in to the magnetism that was gradually drawing us closer.

I couldn't spend too much time thinking about Kyle. The thought of his chocolate brown skin touching mine was beginning to create an uncomfortable moistness between my legs that was unwelcome at the moment. My desire for my man was simply inappropriate at a time when the people closest to me, Carmen and Danny, were in such turmoil. As I lay across the bed, I forced out all thoughts and images and allowed my mind to go blank. I placed my forearm over my face to shield my eyes from the bright light fixture on the ceiling.

When I stretched my right arm out at my side, I felt the silky fabric of my mother's scarf between my fingers. I was almost immediately entranced by the soothing sensation the scarf gave me, and I pulled it gently toward me. Since that night at the Lounge, I always kept it nearby. I placed the scarf across my chest and continued to fondle it, imagining what my mother must have worn with this accessory. From what GiGi told me, my mother was quite fashionable; Carmen said she was "hood rich." I'd heard stories about her strutting around Westside Detroit in Gucci heels and an assortment of furs. I envisioned her whipping the decorative scarf around her neck and tilting her chin upward with an air of pride. Her perfectly made up face, auburn-dyed hair, and bold curves were known attractions to anyone that frequented the vicinity. Living in one of Detroit's most notorious ghettos wasn't the slightest deterrent to her grandiosity. She was fabulous, and she made sure that everyone knew it.

GiGi would scold her for her flamboyance, worried that she was drawing too much attention to herself, just begging for a police investigation. I envisioned my mother brushing off GiGi's overbearing comments with a giggle and a reassuring pat on the arm. She knew she was playing with fire, but the possibility of getting caught only heightened the excitement. I didn't know her beyond third party descriptions, but I loved her. It didn't matter to me that she was a drug dealer. She was my mother, and I missed her dearly. Carmen was bitter that she never got to live with her at all. I think that's why Carmen hates me so much. She's jealous that our mother decided to raise me instead of giving me away. It's not my fault though. Besides, I didn't even remember the short part of my life I spent with our mom, so I felt just as unfulfilled as she did. Of course, I could never explain this to Carmen. That girl is determined to despise me until the day she dies. I didn't know that I would ever earn her love or affection. Gradually, I was learning to tuck away the pain and deal with the disappointment.

Danny was a different story. Danny didn't care one way or the other about mom. He didn't care for mom's occupation and was happy to be out of harm's way, in the safe home of a foster family. Danny loved our mother, but he also understood the circumstances of the life she created. To Danny, acceptance was freedom.

I envied both Carmen and Danny. They each had vivid memories of our mom: her laugh, the songs she would sing, and the jokes she would tell. I had nothing more than scattered visions of her brutal murder. I wanted—needed more. It took twenty years to get me this far; there was no telling how much longer it would take to recapture those times in my childhood when I had the loving relationship of a mother to her youngest child. I wondered if I would ever get the memories back at all. With my eyes still closed, I pulled the scarf right under my nose and inhaled my mother's fragrance. I wondered if she was as sweet as her smell. I wondered if she missed me, wherever she was.

A cold chill invades the bedroom. The windows are closed and the heat is on, but there is still an unjustified frost nipping at Rain's skin. She lies snuggled in her twin-sized bed under her Sesame Street blanket. It is eerie. It's not the faint sound of screaming in the near distance or the echo of heavy footsteps pounding the linoleum floors that makes her wake up. It is the creepy, cold air that bites at her ears, fingers, and toes. She rubs her eyes and lazily throws the covers off her body. Her feet dangle from the side of the bed. It's dark in her room, and she can see the light from the hallway creeping under the door. She can tell it's still nighttime. She opens her curtains and sees the steel moon staring back through the pouring rain, so now she knows it's still the middle of the night. Then she hears it again, thundering footsteps followed by a shrill scream. She knows it's her mother.

My eyes popped open and I sat upright at the end of my bed. I shook my head vigorously, trying to remove the scene that was playing out behind my closed eyes. I didn't want to see it, not then. I was too drained to watch that little girl— me—walking in on the tragedy that would forever alter her life. My head was pounding and my body was aching with exhaustion. I just couldn't handle it at that moment. I needed to rest, but the fear of that returning scene kept me wide awake. Afraid of triggering any more visions, I kept a narrow focus on the bare wall in front of me. There was nothing there, nothing to drive me deeper into this lunacy.

The comfort I found in that emptiness suddenly dissolved. I watched in horror as the pale pink paint of the walls began the drip slowly to the floor, revealing an eggshell white coating from underneath. The paint oozed from every corner of the walls like rain running down a window. I was stupefied, unable to move or utter a sound. The panels of the hardwood floor cracked beneath my feet, snapping open against the grain of the wood. Each panel uprooted itself, making a horrifying bursting sound that made me jump. The taupe carpet hiding underneath the hardwood was exposed. Unsure of what to do to stop the supernatural transformation that was taking place before me, I clasped my hands over my eyes, hoping that everything would be back to normal when I reopened them—but it wasn't.

Cautiously removing one hand at a time from my face, I saw several toys scattered about the floor. An Oscar the Grouch stuffed doll, a red Barbie Corvette, and an Etch-A-Sketch lay at the foot of the bed. An oversized toy box rested in the far left corner of the room that was about half the size it was just seconds ago. The now off-white walls were decorated with posters of Sesame Street and Muppet characters. A small vanity, covered with Crayola graffiti, sat to the right of my bed. My bed, no longer a spacious queen-size, was topped with pink and purple blankets and small pillows covered in frilly, laced pillowcases. I gasped loudly and covered my mouth as I looked down at the floor and saw my feet dangling from the edge of the bed, not nearly touching the floor. I patted myself in disbelief and found that my flat chest and three-and-a-half foot body were dressed in a pink Barbie nightgown.

I jump out of the bed and rush into the hallway. I start out running, but quickly slow my pace to a slow and careful walk. I know Mommy is in danger and I might be too. But I want to know what's going on. I hear her voice. She is talking—begging.

I hear a smack, then a crash. The deep voice of a man is shaking the walls. He sounds just like a monster. Like Skeletor. His voice sends a cold shiver down my back that makes me cry.

"Rock dead. You ain't heard?" The man's cruel laughter makes me cringe. "Yup, got shot in the head and set on fire."

The door to my mommy's bedroom is open just a crack, not wide enough for them to see me, but I can see them—the whole scene. A tall, dark man is standing over my mother. I can see his face. He has big lips and a square chin, and he's making a mean face. His nose is getting wide and he looks mad. Mommy is on her knees crying, and he's pulling her hair. He is hurting her. I never saw Mommy cry before.

"You know what's 'bout to happen next, don't you? You know what happens when people fuck with my money."

Mommy shakes her head. "Please. We got history. You know me. You know I'm good for it."

"Shut up!" He pulls a big, black gun from the back of his pants and points it at her forehead, right between her eyes. This man is about to kill my mother! I can't let him do it! I have to do something to stop him! I don't know what to do.

I run into the messy room screaming, "Mommy!"

They look at me, and he drops the gun to his side as I run to Mommy and hug her; I have to protect her.

"Rain, baby, please go back in your room, sweetie. Everything is going to be alright. We're just playing a game right now, okay?"

"No Mommy. I'm not leaving you. He needs to leave you alone!" I point a short, stubby finger at the man.

"Baby, listen. Nothing bad is going to happen. Go in your room and count to a hundred and I'll come in there and check on you. Everything will be fine."

"Yeah, Rain. Listen to yo' mama. Go to your room."

I give him a mean look and then look back at Mommy. "Do you promise? You promise you'll come get me after a hundred?"

"Yes, baby. I'll be there."

"Go ahead, baby." She begs me with her eyes, "Do this for Mommy. Do this one thing for me. I promise when we wake up in the morning it will be like none of this ever happened. Just like a bad dream."

I don't want to leave, but I let go of her and walk backward to the door. I keep looking at them until I close the door behind me.

I'm walking back to my room, crying. A bump, scream, and

crash make me jump. I hear a second scream, and I turn and race back toward my mother's bedroom. He is going to kill her! I know it.

I barge through the door again. This time, the man has the gun lodged in Mommy's mouth and he pulls the trigger. I see my Mommy's eyes roll to the back of her head and blood splatter all over the wall behind her. Her body drops to the floor.

I scream, staring at Mommy's bloody body, I keep screaming. I knew he was going to kill her!

"Rain! Rain! Come back, Rain. Come back." Kyle's voice, laced with distress, roused me back into reality. I was sitting on the floor in the living room with my knees folded into my chest and my back against the wall. Kyle quieted my screams, wrapping his strong arms around my shaking body. He couldn't stop the rapid flow of tears that darkened his shirt as I rested my head on his shoulder.

"Shhh," he calmed me, rocking me softly back and forth. "I called GiGi; she's on the way."

I tried to speak, but nothing escaped my lips. I was trying to tell him that I saw him; I saw the man that took my mother's life, but words failed me again. GiGi burst through the door, slamming it shut urgently. She rushed toward us with heavy footsteps.

"What happened?" GiGi demanded as she lovingly stroked my head.

"I didn't come up until the end, but I'm pretty sure she just remembered the murder. From what I heard, it seems like she saw and heard everything that happened that night."

GiGi stormed into my bedroom. When she came back, I looked up to see her holding the photo of my mother before my face. "Tell me what happened, Rain. Let it out!"

The sight of my mother's face instantly sent me into a state of hysteria. I started to scream and thrash, slumping my body against Kyle's. GiGi hurriedly snatched the photo out of sight and placed it face down on the floor behind her. Kyle held me with one arm, then reached into his shirt pocket to retrieve a syringe with his free hand. I didn't know what he was planning to do with it, but I was too weak to resist anything.

GiGi halted him when he removed the syringe cap, just as he was preparing to inject my arm. "Whoa! Hold off on that, Kyle. I want her to be alert for this. I need her to tell me what happened. She has to let it out, or she'll never get better."

"Are you sure?" he asked.

"Yes, leave her be for now." GiGi turned her attention toward me again. Gently stroking my arm, she asked again, "Rain, tell me what happened."

"What the hell is going on in here?" Carmen's slurred voice crudely interrupted the three of us.

"No, Carmen." Kyle held his hand up to her. "Now is not the time. We are talking to Rain right now. It's important." Kyle intercepted.

"Well, she's *my* sister and I want to know what the hell is going on!" Carmen exclaimed.

GiGi spoke slowly, almost whispering. "Carmen, please. Please, just go away for now. We need to talk to Rain. Please understand. This is serious."

"What-the-fuck-ever." Carmen smacked her lips. She rolled her eyes like our mere existence pained her. "Y'all acting funny as hell. You can't tell me nothin'? I don't have time for this crazy shit anyway."

"You watch your mouth, little girl!" GiGi scolded her. Carmen just rolled her eyes.

Kyle huffed and smacked his hand on the floor with frustration. "I don't know how much more of this I can take," he muttered.

I sat silently and motionless on the floor. GiGi turned to Kyle, her face showing her concern. "Don't give up on her, Kyle. We're almost there. I can see it. We need you now more than ever."

He sighed, placing a reassuring hand on GiGi's shoulder. "I know, GiGi. I know. I'm sorry."

Carmen yawned loudly. "What is this, a soap opera? You guys kill me with the dramatics. I'm out." No one said a word as she left us on the floor in the middle of the hallway.

I don't remember what happened next.

16 *Carmen* / *Friday, May 6th*

KYLE and GiGi are really getting on my damn nerves. They baby that chick like she's a fucking ... well ... a fucking *baby*! Every time GiGi is up in here, she manages to make me feel like a stranger in what's supposed to be my own home. I hate living here. Danny is tolerable most of the time, but living with Rain and having to dodge Kyle whenever I need to leave the house is becoming unbearable. I'm liable to snap any minute, and when I do, all hell is sure to break loose. That's why I can't wait until I finally move in with Jay-Jay. I know it's going to happen soon. I've hinted about it a couple of times. Every night I spend with him, I plant the seed in his mind about our future living arrangement. Usually, he just pretends to blow me off, but I know it'll only be a matter of time before I get through to him.

I saunter to the kitchen to get a glass of juice for my dry mouth and scratchy throat. Lately, it seems as though I can never get enough to drink. My lifestyle is draining me and I know it, but I can't stop—not when I am so close to where I need to be. *It'll only be a little while longer*, I tell myself as I pour a hefty amount of cranberry juice into the glass I removed from the dish rack. I raise the glass to my lips and take a generous sip, but frown and quickly place it back down on the counter. *Am I really having a virgin drink?* I crouch low in front of the kitchen cabinet. After rummaging through a few pots and pans, I finally feel the cool, slender neck of the vodka bottle I keep stashed here. I pour a little less than half of the juice out in the sink, then refill it with vodka, smiling at my spiked beverage.

I hear shuffling and hushed voices floating from the back hall. The reminder that Rain, Kyle, and GiGi are still in the house makes me roll my eyes before I take the next sip. The cocktail quickly refreshes me, making me feel a thousand times better than I had just a few seconds prior. I take a deep breath and close my eyes as the liquid warms my throat. "Ahh!" It's just what I need.

I see GiGi and Kyle walk past the kitchen entryway toward the front door through my peripheral vision. I quickly shift my position in front of the counter to block their view of the half empty vodka bottle. I don't dare turn to face them, for fear of provoking some unwanted conversation. I say a silent prayer that they will just leave without saying a word. God must be on my side for once, because the next thing I hear is the front door open and close with not so much as a comment from either of them. They must have doped Rain up like they always do when she's off into that psycho shit. I don't hear a peep from her either.

After carefully placing the vodka bottle back inside the

cabinet behind an oversized mixing bowl, I leave the kitchen and make my way to the living room. Before I can sit down on the couch, I notice my cell phone vibrating on the table. My heart skips a beat when I look at the caller ID and see that it's Jay-Jay.

The conversation is short. The usual. He tells me what to do, I pout and eventually comply, he coaxes me with promises of money and love, and I turn into mush—simple. The sudden silence on the other end of the line tells me that he hung up on me. With a sigh, I place the phone down on the coffee table and reach across the table to retrieve my purse. The brief exchange with Jay has induced a serious craving. I dig through the new designer handbag he bought me on our last trip to the mall. After sifting through a few stray dollar bills, some makeup, condoms, and rolling papers, I feel the small plastic baggie I'm searching for. A smile creeps across my face as I open the baggie and dump the pill in my hand. I'm starting to love the drug almost as much as I love my man and making money—almost. Me and E, we have a real passion for one another—a bond that can't be broken. We'll never break up—never. I pop the small pill in my mouth and wash it down with a gulp of cranberry and vodka. Allowing the pill to find its way down my throat, I lay my head on one of the oversized cushions of the couch behind me.

I close my eyes, unintentionally allowing thoughts of Rain to cloud my mind. Just what is her deal lately? Do I need to be concerned about Rain choking me out in the middle of the night? Nah, she still don't have that much heart. But her little episodes are starting to get out of hand, and I don't know how far she'll take it. What if she is really starting to remember everything? Then what? Will she be normal again? Was she *ever* normal? The twinge of concern and sympathy I suddenly feel for my little sister stuns me. I shake my head to free myself of those thoughts and feelings. I hate her—always have—always will.

Or do I?

I pop my eyes open and sit back up as a rare epiphany strikes me. I stand, swiftly stuffing the remainder of the stash in the pocket of my skinny jeans and head back to the kitchen. I know just how to make this right.

Moments later, I emerge from the kitchen with another glass of juice—no liquor. I tiptoe out of the kitchen, careful not to spill a drop out of the glass and trying to avoid causing the floorboards to squeak. I'm beginning to feel the effects of the dose of Ecstasy I took as the high rushes to my head, causing me to pause in mid-step to balance myself and regain composure. As I walk carefully past the coffee table in the living room, I bend slowly to grab my other glass. I take a quick swig, continuing my journey to the back hall. I tiptoe past Danny's bedroom, and it occurs to me that I haven't seen Danny's face in about a week. It's a bit out of character, but a wave of concern comes over me as I pause to knock lightly on the door with my elbow. Danny gets on my nerves more often than not with that overprotective meddling, but this sudden withdrawal from the world bothers me. I lean in until my ear is touching the door so I can hear a voice or movement on the other side. When I hear nothing to indicate that anyone is alive in there, I balance both glasses in one hand and crack the door open just a bit so I can take a peek inside. Danny is lying under a mound of blankets, sleeping with a soft snore. I don't want to disturb him, plus I don't have the time; I'll find out what's going on when I get back—whenever that is.

I continue down the hall to the next door on the right. Rain's bedroom is just opposite mine. Figuring that she's also sleeping, I slowly turn the knob and let myself in. We startle each other. Standing in front of her dresser mirror playing with her hair, Rain jumps at the unexpected sight of me; her expression of surprise triggers the same reaction from me as I jump back a little, almost dropping the drinks.

"Shit," I curse as juice spills over the brim of one of the glasses.

"What is it, Carmen?" Rain asks reluctantly, preparing herself for our usual combative exchange.

"Nothing. Just checking on you, that's all." I ease my way into the bedroom, closing the door behind me with a swift push of my hip.

"What?" Rain scrunches her face into an unflattering look of confusion. She turns toward me and places a defiant hand on her hip.

"Don't look at me like that," I rebut. "Ain't nobody trying to get all mushy on your corny ass. But even though I can't stand you, you are still my sister and I don't want see you get locked into a crazy home with all that delusional shit you be going through."

"Whatever, Carmen. Nobody's getting locked up, okay? I'm fine." She turns away from me, dismissing my comment and turning her attention to her reflection in the mirror. I casually walk over to the bed behind her and have a seat on the right side edge. After sliding some papers and a dirty plate to the side to make room, I set both glasses on the nightstand, careful to keep mine separate from hers; my glass is on the left and hers is on the right. I push some of Rain's stray clothes away from me as I get cozy on the bed.

"So, Kyle and GiGi didn't dope you up this time?"

"What are you talking about, Carmen?" Rain asks with exasperation.

"You. Crazy. Shot."

"You know what, if you just came in here to get under my skin, you can save both of us the time and just get out. I'm not in the mood for your attitude today. And, no. Nobody 'shot' me up! That's *your* thing."

"Get off the defensive, Rain. Damn, I'm just trying to talk to you. That's all."

"About?" She doesn't try to hide the cynicism in her tone.

"Well, I've been thinking ..." I pause as I try to come up with the appropriate words.

"You've been thinking."

"I mean ... I know we aren't close and all. And I know it's my fault. I was um ... talking to GiGi the other day and she really got on my case, you know."

"GiGi's always on your case." Rain rolls her eyes at my reflection in the mirror.

"Yeah, I know." I fake a light-hearted laugh. "But this time we got to talking about deeper stuff, you know. She made me realize that I have some resentment toward you and, for the first time ever ... I was able to talk about those feelings. It was kind of weird."

Rain slowly turns her head toward me, keeping her body oriented toward the mirror. Her brow is raised with an expression of suspicion and curiosity. I rub my hands together nervously and struggle to speak my thoughts sincerely. "Yeah. Sounds strange coming from me, right?"

She keeps her voice monotone and her face straight. "That's an understatement." After teasing out her blow-dried hair, she finally turns fully toward me, folding her arms across her chest.

"I'm serious, Rain. I just want to talk to you. Get everything out in the open, so we can be like real sisters. I told you, I've been thinking and this is long overdue." My eyes skirt around the messy room, never resting on Rain's skeptical face for more than a second. I wipe my forehead as I try to shake the high that's creeping up on me. I need to focus.

"You're high," Rain observes.

I drop my head in mocked shame, squeezing my eyes shut tightly. "Why do you think I get high so much, Rain?" I whisper through quivering lips, "I have so many issues, my own *mother* didn't love me. GiGi hates me, plus the jealousy I have for you—I can't handle it all with a clear mind." One lonely tear skips down my cheek.

Disarmed, Rain drops her comb and comes to sit next to me on the bed. "So ... you wanna talk?"

I can easily sense my little sister's desire for a connection with me. It's kind of sad—her desperation. "Yeah, I do." I reach for the glass sitting on the nightstand, the one on the right. "Here, I brought us some drinks, so we can relax and talk for once." I smile weakly before swiping the tear from my cheek.

"No thanks, Carmen. I'm trying to lay off the alcohol. Kyle gets on me about it, and I'm starting to think he's right about the effect it has on me."

"I know. I thought about that. That's why I didn't put anything in your juice."

She reaches out a hesitant hand.

"Rain, it's only cranberry juice. Damn!" I cop a quick attitude, momentarily regressing.

"Okay, okay. Thanks." She finally retrieves the glass from my trembling hand. "So, what did you want to talk about exactly," Rain inquires with an eagerness that echoes through the softness in her eyes and her welcoming body language.

I take a sip of my drink before speaking, subliminally

encouraging Rain to do the same. "Well, this is kind of hard for me," I start, placing my hand lightly on my chest, "but I've grown up resenting you. Hating you because, well … because …" I drop my head, trying to formulate my next few words and ease the head rush that is enticing me to lie back on the bed.

"You can let it out, Carmen. You can tell me." Rain places a comforting hand on my shoulder to let me know it's okay to confide in her.

I turn my watery eyes back toward her. "I've always thought that Mom loved you more than she loved me. She just threw me away like … like I was trash!" I throw my hand in the air for dramatic effect. Rain remains silent, finally taking a sip from her glass.

"Why did she love you and not us? What made you better than us? What made her love you more than she loved me?"

"You know what Mom had going on in her life. She didn't exactly have the traditional job. You wouldn't find her at home making milk and cookies. She probably did what she thought was best at the time," Rain reasons before taking another sip of juice, this time drinking a lot more than she had before.

"Then what changed when she had you, huh? We're only two years apart. What was so different after two years? Why didn't she come back and get us? She just left us there with a foster family without giving us a second thought. Why wasn't I good enough; why not Danny? Why you?" I'm slightly thrown off and momentarily silenced by the wetness of tears running down my cheeks and nose. I'm crying for real, and I can't stop it. I don't want to stop it; I need to let it out.

"Oh, Carmen." Rain places her glass on the floor near

her feet and embraces me with an almost-motherly hug. Forgetting my disdain for her, I allow her to hold me, but the embrace only makes my tears flow harder and faster. My loud sobs are muffled by her shoulder. "We may never know why Mom made some of the decisions she made. What I do know is that we have each other—you, Danny, and I. I understand why you took it out on me, but I've always loved you. All I wanted was for you to love me back."

Suddenly realizing how far off track I've traveled, I slowly pull back and shake myself from Rains arms, wiping the salty tears from my face. I can't believe I've allowed myself to get sucked into the moment so easily. I didn't even know I had that bottled up inside me, but I refuse to give in to my emotions. Quickly getting my feelings into check, I ask, "And what about GiGi?"

"What *about* her?" Rain gently brushes my cheek with her fingertips. My immediate reaction, to wince and smack her hand away, is calmed by my commitment to make this work.

"She doesn't like me either."

"Well, we'll just have to fix that won't we? Don't worry, I'll talk to her. Everything will be fine. You've got me."

You have no idea.

"Wow, sis." The endearing name is one so foreign to my lips that I almost grimace at the sound of it. "I'm glad we finally talked about this."

"I am too." Rain sings with a broad smile. She looks like a grinning fool.

"Well, this is cause for a celebration." I raise my glass in the air. "To a new beginning. To us."

Rain reaches down to grab her glass of juice from the floor. "To us," she repeats.

With matching smiles, we clank our glasses together.

"Cheers," we shout in unison.

I throw my head back and gulp the contents of my glass until it's empty. The potent mix of vodka and cranberry races through my insides and causes me to sway slightly back and forth from the woozy feeling that has overcome me. Rain watches me, waiting until I've downed my drink, and asks, "You sure you didn't put any liquor in here?"

"Yeah, I'm sure." I answer, slightly annoyed. "How do you think we can start this new sisterly relationship if we don't have trust?"

She brings the top of the glass to her nose and sniffs the juice for confirmation. Satisfied that I'm telling the truth, she follows my example and drinks the juice like a triple shot, throwing her head back and gulping loudly.

We hug for the first time in twenty years.

17 *Carmen* / *Friday, May 6th*

I struggle to hold Rain up, huffing loudly, gripping her right forearm and elbow. She drags the left side of her body along as if it's dead weight. Neither of us weighs more than 130 pounds, but tonight her body mass seems to double mine. We trudge along the floor, heading toward the front door of the flat, but I fear that we'll never make it at the pace we're going.

"My face, Carmi. My face!" Rain whispers loudly as she smacks and grabs at her face, checking to make sure it hasn't disappeared from her head. I know she is wasted when I hear her call me by the childhood nickname I've long since forbade her from using.

"Your face is there, Rain." I give her a nudge with my

hip to readjust my leverage and get a better hold of her. "Now, come on. I need you to move your feet. One at a time … here we go. Left, right … move your right foot, Rain. Okay, good. Now, left."

"Ooh. Oh my Goodness, Carmi. You have to feel this. My skin … it's soooo smooth. It's beautiful. Like … like, silk and, and … milk." She giggles like a mischievous school girl, placing a coy hand over her mouth. "Did you hear that? I just made a rhyme. Silk and milk. Get it? I guess that's why I'm such a dope poet." She giggles again. I shake my head in frustration. This is going to be a long night.

"Listen, I need you to shift a little to the left. Just so—"

"Aww!" Rain gasps loudly and stops suddenly in mid-step. "Do you see that?

"What?" I ask, my tone dripping with irritation.

"Look at that picture." She points to an old oil painting of four black children running through a meadow peppered with dandelions. It hangs on the left wall just above the couch in the living room.

"What about it? GiGi gave us that painting years ago."

"The colors. They're so … so pretty! The white, it's so bright." She snickers. "Another rhyme."

I suck my teeth loudly.

"And look at the yellow flowers. It's like looking at the sun. Is it three-D?" She reaches her arm out and leans her body toward the wall, trying to grab the figures in the painting. I snatch her arm back before she makes both of us fall flat on our faces.

"Come … On … Rain!" She's beginning to piss me off. Not only do I have to damn near drag her out of the house, she's blowing my high—and nothing pisses me off more than being sober when I don't have to be. I don't have time to enjoy the colors or the silky touch of my skin. No, I have to babysit this dumb-ass amateur who doesn't know how to handle her shit.

I flinch as I feel the vibration of my cell phone in my pocket. There's no use in trying to wriggle my hand free so I can answer it. I know exactly who it is and he will just have to wait. Shit, if it weren't for Jay-Jay, I wouldn't be going through this bullshit in the first place. I can just hear his mouth as soon as he sees my face, "What the fuck took yo' ass so long? What I tell you about making me wait?" His rough voice rings in my ears as if he is right here in the living room with Rain and me. Even though I know he isn't in the room, I turn my head quickly in all directions to scan the premises. Jay-Jay is still downstairs waiting on us in the truck, not watching us inconspicuously from some dark corner in the house. My irrational fears eased, I continue to drag Rain along until we finally reach the front door.

Suddenly, Rain stops again and crouches to the floor, covering her face with her hands. Her breathing is heavy, audible. "What? What is it now?" I ask, exasperated and nearing my wits' end. It has only been an hour since she drank the juice, and she's already tweaking. *Maybe I should've only given her a half dose*, I think to myself as I bend down next to my sister.

"Whoa, Carmi ... I mean Carmen. Something is wrong with me. I don't feel normal." Rain shakes her head slowly from side to side, her face still covered by her hands.

"Look," I whisper, "Let's just make it outside and you'll feel a whole lot better. Okay?"

"I'm hot!" she exclaims as she begins to wipe imaginary sweat beads vigorously from her forehead and neck.

"I know. It's hot in here. That's why we need to get outside. You'll feel better once you get a breeze." I'm trying hard to keep the gathering frustration from seeping into my words. Slowly, I rise from a kneeling position, pulling Rain up with me by her arm. She remains silent as she allows me to lead her swaying body out the front door and clumsily down the stairs to the flat.

"Where's Kyle?" she asks, leaning her body toward his door. I grab her fist before she gets within knocking distance. Where *is* Kyle? That's a good question. He left the house just minutes before I managed to get Rain outside. I made sure he was gone before I would even dare try to sneak out. But I know wherever he is, he isn't going to be gone long. We have to hurry; I just wish I can get Rain to realize that and bring her ass on. We step out onto the porch.

"I don't know where he is. Look," I say, pointing to Jay-Jay's running SUV parked at the curb in front of the house. "Look at the pretty, sparkly truck!" Its newly refreshed silver paint glistens in the sunlight, sending a long glare toward the porch. Rain's eyes widen with childlike awe.

"Woooow!" She reaches out and grabs at the air, waving her arms, trying to catch the shiny rays as they reflect from the SUV. Jay-Jay honks the horn to rush us along. Placing my hand firmly at the small of her back, and keeping her right arm securely locked into mine, I guide Rain down the steps of the porch, coaxing her the entire time with soft words of encouragement. I feel like I'm talking to a dog, persuading her to do some silly trick for a doggy snack. I sound ridiculous, but it seems to work as we cross the front lawn and approach the SUV. When we reach Jay-Jay's driver side window, he rolls it down and greets me with a look of perplexity.

"What's wrong with you? Why you taking so long?"

"Whatchu mean?" I match his look of bewilderment with a twisted face, feeling aggravation and angst. An overwhelming sense of anxiety washes over me as I struggle to keep Rain in place. I don't like the fact that he wants to meet my sister, and the lingering question "why" is causing my stomach to twist into bow-ties.

"What do I *mean*? You walking like you crippled or something. What the fuck is wrong with you?"

"You see I had to damn near carry her ass out the door. This shit ain't easy, you know."

Jay-Jay nods his head as a moment of clarity seems to transform his grimace of confusion to an expression of understanding. "Yeah, yeah, of course I see that. You uh … did what I told you to do?"

"Yeah, I think I gave her too much though. She a first-timer. A whole pill may have been too strong for her. She can barely stand up." I readjust myself, shifting my weight from my right hip to the left.

"Ooh Carmi … you smell sooooo good." Rain moves her face close to my neck; she's resting her head on my shoulder as she sniffs my perfume loudly. I feel her hand sliding down my back.

"Hey, Daddy, we need to hop in the car real quick. I wanna get outta here before Kyle pulls up."

Jay-Jay stares at me for a few moments without saying a word. His chiseled, dark face shows amusement. "Hey, did you hear me?"

"Uh … yeah, get in. Shit, I don't know what you waiting on."

I shuffle my way to the back driver-side door and manage to pull the handle with Rain's distracting hand sliding up and down my back. I turn to see her caressing her left breast with her free hand and I snicker at the sight of her self-pleasuring. She is so high! After a few uncomfortable moments of shifting and pushing, I'm finally able to get her ass into the back seat. She smoothes her hands over the imported leather that covers the seats. "Oh, this feels so good." She sighs and lets her body go limp, slumping into a half-seated, half-reclined position. I reach over and clasp her seatbelt, knowing she'll probably slip to the floor if she isn't secured.

I smile and shake my head with a tsk, thinking back to my first time rolling off the pill. A veteran now, I doubt that I'll ever get that feeling back again. It's been over an hour since my last hit and I know I'm far from my peak. The beauty of the lights and glare are minimal compared to Rain's view of them right now.

I kinda like her like this, I think to myself as I trot around to the other side of the truck to climb into the passenger seat. I notice Jay-Jay chuckling to himself after I snap my own seatbelt together. "What?" I ask.

"Umm … she aiight back there?" He raises an eyebrow and eyes the backseat through the rearview mirror.

"Yeah, she good. Let's go. I wanna get up outta here." I answer, looking behind me, paranoid.

Jay-Jay punches the gas and we ride to his house in Redford, about three minutes outside Detroit. Thankfully, Rain remains silent for the duration of the trip. Jay-Jay and I are too. I catch him stealing side glances at me from time-to-time, prompting me to check my teeth for lipstick stains and my hair for strays through the visor mirror. I don't see anything out of place, so I figure he is just admiring his woman. Shit, I can barely keep my eyes off his fine ass, so I know the feeling.

When we pull up to Jay's house, I hesitate before getting out of the truck. He opens his door halfway, before turning to me. "What? Get out!" he barks.

The bow ties in my gut began to tumble. "Umm … now, I'm not trying to question you or nothing, but are you gonna tell me what this is about? Why did you wanna meet Rain so bad? So bad I had to drug her to get her out here."

"Hey, I only told you to do that because you said she wouldn't agree to go freely."

"Well, she wouldn't have."

"So, what's the problem?"

"She *is* my sister, Jay. I just wanna know what the plan is so I'm prepared."

He closes the door and slides all the way back into his seat. "Look, I told you. I just wanna talk to her, aiight? Nothing deep. Just see where her head is at. You gotta problem with that?" His last question is accompanied by a look that dares me to oppose him, but also warns me not to.

"Nah, no problem, Daddy." I look away to evade his hardened glare. I hop out of the passenger seat and open the back door to let Rain out. "Come on, girl!" I scream at her, no longer able to keep my impatience at bay.

She licks her lips and slides across the backseat until she's within my reach. "You're so pretty, sister," she coos as she slithers her way out the door.

Rolling my eyes, I grasp her arm tightly and nearly yank her out of the truck, careful to make sure she doesn't fall on her way out. As we walk, my arm around her neck, looking as though we're attached at the hip, Jay-Jay lingers behind us. When we reach the porch, it takes him several strides to catch up and unlock the door.

Once inside, I drop to the couch, bringing Rain down with me. Jay-Jay, keeping a suspiciously watchful eye on both of us, walks in front of us, around the couch and takes a seat a few spaces away from me. I place my head on the cushion behind me and exhale deeply, ready for my high to reinstate itself and hopefully escalate.

Rain is the first one to break the silence. "This is a nice

house," she says softly, rubbing her neck.

"Thanks," Jay-Jay quickly replies. I keep my eyes closed and my body relaxed.

"So … you must be the infamous Jay-Jay," she says, flirtation oozing from her purposely pouted lips. I sit up abruptly and shoot her a look. She's smiling and places a hand on my thigh. I brush it right off.

"Yeah, that's me." He squints his eyes and leans his body forward, looking into Rain's eyes.

"You know me?" He asks the question slowly as if her answer might leap out of her mouth and attack him.

"Mmm …" she moans. "You look a little familiar. Maybe I need a closer look." Rain laughs and gets ready to stand up. I violently yank the back of her shirt to slam her back down on the couch. I don't know what the hell is going on in that schizoid brain of hers, but if she thinks I'm about to let her seduce my man, she's begging for an ass whooping.

"What are you doing?" Jay-Jay frowns at me.

"I know you don't like people you don't know all up in yo' face. I'm just watching yo' back, Daddy. Don't wanna let her get too close."

"Nah, let her come over here."

I turn my head slightly so he won't see me roll my eyes. "Go on 'head." I reluctantly permit my little sister to get closer to my man.

One wrong move and I'll kill you.

She sashays her way past me, careful not to lose her balance between the sectional and the round cocktail table that sits inches from her feet. She eases back down onto the couch in what I'm sure she thinks is a sexy motion, but it ends up looking more like a drunken, uncoordinated stumble. Jay-Jay smirks. I grimace.

"Look at me," he commands her. She does, gazing into

his dark brown eyes and placing a seductive hand on his shoulder.

"Do you know me, Rain?"

She moves her face within kissing distance of his and I nearly have a conniption.

"What the fuck is going on?!"

"I need to talk to Rain." he interjects.

"I'm here." Rain answers, whispering in his ear. "I don't believe I've ever seen your handsome face before. I've heard a lot about you though. A lot of good things." She smiles, tilting her head slightly.

He returns the smile. I think I'm going to hurl on the floor.

"You know *me*?" She inquires.

"Hmm …" He pauses, laughs. "Not like I want to." He leans in and grabs Rain at the back of her head, pulling her face even closer to his. They look at each other for a moment before they kiss, making loud smacking sounds as their tongues twist around each other's. Rain squirms in her seat, his aggression making her hot.

I jump up from the couch.

"What's wrong?" Jay-Jay asks.

"What … what's wrong?" I scream.

"Nothing's wrong, baby." Rain jumps in.

"Wait … Rain." Jay-Jay calls Rain's name, but he's standing before me, looking into my eyes.

"Yes?" she responds.

"Carmen?" he asks, looking back at me.

Seething with anger, I'm too flustered to say anything. I just stare at him intensely.

Rain rises from the couch. "You were saying?" She reaches out and cups his face in her hands. I don't know what's happening, but I know I'm not prepared to see what could come next. Did he have me bring my sister here just to fuck her? Why would he do that to me? We're in love.

That's what he told me.

They kiss again. This time standing, she wraps her arms around his neck and he grips her ass. I think I'm going to be sick, as the nausea ravishes my stomach, causing me to clutch my abdomen and double over in pain.

I hear Jay-Jay's sinister laugh. This dude thinks everything is a fucking joke. "This shit is crazy," he expresses to no one in particular.

"Baby, don't stop." Rain pleads.

I don't give Jay-Jay a chance to respond to her. "I can't take this."

"Can't take what?"

"You … her! This is some bullshit, Jay. Why would you *do* me like that? You choosing my sister over me? What kind of shit is that?" Unanticipated tears roll from my eyes as I scream and sob.

Jay-Jay stops, looks at me with smugness. "I'm not choosing," he reasons, "I want both of y'all."

"Sounds good to me," Rain sings.

"Fuck that, Jay—"

He cuts me off. "How many times do we have to have the same damn conversation?" He's hissing through his teeth like he does every time he scolds me. "You do what the fuck I tell you to do if you wanna be on my team."

"I do, Daddy. I do. But this is my sister! This is too much."

"So, what you tryin' to say. You ain't down fo' yo' man no mo'? After all the shit I did for you? All the money we made? You lyin' ass bitch, you said you was down—loyal. Now you tryin' to play me?"

I remain silent.

"Huh?"

"No," I answer, head down, almost whispering.

Rain giggles. "Aww, come on Carmen." She fondles Jay-Jay's belt buckle. "Let's have some fun."

Negotiations are over. Jay gently moves Rain's hands from his belt and turns toward the bedroom. Without a word of instruction, I know we are expected to follow. I look to the ceiling in an attempt to summon the strength it will take to have a threesome with my sister and the love of my life without killing her in the process. I know I won't find any comfort from above, so I pat my pockets frantically looking for another pill.

Dammit! I left them in my purse at home!

"I got drinks and E in the room." Jay reads my mind as he addresses me without turning back around to see the envious rage in my eyes. I have to be soaring if I'm going to go through with this, and one pill just isn't getting it.

Rain is the first to follow Jay, sauntering behind him seductively. I'm a close second. Minutes later, the modest-sized bungalow is filled with screams and moans of ecstasy as he sexes us both.

18 *Rain* / *Saturday, May 7th*

I tossed and turned in the bed for several minutes before ending up on my back. My eyes twitched before fluttering open, the morning crust gathered in the corners of my eyelids. I wiped it away with a quick swipe of my forefinger and shook my head in an attempt to orient myself. Fully awakened, I gasped and held my breath. The piercing rays of the sun squeezed between the window blinds on the opposite wall. There was enough natural light in the room for me to determine that I was in an unfamiliar place. I was in someone else's home. The décor told me it was a man's house: an erotic sketch of a naked woman, a large flat-screen TV with a game system and an elaborate surround sound system, along with a couple of free weights sitting in the corner—a man's bedroom.

Where am I, and how in the hell did I get here?

Feeling a body to my left, I was too afraid to turn my head and confirm that I was indeed in the bed with a stranger. A subtle shift of my legs against the cool sheets beneath me affirmed my nudity. He—whoever he was— snored heavily as he changed positions, rolling onto his side and stuffing his hands underneath the pillows. I watched his movements in my peripheral vision, refusing to move my body in any way that might disturb or wake him.

How am I going to get out of here?

I quickly realized that my original plan—to be as still as possible until he just disappeared—wasn't going to work. I had to come up with an exit plan. Quickly. I eased my right leg slowly to my side until I felt a draft of cooler air on my foot. I did the same with my left leg, making sure I didn't pull the covers. Then, I started to scoot my upper body toward the edge of the bed with short, discreet pushes until my entire body was aligned with the edge of the bed. The man stirred slightly in his sleep, making a grinding noise with his teeth. I froze until I was sure he was done moving. Conscious of my naked body that was soon to be exposed to this stranger and whoever else roamed this unknown place, I grabbed the comforter and pulled it up to my neck. I paused again when I thought I was being too loud and moving too much. His snoring grew louder, accompanied by an occasional snort. My breathing was heavy and I tried my best to calm it, but my nerves wouldn't allow that.

Suddenly, the shrill sound of a ringing cell phone blared loudly from the nightstand on the opposite side of the sleeping stranger. He awoke immediately. I jumped, losing my balance at the edge of the bed. Arms flailing and feet kicking, I dropped off the side of the bed and landed on the floor with a loud thud, taking the comforter with me. The phone continued to ring. Embarrassed and still desperate to cover my nudity, I pulled the cover over my head to conceal myself. The phone went silent after about the fourth ring.

"What up?" I heard the man answer his cell as I lay face up on the floor, growing uncomfortably hot inside this comforter cocoon. "Yeah, yeah. I got it. Meet me at the spot in about an hour." He ended the brief conversation, placing the phone back on what I guessed to be the nightstand. He fell silent for a moment. Then I heard rustling on the bed. "You gonna stay on the floor looking like a fool?"

I didn't say anything.

"I heard you fall. Get yo' ass up," he ordered.

I refused to move, secretly hoping that he would somehow vanish and I would miraculously float back to the safety of my own home. I heard him sliding over to my side of the bed, the springs of the mattress creaking under his weight. Once again, I held my breath and clutched the blanket even tighter.

His voice was a lot closer now. "Yo!" I felt him grab the top of the blanket and try to yank it down to reveal my face. I resisted as much as I could, countering his downward tug with an upward pull. After just a few seconds, I lost the blanket tug-of-war. I looked up to see his head and torso hanging off the side of the bed, hovering over me.

My eyes grew wide and the air left my lungs as a flush of realization washed over me. I scampered frantically, trying to free myself from the comforter's entanglement. When the man reached down to stabilize me, I started to scream as loud as my throat would allow as if I was under attack—who knows, maybe I was.

"Calm down! What the hell is wrong with you?" I heard him yelling, but I couldn't process his words. The only thing running through my mind was, *Get out alive. Break free. Get out!* Still screaming, I kicked, twisted and turned until the covers fell off me, exposing my bare body. My screeching ceased only when he stopped moving toward me. I scooted toward the wall behind me and used it as support to get to my feet. He stared at me with an incomprehensible look that sent chills down my spine. His glare made me aware of my nakedness once again. Spotting my clothes, thrown against the opposite wall where the TV was mounted, I bent to retrieve the covers, so he could no longer enjoy the peep show. But he was quicker than I, using his leverage on the bed to swiftly snatch the blanket out of my reach. Out of options, I placed my left arm across my breasts as my right hand covered my genital triangle.

His icy stare never left my body. "Don't kill me."— It started out as a hoarse whisper. "Please, Don't kill me!"— but ended up as a nearly unintelligible wail.

I saw his frown through tearful, blurred eyes. "Rain?"

I felt as if someone had suddenly punched me in the gut. My heart rate picked up speed and my mouth went dry. He knew my name.

"You're … you're—"

"Jay-Jay."

"… nothin' bad is going to happen to you as long as you don't say nothin' about what you just saw. Do you understand?"

"Oh, God. I never told. I never said anything. I never said a word! You have to believe me. Please don't hurt me … please!" My words seemed to jumble together, toppling on top of one another as they fell from my trembling lips.

He smirked and repositioned himself into an upright position on the bed. He planted his feet firmly on the ground and rested his elbows in his lap, his hands clasped together. "I don't know what you covering up for. It ain't nothing I haven't seen before."

"No …" My voice trailed off as I shook my head. All sense and reasoning evaded me. All of a sudden I felt as if I'd bathed in feces. The thought of him touching me, being inside me, made me want to peel my skin from my body. I closed my eyes, not able to stomach the site of him. "How … how did I get here? Did we …"

"You know? I think I like Carmen better." Jay-Jay took his time getting to his feet, making sure to locate his house shoes under the bed first so he could slip them on with ease.

The mention of my sister's name reignited my panic. "Where is Carmen?"

"You tell me, Rain." He finally stood, his massive frame just inches from my trembling body.

"As long as you stay quiet, no one is going to hurt you, okay?"

"Please. I didn't tell. Not even Carmen," I bowed my head and whispered as he walked closer.

"I know you didn't. I just wanted to see how far this shit was gonna go."

"What?"

He laughed. "I mean, I'd heard you went crazy. I was just waiting to see when the shit would blow up."

"I don't know what you're talking about." My head was still down.

He chuckled. I was surprised to open my eyes and see him half way across the room, no longer directly in front of me. He moved smoothly across the carpeted floor with clear confidence. His solid build revealed a once-chiseled physique that had missed too many days at the gym. His large manhood swung from his left thigh to his right as he made his way to the closet door to retrieve his robe. I watched in silence. "I don't know. Maybe I'm the one that's crazy. You had me going for a little while, lil' mama. But,"—he shook his finger at me after slipping on a thick terrycloth robe—"You know exactly who I am." He threw an oversized t-shirt in my direction. Desperate to cover my indecent exposure, I caught it in mid-air and quickly slipped it on.

I flinched and hugged my arms together when he began to move back toward me. My muscles tense, I couldn't move. He stopped right in front of me. My legs began to tremble lightly. "Thank you." His tone was deep, his voice breathy.

"For what." I cried shamelessly.

"For keeping our secret." He raised his hand and cupped my chin.

I violently jerked away from his touch and swung my arms—fists closed—wildly in front of me. Screeching and sobbing, I twisted and turned my body into near convulsions. "Don't kill me. Don't kill me." I repeated in between screams and tears.

He grabbed my shoulders firmly, shook me, and pushed me against the wall. "I said … calm … down!" He held me in place until I stopped resisting. We stood silent for several moments, our eyes locked on each other's. Our chests rose and fell in sync.

"Why did you kill her? Why did you kill my mother?" I finally broke the silence.

He backed up, trusting that my crazed tirade was over. His eyes hardened. "Yo' mama was a lying bitch! She deserved to die, and you should be happy about that." His shameless confession made tears pour down my face. He continued, "I loved her too. She was my bottom bitch. Never thought she would play me like she did." He sat back down on the bed, shaking his head as if he was reliving the past.

"You *loved* her?"

"Hell, yeah. Me and Corrine went way back. I taught

her everything about the dope game. I raised her in these streets. Made her my woman. Then she—"

"Whatever she did, she didn't deserve to die the way she did!" I cut him off, yelling, forgetting about my fear of death at the hands of Jay-Jay.

He jumped back to his feet. "Two hundred and fifty thousand dollars ain't enough to die over?!" When he yelled, sprays of saliva speckled my face. I jumped, but didn't bother to wipe the spit away. "That bitch set me up. Her and my boy, the one she was fuckin', set me up. After everything I did for her!"

"Why are you telling me all this?"

It seemed as though that question momentarily removed him from his trance. "Because you need to know what a triflin' bitch yo' mama was." He leaned in closer to my face. "Don't you wanna know?"

I shook my head 'no.'

He walked away from me again, easing toward the dresser. "Shit was all good until this new nigga, Rock, came around. Corrine was my girl. We ran the streets together. She was the only woman I allowed to get that close to me. I loved her ..." His voice trailed just as he reached the dresser. He grabbed a brush and began smoothing his wavy hair into place. "But, Rock ..." Jay-Jay stopped again, taking a deep breath and shaking his head in exasperation. "I knew something was up with that dude the first time I met him. I never shoulda trusted him, but Tre talked me into it. Said the nigga was good people. So, I let him in."

"So what does any of this have to do with my mother?" I was anxious to hear more and growing impatient with his lengthy journey down memory lane.

He smirked, seemingly more to himself than at me. "Everything. Corrine started to act funny after a coupla weeks. She would jump to Rock's defense too quick when money came up short, or she'd try to cover for him when she knew I was looking for him. Those shoulda been my warning signs right there, but she had my heart, so I ignored them. I coulda stopped them; I knew they was fuckin'."

"Why did you kill her?"

"She deserved it."

"No!"

Jay-Jay ignored my outburst. "I hated to see what he was doing to her. She was changing right in front of my eyes and I didn't know how to stop it. I tried to talk to her about it over and over again. We'd get into fights, but all she cared about was Rock." He punctuated his sentence by pounding his fist on the dresser. "After everything I did for her!" He seemed to forget that I was in the room as he continued his monologue. "I didn't know what else to do. The only thing I could think of was to hit a lick for a lot of cash and move away from the city so we'd never have to come back. I tried to get her away from Rock, away from the 'hood, so we'd never have to work the streets again. I had an airtight plan, and she was down for it. Now that I think about it, she was a little *too* eager."

I shifted my weight from my right hip to the left, not sure of what to do with myself while he continued to ramble.

"We hit the First National Bank over on Grand River. Caught the manager before opening time and raided the vault. It went smooth too. In and out in five minutes. Clean. Corrine drove one of the getaway cars. I rode with Tre. All we had to do was meet up at the eastside spot in exactly two hours so we could divvy up the cash and get out of town. Four hundred thousand dollars. Corrine had two fifty in the car with her."

"She never showed," I whispered.

"Never trust a bitch. The next day we found the car she was driving crashed into a tree about a block away from Rock's house. It had been set on fire. No bodies. I knew then that she and Rock had run with the money. Two hundred and fifty grand. Gone. I didn't see them again for two months." He continued to brush his hair rhythmically and mechanically. I doubted he even realized he was still doing it.

"Why did she come back?" Jay-Jay had me deeply engaged in the story, thirsty for more.

"Rumor was, she'd hid most of the money in the city before she left. Her and Rock blew the stack they kept on flashy bullshit. I caught them when they came back to get the rest of the money—and you."

I felt my heart rate quicken as he began to segue into the story of my mother's murder. Most of me didn't want to hear it, a narration of my visions and pieces of memory, but part of me needed the closure. He stopped brushing his hair and set the brush down on the dresser. He grabbed a black do-rag and placed it carefully on his head, tying it with precision.

"I got to Rock first. Caught his dumb ass coming out of his mama's house in the middle of the night. The back door. Corrine was next."

I shook my head slowly from side to side, silently pleading with him to spare me the details. I knew what happened, it was all a vivid movie that haunted me regularly. He walked carefully back toward me. He couldn't seem to keep still.

"I never found out what she did with the bulk of the stash, but I always thought maybe your GiGi was holding onto it. But I got locked up, had to do a ten-year bid before

I could find out."

I began to process what he was telling me. The spacious, three-bedroom, two-unit flat—owned free and clear, every bill and expense taken care of; the expensive psychotherapists throughout the years, and the wads of cash paid to Kyle. GiGi had that money, and she used it to take care of me—of us. I didn't let on that I'd cracked the case. I kept my mouth shut.

Jay-Jay continued to walk toward me until he was standing only about six inches away. "When I got out, I put that shit behind me. Until ... I met Carmen."

The tears started to flow again. "What do you want from me? You already took my mother from me. What else do you want?"

"I'll never get that money back." He placed a gentle hand on my shoulder. "But I've got something better. I have a piece of Corrine standing right here in front of me, and I'm not letting her go." He squeezed my shoulder until I winced in pain.

"Let go of me!" I yelled, twisting my body awkwardly to free myself from his hard grip.

"You're mine." He declared, never loosening his hold.

I looked to my left and quickly spotted an empty champagne bottle on the edge of the entertainment center. I grabbed it, raising it high in the air before striking Jay-Jay on his head with every ounce of strength I had. He stumbled backward clumsily, losing his balance and releasing me. I took advantage of the space between us and swung the bottle again, this time hitting him in the back of his head. He groaned in pain, holding the sides of his head as he tried to keep his balance. Satisfied at the sight of a thin line of trickling blood, I darted around him and raced out of the bedroom door. Wearing nothing more than an oversized t-shirt, I ran out of the house and down the block, doing my best to avoid the sticks, rocks, and debris that decorated the sidewalk, slicing into my bare feet. I didn't know if Jay-Jay was behind me. I didn't hear him; then again, I wasn't trying to. The only thing on my mind was finding safety. Eventually I did, at a small carryout soul food restaurant about four blocks away from the house.

"No shoes, no service!" The husky black man behind the counter scolded me as soon as I stepped foot into the restaurant.

"Please, I'm in trouble." I raised my hands in surrender. "I just need to use your phone."

The restaurant was empty, but he glared at me like my disheveled appearance was making him lose customers and money. "Please," I repeated.

He rolled his eyes and twisted his face. "Hurry up." He sighed and pushed the phone in my direction on top of the counter.

"Thank you." I dialed Kyle's number. Then, I waited fifteen minutes for him to pick me up.

19 Rain / *Saturday, May 7th*

"WHAT in the hell happened to you? Where have you been?" Flustered, Kyle fussed over me as he eyed my tattered hair, bare legs, and bleeding feet.

"I can't talk about it right now, Kyle. I just can't." I started to cry all over again, trying and failing to swipe away the tears that raced down my face.

"Rain, you have to tell me something. You can't just disappear for the night, then pop up at Uptown Café, calling me to come get you. How am I supposed to do my job, look after you, protect you, if you're constantly running on your own agenda?"

"My own agenda? Kyle, you really don't know anything, do you? Hell, *I* don't know anything. I don't know how the hell I got there. Please, I just wanna go home."

"Okay, you don't have to talk to me, but I know someone you *will* talk to—"

"No!" I shot up to a ninety-degree angle in my seat. I wasn't ready to face GiGi with all I knew. I wasn't ready to ask her about the money that she hid from me for twenty years.

"Rain, you're not making this easy. We're just trying to help you."

"I don't need your help! All you wanted me to do is remember what happened, and I do. I remember everything. I remember my mother. That's what you wanted, right? I remember!" As I yelled, I felt the heat rising inside of me. "Poof, I'm cured, okay?"

"It's not that simple, Rain."

"Nothing's simple. I'm finding *that* out the hard way. Why couldn't you leave well enough alone? Why couldn't GiGi? I was *fine* living in the dark. Everything was okay until she came back to me. Why did you make me remember?"

Kyle took his eyes off the road for a moment, looking at me with softness in his eyes. "Rain, we still have a ways to go. You weren't fine before, and everything is *not* okay now."

I rolled my eyes and grunted loudly.

"GiGi loves you. That's why she does what she does. That's why I'm here."

"Do you love me?" There, I'd finally asked the one question that constantly lingered in the back of my mind.

"Don't start, Rain. You know the answer to that. I'm here to look after you, to nurse you back to health."

"Whatever! Just take me home, okay?" I swallowed the lump in my throat and hid the hurt of his rejection in my tart tone. "I'll talk to GiGi later."

He gave me a skeptical look.

"I promise. I will. I'll tell her everything. Just not now.

Then you two can dissect me like a science project until *you* think I'm okay." That seemed to shut him up. I sighed and laid my head back, arms folded across my chest.

We rode the rest of the way to the house in complete silence. Surprisingly, Kyle walked me into the upper flat in peace. I was thankful for the relief—even if it was only temporary. I knew that as soon as he got back downstairs, he'd call GiGi and she'd be on me in no time, pressuring me to tell her everything. Kyle walked back down to his flat, leaving me alone—or so I thought.

"I hope you enjoyed fucking my man. Did you taste my pussy on his breath, bitch?" Carmen stormed into the kitchen, charging toward me as I stood next to the dinette.

"Carmen! I was worried about you. What happened?" I ignored her rage and responded with sincere concern.

"Don't play coy with me, hoe." She pointed a hot-pink polished fingernail between my eyebrows. "You know *exactly* what happened. You couldn't *wait* to take what was mine. The only thing I have!"

"No Carmen, I swear. I don't even remember what happened. I don't remember how I got there. I would never do anything to intentionally hurt you. I swear—"

"Shut up! You don't give a *fuck* about me. You never did. You walk around here like you're America's fucking sweetheart. Everybody loves Rain. Mama! GiGi!" Carmen screamed.

I reached out to place a hand on her shoulder, trying to calm her, but she slapped it away. "Don't fucking touch me! I hate you. I hate everything about you."

Her words pierced me like a dagger to the heart. I took a deep breath; I needed a moment to gather my words. "Carmen, you don't mean that. We're sisters. Remember the talk we had? I love you."

Carmen laughed balefully. "Ha! You're so damn stupid. I didn't mean any of that shit. I just said what I needed to say to get you to swallow the pill I dropped in your glass. You fell for it too. Gullible bitch!"

"What? You drugged me?" I could feel my concern quickly morphing into fury. "How could you do that to me? Why?"

She snickered. "Oh, shut up; you act like it was crack or something."

"Carmen!"

"Jay said he wanted to meet you, so I did what I had to do to get you to him. I didn't know you were gonna try to steal my man though. I left when I couldn't take it anymore."

The mention of Jay-Jay's name catapulted me back into the reality of what I'd just learned. "Oh my God, Carmen. There's something you need to know about Jay-Jay—"

Carmen took a step back and folded her arms across her chest. "What? You spend one night with him and all of a sudden you know him better than I do? You can't tell me shit I don't already know."

"No, Carmen. Listen." I tried to soften my tone and prepare my sister for the blow I was about to hit her with. "He killed our mom. He killed her! He told me the whole story."

"What the *fuck* are you talking about? You have no idea who killed her. Your crazy ass don't know the difference between a stupid vision and reality. If you think making up lies is going to get me to stop being with Jay-Jay, then you're dumber than I thought. He loves me."

"Carmen, I'm not making this up. I did see his face in a vision and I knew it was him when I woke up at his house." I paused, tried to gather some cautious words to say. "The only reason he got close to you was because he has some sick obsession with mom. He wants you and me because we are a part of her."

"You sound ridiculous!"

"He doesn't love you, Carmen." It was almost a whisper; I feared her reaction to the ugly truth. She didn't respond—not verbally. The next thing I felt was the harsh sting of her palm as she slapped me across my left cheek. The blow made me stumble backward, knocking one of the dinette chairs against the table. I grabbed it to brace and balance myself before I went crashing to the floor along with it. I was momentarily stunned by the impact. Not fully realizing that my sister had just struck me in the face, I held my cheek with my left hand. But my daze didn't last long. Before she had time to strike me again, I threw myself into defense mode and charged at her with anger and resentment I didn't know I possessed. My closed fist hit her left temple. Blinded by tears of rage, pain, confusion, and yearning, I followed the first punch with a second to her gut. Winded, she staggered backward, clutching her stomach and coughing. I shifted my weight uneasily from my left leg to my right, anticipating her next move. Ready for anything, I kept my fists closed tightly in front of me and my eyes narrowed over her hunched body. She looked up at me with what I thought was a hint of surprise in her eyes. Carmen never thought her weak little sister would come at her with such force—I guess it was time for her to think again. Screaming unintelligibly, she pulled herself upright and rushed me, and her head plunged into my midsection as her arms wrapped around my waist. She knocked me off my feet and we went flying into the wall behind me. The impact sent The Lord's Prayer crashing down to the floor. I managed to keep myself from falling. I knew if I fell, I would give her the advantage to fully kick my ass. As she maintained her grip on my waist, I began to wail on the back of her head and back with powerful blows. When I felt her trying to stand erect, I snatched her head back down quickly and kneed her in the chin. She fell backward, but she took me with her. Breathless and losing momentum, I fell on top of her with strength to do little more than smack her face. Our grunts and moans were the only sounds that filled the house as Carmen struggled to free herself from under my weight. Before I could determine what to do next, her hands were around my neck, squeezing relentlessly. I scratched at her hands, trying desperately to pry her fingers from my throat. Carmen had the upper hand now, and she used it to roll me over on my back. She straddled me and looked fiercely into my eyes as she choked the life out of me. Gagging and coughing, I looked up at the woman I thought was my sister, but I saw a stranger. Carmen was gone, replaced by a crazed woman who had nothing more than vengeance flowing through her body.

"Stay the fuck away from my man! He didn't kill anybody, but *I* will, if you *ever* disrespect me like that again," Carmen huffed through clenched teeth.

"Carmen, please." It was all I could manage to say as she strangled me. At that moment, I knew we weren't sisters anymore. We were enemies, and nothing could change that. She despised me with every ounce of her being. The hurt I felt was infinite.

Without another word, she suddenly released me and stood up. Relieved to be able to breathe again, I held and massaged my neck in my hands and turned over on my side. Breathing heavily, Carmen charged out of the kitchen. I watched her snatch her purse hastily from the closet door before leaving the flat, slamming the door behind her. I couldn't move—I could only cry.

Why is this happening to me?

I slowly gathered myself and managed to get to my feet. Staggering, I tried to make my way out of the kitchen, but I nearly collapsed by the counter before I could make it out. My head was spinning and my stomach was nauseous. Head down and knees bent, I held myself up with my hands on the countertop, so I wouldn't hit the floor. It was all too much to digest—Jay-Jay, Carmen, GiGi, the money. How was I supposed to handle all that on my own? Why did they make me remember? Why? I feared that Jay-Jay was going to come after me—would he kill me? Would the brutal images of my mother's murder ever stop haunting me? All questions—no answers.

My loud sobs echoed through the house. I just wanted it all to go away. "I don't want to remember anymore!" I screamed to the ceiling. "I don't want this. Please ..." My voice went hoarse as the words trailed off. My tears hit the countertop in rapid succession, falling like raindrops in an unending storm. Slowly, using what little strength I had left, I pulled myself up to a standing position.

No! I refuse to let this consume me!

All of a sudden, I hated my mother. I hated her for leaving me, and I hated her even more for coming back—for disrupting my life. I gathered myself, then I marched out of the kitchen and into the hallway toward my bedroom. I pushed the door open forcefully; it slammed against the wall in response. Angrily wiping the unwelcome tears from my face, I stomped around my bedroom, rummaging through the belongings scattered about the bed, dresser, and floor. I opened the top drawer of my nightstand and found the scarf—*her* scarf. I snatched it up, balling it up in my fist. My mother's picture was just beneath the scarf, her black eyes speaking to me—begging me not to do what I knew I must in order to have normalcy in my life. Ignoring her pleas, I grabbed the picture and slammed the drawer shut.

I don't want to remember anymore!

Fueled by determination, I rushed back to the kitchen, both items clutched tightly in my hands. Dried tears streaked my face, retraced by fresh ones. I was crying so hard I began to cough, and my nose was running. I didn't bother to wipe a drop away; the tears propelled me forward. "I can't do this anymore. I can't handle it. Please!"

Stepping on the lever at the bottom of the trashcan to open it, I threw the scarf and the picture inside. "I'm sorry, Mommy." I sobbed to my mother's beautiful photo. "I'm sorry. I have to do this. I just want you to go away. Please, go away!"

Rummaging through the kitchen drawers, I spotted a book of matches among the random tools, papers, batteries, and other junk. I grabbed the matches and quickly struck a match. I was no longer thinking. Pure impulse and instinct to protect myself took over. Standing perfectly erect, with a stoic look on my face and tears and snot draining from my eyes and nose, I dropped the match in the garbage can. The flames rose out of the open can, reaching for me, dancing to the broken rhythm of my cries. The fire seemed to pull all my energy, breath, and balance as my body slumped and I dropped to the floor. The flames continued to dance wildly, sending smoke and fumes past the sensors of the smoke detector mounted on the ceiling in the hallway. Consumed by mixed feelings of relief, regret, guilt, and dread, I ignored the screeching beeps of the smoke detector and rested my head on the kitchen floor, curling myself into fetal position. I didn't care if I died, didn't care if the whole house burned into a pile of ashes. I just needed her to go away.

20 *Danny* / *Saturday, May 7th*

"RAIN! What the hell are you doing?!" I barge into the kitchen, my voice charged with panic. Smoke is drifting and spreading from the kitchen to the rest of the house. Rain isn't responding to me, and I can't tell if she's okay. Worried, I try desperately to clear the smoke from my line of vision to no avail; it has consumed the small kitchen. I can't see a thing, so I crouch low to the clean air below the smoke and creep the rest of the way in. That's when I spot Rain on the floor, curled in a ball.

"Rain! Rain!" I yell, trying to shout over the blaring smoke alarm. She looks up at me from the floor with a tear-streaked face and swollen eyes. Satisfied that she's still alive, I quickly scan the kitchen to determine the origin of the fire. I spot reddish-orange flames rising from the trashcan in the back corner. "Oh my God! Are you trying to kill us?" I don't wait for a response. I'm pretty sure I'm not going to get one anyway. Coughing and covering my nose and mouth with my forearm, I rush to the stove and grab an empty pot from the back burner. Rain watches me silently as I fill the pot with water from the sink and dump it into the trashcan. When the first pot of water doesn't completely kill the fire, I refill the pot twice more, and I'm finally successful in putting out the flames. Out of breath and confused, I stand next to the trashcan, taking a moment to digest what just happened—and what almost happened.

I hear pounding at the door. I stare down at Rain on the floor for a moment and shake my head in pity and bewilderment. "Oh shit, here comes Kyle," I sigh.

Kyle doesn't wait for anyone to answer his knocking. He rushes into the flat, causing the door to slam hard against the wall. I meet him in the front hall before he has a chance to venture too far into the house. I don't know what the hell is going on, but I know that I don't want too much of Kyle's interference until I find out. Hell, I'm no shrink, but I know my sister is losing it and his tactics haven't been much help so far.

"What's going on? Is everything alright?" Kyle waves his hands in the air to clear the smoke. I'm blocking his view into the kitchen so he can't see Rain lying on the floor.

"It's nothing," I yell so Kyle can hear me over the loud beeps of the smoke alarm. "I was cooking some bacon and got distracted when the phone rang. Started a grease fire. I put it out though."

He coughs, covering his mouth with his fist. He eyes me suspiciously, tilting his head slightly to the left.

"It's no big deal, Kyle, really. I was just about to turn the smoke detector off when you came up."

"Where's Rain?"

"I had her go to her room so she could stay clear of the smoke. She's in there now, waiting for me to tell her when it's safe to come out."

"Carmen?"

"I don't know. Who ever knows where the hell she is?" His line of questioning is beginning to irritate me. I'm anxious to find out what the hell is going on with Rain, and he's wasting my time.

"Well, you look fine," he says cautiously, examining me from head to toe.

Yeah, man." I offer a lighthearted chuckle. "Who ever heard of death by bacon?"

He doesn't join in on the laughter. I place my hands over my ears and look up at the ceiling to cue Kyle to stop the damn alarm from screaming. He steps around me, so he can look at the smoke detector. "I guess I'll just turn this off for you."

I steal a peek behind me and see Rain still on the floor, now sitting up with her back against the cabinet. Kyle grabs a stepping stool from the broom closet just outside the kitchen and proceeds to disarm the smoke alarm. The house falls silent.

"Whew! Thanks so much, man. I thought I was going to go deaf in here with all that damn noise."

His expression is distrustful. I ignore it, not giving him a chance to dig deeper. "Anyway, I'm about to clean up the mess in here and just relax. Nothing exciting going on with the girls." I place my hand on the wall beside me and cross one leg in front of the other. I tilt my head to the side, waiting for him to make his exiting remarks.

"You sure there's nothing going on here?" Kyle stretches his neck so he can see above my head and into the rest of the house.

"Nope." I drop my hand and straighten my posture. "You wanna do a look through?" I step a little to the side raising my arm shoulder length, giving him an invitation to walk through the rest of the house. I'm still blocking the entryway to the kitchen.

He leans forward slightly, but backs up. "Naw, I'll head back downstairs. I have a few runs to make. I won't be gone long though. GiGi said she'll be by later tonight to talk to Rain."

"Okay. I'll let her know."

"Okay."

"Okay."

Kyle walks backward until he reaches the door; then, he turns and leaves, closing the door softly behind him. I rush into the kitchen to find Rain still sitting on the floor, rocking back and forth to a melody that's playing only in her head.

"Rain?" I approach her cautiously, not sure of what she's thinking or feeling. She doesn't answer me, just continues to rock.

I kneel down so that we're eye level with each other. I gently take her face into my hands, lifting her head so she will be forced to look at me. "Rain, baby. Are you alright?"

Her body jerks as if she's suddenly brought back to life. She gasps. "Danny! Oh my goodness, I'm so glad you're here!" She reaches out and hugs me tightly. Confused, I return the embrace.

"Tell me what's going on." I speak into her neck.

"Carmen. She ... she attacked me."

"She *what*?" I lean back, putting space between us. I take a good look at Rain's face and can see the signs of a physical confrontation. Her left cheek is red. And I see what I determine to be a handprint on her neck. I know the telltale signs of abuse all too well, and the realization brings me to a state of momentary shame. I silently restate my vow to never harm Maya again. "I'll get in her ass for you. Tell me what happened."

Rain shakes her head as if she's trying to rid herself of unwanted thoughts. "She hates me. And ... and I can't blame her. I brought this all on us."

"What are you talking about?" I wipe the tears from her eyes.

"Everything would be okay if I'd never started to remember."

"Remember? What? You mean, you remember what happened to mom?"

She grimaces and looks at me for what seems to be the first time since we've been talking. "Where have you been? Where were you?"

"Don't worry about that. I had to put some things into perspective and pull myself together. I'm fine now. Just tell me what you remembered." I can see her hesitating, can tell she's contemplating whether or not to let me in on the confusion of her life.

She frowns. "You didn't hear us out here?"

"No, I didn't! Now tell me what the hell is going on!" I'm growing increasingly impatient and I'm beginning to think it isn't worth it, but one glance over at the smoking trashcan changes my mind.

Rain's eyes go blank, staring at nothing. "I saw the whole thing. I was there. It was like it was happening to me all over again. I tried to stop him. I tried to save Mommy's life, but I was too late. He killed her!" Tears stroll silently down her face as she recounts the murder. "I remember everything like it just happened. He looked right at me. I saw him."

"You saw him? What did he look like? Do we know him?"

Rain falls silent, clamps her mouth shut and starts to shake her head again. Whatever it is, whoever it is, she's afraid to tell me.

I take both her shoulders in my hands and shake her. "Come on. If you know, you have to tell me. She was my mom too!"

"Oh my God, Danny! I can't take this!"

"Why did Carmen attack you? Did you tell her who it was? Tell me!"

"It was …"

"Tell me!"

"It was Jay-Jay! It was Jay-Jay!" she screams with panicked eyes and a shaking body.

"*What?*" I think maybe I didn't hear her correctly. Our mother's murderer couldn't have been right under our noses this whole time.

"Jay-Jay!" she screams again.

I still refuse to let the truth sink in. "*Carmen's* Jay?" Rain doesn't answer; she doesn't have to. She knows that I know exactly who she's talking about. I rise slowly from my kneeling position. Stunned, I try to make some sense of the words she's speaking. "Jay?" I repeat, as if saying his name again will change reality.

"He told me everything."

"You talked to him? How?"

"I don't know. Carmen said he wanted to see me, so she drugged me and took me to him."

"She did *what?*"

"I don't know what happened, but I woke up in his bed."

This story is beginning to spin out of control at a rapid speed. I don't know how to process what my little sister is telling me. Nervously, I begin pacing the floor, my hands in my pockets.

Why in the hell did I come out of my room?

"He told me everything," she repeats. "He told me why and how he ..." Rain's voice trails off into sobs.

"Jay-Jay." This time his name shoots out of my mouth with conviction. My mind races back to our brief phone exchange the previous week.

Yeah, you'll be around until you meet me, nigga. You think I'm playing? I don't like people fucking with my family, so you better pray you don't run into me.

I feel the heat rising inside my body, through my blood. I tighten my fists by my sides and clench my teeth. Confusion transforms to anger, then to outrage. This dude had single-handedly ruined my family. He killed our mother, turned our sister into a whoring drug addict, and the other is a psychotic mess. I wouldn't be surprised if I found out he had something to do with what those homos did to me. Within seconds, I convince myself that he had. I allow the fury to boil up inside me like lava.

Still pacing the kitchen floor, I punch the wall. Rain jumps. "Danny, what are we going to do? What if he comes after me? He knows I know now."

"He ain't gonna do shit to you. That nigga ain't fuckin' with nobody else in this family. I'll make sure of that." I storm out of the kitchen and into my room, slamming the door behind me.

21 *Carmen* / *Saturday, May 7th*

JAY stares at me intently through narrowed eyes. He watches me as I walk back and forth between the living room and the adjoining dining room. I can't keep still. My mind is racing and my feet have to keep up with the pace, or else my thoughts will come crashing down on me. I know that Rain just fed me a bunch of bullshit to keep me away from him. I know none of it is true, but that doesn't stop the thoughts from seeping into my head.

He killed our mother!

No! No, he didn't. That bitch just wants to take the only person in the world who loves me away. *That's* it.

He doesn't love you, Carmen.

Yes, he does. Why else would he do the things he's done for me? He loves me, takes care of me. We're going to be together forever. Fuck Rain! I grab handfuls of hair on either side of my head and continue to walk back and forth, back and forth.

"You gonna tell me what the fuck your problem is? Or you gonna keep walking around this house like a psycho?"

I keep moving; I can't stop. "I just don't know anymore. I don't know how to take this shit."

"Take what? I told you what the deal was."

"Why was Rain talking that shit? Why would she say you did it?"

Jay-Jay stands up, but he doesn't make a move toward me. "How many times we need to go through this? You know why. She wanna take you away from me. She told me this morning."

"I can't let her do that. *You* can't let her do that!"

"I don't want her."

"Why did you fuck her?" I finally stop pacing and scream at him.

"Hey watch yo' mouth. Don't forget who you talking to."

I start to cry, my shaking hands roughly massaging my temples. "Sorry. I'm sorry." Jay-Jay walks toward me, reaches out a closed fist. I know a pill is inside. "No, I don't want a pill." He frowns; I do too. Did I just say what I think I said? Yeah, that's right. I don't want to be high. I need to process this shit so I can get through it. I need to get to the bottom of this Rain business.

He pushes the pill back down into his pocket. "I don't want Rain. I want you, baby. You're mine. You always will be." I look up at him, searching for sincerity in his eyes. It is there. I know he loves me. "It's time to take you off the streets, take you out the game, away from this life. You proved yourself to me, and now I can make you my wife."

The tears stop. I drop my hands to my sides, sniff. He

just said the words I've been waiting to hear since we met. I've made it. "Really, Daddy?"

"Really." He wraps his arms around my waist, pulls me in closely. "Me and you, nobody else." I smile shyly, raising my arms and clasping my hands behind his neck. He kisses me with a passion only two lovers can share. My heart is racing, pounding relentlessly as he slides his tongue across my lips. I suck his bottom lip and move my body in closer to his erection. "Mmm." He moans at the feel of my hand as I massage his manhood. I lose myself in our passion, melting against his body, letting him handle me with his aggressive masculinity. I play with his belt buckle, trying to wriggle it loose. He pulls back slowly, ending our kiss.

"You know I only wanted to see Rain so I could see where her head was at. See what she had going on inside that crazy little mind of hers. Now that I know, we need to come up with a plan."

"What you mean, Daddy?"

He backs up, turns, and takes a seat on the couch. I follow, sitting sideways on his lap. He clasps his hands around my hips. "Rain is out here throwin' dirt on my name. Sayin' I killed yo' mom and shit. She tryin' to come between us. We can't let that happen."

I'm only half listening as I suck on his earlobe. "Mmm hmm."

"I can't have her out here making false accusations. I get locked up, we can't be together."

"No, we can't have that." I mumble between licks.

"You gotta take care of that bitch."

I stop, lean back, and look Jay-Jay in the eye. "Take care of her?"

"You know what I mean. She can fuck this whole thing up. You know I ain't do that shit. You know the only reason she saying it is 'cause she wanna take you away from me. You gotta stop her." When I don't say anything, he continues. "I love you, and I can't have anything or anybody keeping me from my woman."

"I love you, too."

"I know you do. That's why you gonna kill Rain."

I try my best to swallow the oversized lump in my throat. It takes several seconds for it to go down. "Kill her?"

"Yeah. There's no other way. Then we can move up outta here. Get out the game, and live the life. That *is* what you want, ain't it?"

"Of course."

"Then make it happen."

Our eyes lock. I nod slowly. I know right now that I'll do what I have to do to secure my future. Rain is good as gone. I kiss my man again before rising from his lap.

"Where you going?" he asks.

"I have to use the bathroom real quick, I'll be right back." I smile at him and head toward the front of the house.

"The bathroom's that way. Why you going up there?"

"So, here we are. I finally get to meet the infamous Jay-Jay face-to-face!" Danny's raspy voice seemingly emerges from nowhere as I step into the hall. I snap my head toward the front door. Danny wears a look on his face that I don't recognize.

"What the fuck?" Jay-Jay jumps to his feet. "Carmen!"

I don't know what to say or do. I'm not sure of what's happening. Why is Danny here? Where did he come from?

"Get over here, Carmen," Danny barks at me. I don't move.

"Danny?" Jay-Jay asks cautiously.

"Yeah, nigga, you know exactly who the fuck I am,"

Danny sneers. He reaches under his shirt and retrieves a .22 caliber pistol and raises it slowly with a straight arm, pointing it at Jay-Jay.

"Danny, what are you doing?" I scream, eyeing the gun fearfully.

Danny keeps his eyes fixated on Jay-Jay. "I'm doing what needs to be done. I'm about to kill this nigga."

22 *Danny* / *Saturday, May 7th*

THE gun shakes in my trembling right hand. I reach up and hold my right hand with my left to calm the shaking. My breathing is steady, but I can feel my heart pounding, sending pulsations through my body. Suddenly, I'm overwhelmingly hot. My shirt is too heavy, my pants too thick. My feet ache. I shake my head back to get loose strands of hair off my sweaty neck.

Jay-Jay stands before me on the opposite side of the living room. A small glass cocktail table is the only thing between us. Even with a gun pointed at him, threatening to steal his life away, he exudes unapologetic arrogance. His eyes dare me to make a move. The corner of his mouth is upturned into a sly smirk. I can smell his cologne, a loud musk, from where I stand by the front door. It stinks.

"Danny, put the gun down!"

I can hear Carmen screaming, but her words pass right through me. I can't see her, can't see anything in the house but my target. Jay-Jay seems to move in slow motion: his blinks, the rise and fall of his chest, his words. Each second stretches into infinity.

"So now what? You gonna kill me?" Jay-Jay's sneering tone is infused with derisiveness. His arms are resting casually by his side, his head cocked to the right.

"You killed my mother." My voice is surprisingly low, husky. I feel as if I have turned into someone else—a killer, thirsty for blood.

Carmen nervously shifts her weight from side to side. I eye her through my peripheral. "No, he didn't! Rain is lying! Danny, put the fucking gun down."

"You turned my sister into a fiend. Got her out here selling pussy."

"Danny." He chuckles, unafraid of me and my gun. Jay-Jay makes two careful steps in my direction. "Now I've met all three of you, and I must say, Carmen is still my favorite." Carmen smiles with satisfaction, momentarily forgetting the seriousness of the present situation. He takes two more steps. The floorboards creak under his expensive shoes.

"You ruined my family."

"Danny, stop it! He didn't do shit. Rain—that *bitch*—she's lying. Do you hear me?" Carmen starts toward me.

"Carmen, Danny, Rain … who knew we'd meet up like this? After all this time. I never thought it would come to *this*," Jay-Jay muses.

"Both of y'all stay the fuck back. If anybody moves any closer, I'm pullin' the trigger." I'm talking to both of them, but I never take my eyes off Jay-Jay. They both freeze in place. "Rain told me everything. You've been fucking with us for too long, and now it's time for you to pay."

"You doin' all that talking about what you gonna do, but you standing there with the gun in yo' hand, scared to make a move. Shit, *Rain* got more heart than you. Where she at?" He's mocking me, calling my bluff. I hate him with every ounce of feeling I have inside me, but even I'm not sure why I'm hesitating to end his life.

"Shut up! Shut. The fuck. UP!" I yell, keeping my aim steady on the middle of Jay-Jay's chest. I envision a red dot dancing on his black t-shirt just above his gaudy medallion.

"Please don't—" Carmen starts.

"You shut up too." I finally turn my heard toward her, but keep my stance centered on Jay-Jay. "What the fuck is wrong with you? He *killed* her! He killed our *mother*. Look at you! Look at what he's doing to you. You like being a hoe? Turning tricks? Huh?"

Carmen starts to cry. "Don't do this. Don't take him from me, please. Rain is behind all this shit. Can't you see what she's doing? She hates me. She's lying about mama. She just wants to take him from me. Please ..." Black mascara streaks Carmen's cheeks and chin. Her hair, a bit frizzy, clings to her face and neck. For a moment, I pity her, wondering whether her dysfunction can be fixed—whether she can ever go back to being my spunky, annoying little sister. In a millisecond, my question is answered by the emptiness in her eyes: no.

A single tear escapes my eye; I let it fall freely. There is no way to go back to the way things were, not after today. We've long since lost the days when Rain, Carmen, and I would have innocent arguments about the little things only stair-step siblings could bicker about. Life had gotten too serious, leading up to this very moment, and the pain of that realization drains warm, salty tears from my eyes. For that brief repose, I forgot what I was doing. With the gun still in the air and my finger resting lightly on the trigger, I'm lost in a feeling of longing and loss for my sister—and for myself.

This is my fatal mistake.

With my attention on Carmen and away from Jay-Jay, he makes his move. Suddenly he lunges at me with his arms outstretched. I hear his heavy footsteps rushing toward me as his six-foot frame surges forward. Without thinking, I turn my head in his direction. Panic makes me clench my fist, a reflex that forces my index finger against the trigger. The first shot rings loudly in my ears, startling me and propelling me backward. The sound bounces off the walls like a ping-pong ball and echoes through the house. Carmen jumps back and ducks, crouching low on the floor.

I see Jay-Jay stagger, holding the left side of his chest. He looks down and gasps while I stand motionless with the gun still suspended in the air. He looks at me with hatred glowing in his eyes. When Jay-Jay takes a wobbly step toward me, I know I need to fire again.

Pop

Then again.

Pop

And again.

Pop, pop, pop!

Carmen screams until she begins to cough and choke on her own saliva. The sight of Jay-Jay's thick body, drenched in blood, falling back onto the love seat behind him, makes me feel tranquil. I stabilize myself, planting my feet firmly onto the floor and allowing a menacing smile to extend across my face. His eyes, frozen in a wide stare of shock and terror, make me laugh nervously. Jay-Jay's blood-soaked t-shirt quickly begins to stain the cream chenille couch.

Blood spreads like spilled milk on a kitchen floor, turning the couch's fabric into a tie-dye of deep red and cream.

Carmen remains crouched in the corner on the floor crying. "Jay-Jay! Baby, NO!"

We both watch as his chest jumps in three sudden convulsions. Startled by his sudden movement, I squeeze the trigger once more to make sure he's dead. *Click!* The gun is empty. He gargles, and a stream of crimson-red blood seeps from the corner of his mouth. The heavy stillness in the room tells me Jay-Jay's life has ended—just like he had ended my mother's life. I've done my job damn well.

Carmen pops up from the floor like a jack-in-the-box. She scrambles to his side, sobbing and gagging the whole way.

"Carmen, get away from him!" I yell as she bends over to cradle his limp head in her arms. She doesn't look up at me; she keeps her eyes locked on his lifeless gaze.

"How could you do this to me, Danny. *Why?*" Her hands are shaking as she wipes the blood spatters from his forehead, cheeks, and chin.

"Don't touch him, Carmen! What are you doing?" I drop the gun on the carpet and run to my sister. She sobs. Her tears stream down his chest, blending with his blood.

"Don't you tell me what to do! You killed him! You *killed* him! Oh, my God! How could you?"

I place firm hands on Carmen's shoulders and try to pull her away from the corpse, but she pushes me off violently.

"Get the fuck off me!" She shoots me a look of pure condemnation. "You took him from me! He *loved* me! He was everything to me, and you took him!" Her cries coalesce into broken, almost unintelligible moans.

Reality begins to set in, and I'm becoming frantic. I don't know whether Jay-Jay had been expecting someone to drop by, don't know if anyone has heard the shots and called the police. We have to move quickly, before we're caught at the scene. I've just killed a man! He has *people*—people I know would come looking for me. What have I done? Why are we still here? I can feel myself coming unglued. My eyes dart from the front door to Jay-Jay's body and back again. We have to get the fuck out of here!

"Carmen! We have to go. *Now!*"

"No! I'm not leaving him!"

"You stupid bitch! He killed our mother! He *deserved* to die."

"No! Rain did this. Rain did this to get back at me. You let her use you. You let her talk you into this shit. I know she did it. I know it."

Carmen's stalling and irrational rants are going to get us caught—or killed. I bend down again, and more firmly this time, yank her away from Jay-Jay's body. She flails her arms and kicks her legs in resistance, trying her best to get free from my hold. I'm relentless as I pry her away from the man she thought to be her true love. Her hands, covered in his blood, grab at me, smearing red streaks down my cream colored shirt. I hook my arms tightly under hers and allow her to twist and turn as I ease her farther away from the love seat where our mother's murderer has met his judgment.

"Rain! I'm gonna kill that bitch. I'm gonna kill her for doing this to me."

"Come on! If these niggas come in here and see us, we're dead."

"I didn't do anything!"

"They don't know that, and they won't care. Let's go!" I'm finally able to get Carmen to her feet. Her body is nearly limp as she finally gives up fighting and lets me guide her toward the front door. I open the door, looking to the left and then the right to make sure the coast is clear—no thugs lurking around waiting to attack me in the name of vengeance. I see only Jay-Jay's shiny silver SUV parked at the curb in front of the house. Carmen steals a look back at Jay-Jay's body as I open the screen door to force her out.

"Run!" I yell, and she darts across the freshly cut lawn and down the sidewalk. I follow close behind Carmen, sprinting like Marion Jones. I hear the screen door shut behind us, but the front door remains open, giving any passerby a clear view of the grisly scene in the living room. Had I had more time to think, I would have closed it, but there is no time. Survival instincts carry me down the sidewalk and away from the house at a breakneck pace.

As we run, an older woman, who looks to be in her sixties, steps out onto her porch only a few houses down from Jay-Jay's. She reaches for her mail in the metal box next to her door, but freezes when she catches sight of Carmen and me running past her. The horrified look that washes over her face makes me conscious of my blood-stained clothes. I wrap my arms around my chest in a vain attempt to hide what I have done. The woman's eyes travel to the house we've just left. I silently pray that she doesn't call the police, and I lengthen my strides so I can catch up with Carmen.

This is it; there's no turning back. We don't slow down until twenty minutes later when we've reached our own front door.

* * *

I scramble onto the porch of the flat, beating Carmen to the house by just a couple of minutes. I open the screen and front doors urgently and step inside, but I pause when

I realize Carmen isn't with me, ready to go in. I spot her jogging down the sidewalk, dragging her feet as if her life doesn't depend on speed right now. Even from a distance, I can see her face twisted in agony. Carmen's tears glisten in the late afternoon sun, and her smeared makeup makes her look like a wicked clown.

"Come on!" I lean out the door and yell at her, aggravated at her nonchalance while our lives are in danger. Carmen ignores me, trudging the rest of the way to the porch. I think she might collapse, climbing the three stone steps and slowing her pace even more, sobbing and shaking. I grab her right elbow and hoist her up, almost dragging her.

We finally get inside, stumbling and nearly falling all the way through the doorway. I slam the door behind us, unconscious of the fact that Kyle might hear us. Shit, this is no time for rational thinking. I watch as Carmen seems to melt in the entryway. She slides slowly down the wall, smearing sweat and blood into long, faint streaks until she finally reaches the floor.

"No! Get your ass up! You want Kyle to catch us out here?" I crouch and hook my arms under hers to yank her up violently. She is out of it, not hearing a word that comes from my mouth. Her eyes, watery and glazed over, are empty and listless. Her limp head hangs to the side. It is as if I shot her and not her raggedy-ass boyfriend. I have to do something quickly so Carmen can pull herself together because there is no way that we'll make it up the steps with only my strength. Thinking of all the old sitcoms I had seen, I slap the shit out of her—first the right side of her face and then the left. Gripping her shoulders tightly, I yell, "Snap out of it! Pull it together, or you'll get us both killed!"

Unaffected by the strikes to her face, Carmen's only reply is hiccupped sobbing as she tries to stop herself from crying. "Now come on!" I take her hand and lead the way up the stairs to the upper flat. As I open the door, I silently pray that Rain isn't inside. I don't want to have to explain what happened before I have time to think through my story. Yes, she has to know, but only after I've figured out what I *want* her to know. I'm not sure how the news will affect Rain in her delicate mental state. For me, killing Jay-Jay is closure. For Rain, my action might tear her apart, or worse, lead to her complete insanity.

I'm disappointed to find my prayer ignored as Rain emerges from the kitchen and walks out into the front hall. Rain's eyes grow wide with terror as she fixes them on Carmen's blood-soaked clothes and hands.

"Oh my God! What in the hell happened?"

Carmen glares at Rain, probably wishing that Rain is dead and not Jay-Jay. I step from behind Carmen and rush past both of them toward my room. "Jay-Jay's dead." I mumble, half hoping that she didn't hear me as I make my way down the hallway.

"What? What did you just say? Jay-Jay … *Dead?*" Rain stammers in utter disbelief.

"Look I don't have time to explain now. Carmen, get cleaned up!"

When I don't get a reply or hear any footsteps behind me, I turn to face Carmen. She doesn't make a move. She just stands opposite Rain in the hall, her tear-streaked face shadowed in anger. Carmen's eyes are reduced to slits, and her fists are balled by her sides. From the way her jaw is shifting from side-to-side, I can tell that she's grinding her teeth, seething, as she stares at Rain loathingly. Rain seems to ignore her as she looks at me and awaits an answer that I'm not ready to give her.

"Jay-Jay's dead?" she repeats. "Who did it? Danny,

please tell me you didn't do something crazy!" I can hear the panic beginning to rise in Rain's voice.

"Look, I did what I had to do to make things right." Carmen still hasn't moved and I don't have time for her inaction. I throw my hands in the air. "Carmen, come on! Kyle told me GiGi is coming by later, do you want her to see you like that?" Carmen's eyes remain locked on Rain. Prepared to give her another slap, I stomp back in their direction.

Then it hit me: the gun! Where is it?

Foolishly, I look down at the floor, turning in circles. I check my pants, the small of my back, but of course it isn't there. I know exactly where it is. *Dammit.* I left it at Jay-Jay's house. "Oh, shit." I begin to pace. "Oh shit, oh shit, oh shit." I have to go back. I have to get that gun or I'm going down for sure. It's a risky move, but I have no choice.

"Danny ... no." Rain shakes her head slowly as if she's reading my mind. "Please, don't go. We have to call the police."

"Call the *police*? Are you out of your fucking mind?" *I guess I'm asking the wrong person that question.* "This is between *us*! We ain't telling nobody. You hear me?"

"But, Danny—"

"But nothing! You keep yo' fuckin' mouth shut. No police, no GiGi, no Kyle. Nobody!"

Rain opens her mouth as if she's going to speak, but she shuts it quickly when I shoot her a threatening look.

"I have to go back to the house." I run into my bedroom and grab a clean shirt from the hamper. I change my shirt and come back out into the hall, throwing the stained shirt to Rain. "Here, throw this in the machine with some bleach."

"But—"

"Now!" I push past both my sisters and grab the

doorknob. "And make sure Carmen gets out of those clothes and gets cleaned up. Better yet, burn the clothes." I know Carmen, still stunned and devastated, will be incapable of carrying out that task on her own. Feeling the adrenaline of panic, fear, and murder, I race out of the house and back to Jay-Jay's to retrieve the gun.

23 *Carmen* / *Saturday, May 7th*

I can't seem to form any thoughts in my mind except one—one word: hate. The hatred I feel for Rain at this moment is so heavy, it weighs me down into statue-like inertia. I watch Rain carefully as she scurries around the house from the front hall to the living room, then to the kitchen. I imagine her head swelling to the size of a basketball then exploding, splattering brain and bone fragments over the walls like an abstract painting. She shuffles back into the hallway holding Danny's bloody shirt in one hand and a bottle of bleach in the other.

She stands before me, about half an arm's length away. Her wild hair seems to be more untamed than usual. Rain's caramel skin is spotted by a few pimples—one on her chin and two on her forehead. Barefoot, she stands just a few inches shorter than me. A quick glance at her mid-section tells me that she needs to tighten up her sloppy stomach with a few crunches. Everything about her disgusts me. She's ugly. Her demeanor, her very presence, offends me.

"Carmen," she starts cautiously, sensing the rage emanating from me, "I know we had a fight, but I think we need to put that behind us now. This is important. I think you should try to get cleaned up before Kyle or GiGi comes." She never looks me in the eye as she addresses me. I can feel her discomfort in every shaky syllable she utters.

"He's dead."

Rain, with her head down, begins to walk away from me, but my declaration stops her in mid-step. "I know, Carmen. I'm sorry your man is gone, but … he killed our mom. You have to believe me."

Her words—all lies—mean nothing to me. I watch her mouth move, see the awkward way she twists one hand around the other as if she doesn't know what to do with them. The heat rises inside me slowly, increasing my temperature, boiling my blood. "*You* killed him." I hiss through clenched teeth.

Rain finally looks up at me, fully turning her body toward me. "What are you talking about? I wasn't even there. I still don't know what happened."

"You're the reason he's dead." My monotone voice grows deeper.

"No, Carmen. I didn't—"

"Danny did it because of your lies. *You* did this." I can't see my younger sister anymore. The only thing in my line of vision is a malignant monster, a demon whose sole purpose is to destroy my world. "YOU. KILLED. HIM."

Nervously, Rain starts to back up, putting more space between us. "Carmen, we can't do this right now. I have to clean up this mess Danny left me with." She turns and heads toward the bathroom. "You should get out of those clothes."

As I watch her disappear behind the bathroom door, I remain still for a moment, allowing the internal tides of indignation to wash over me. How can she just walk away like it's no big deal? How can she speak to me so casually, so calm, indifferent about ruining my life and killing my love? She knew exactly what she was doing—the ultimate revenge. She took the only thing I had. She snatched my future and acted as if it meant nothing. Jay-Jay is dead and she is the reason.

My rage, rising strongly and quickly, carries me to the bathroom. The door is open just a crack. I can hear the running water in the tub, the scratching sound the rough sponge is making as Rain scrubs Danny's t-shirt. The smell of bleach is putrid and imposing as it wafts through the air, stinging my nose and eyes. I ease the door open a little more and watch Rain as she kneels before the tub, working vigorously to clean the blood from Danny's shirt. I step softly as I creep into the bathroom and stand behind her. My flat iron is resting on the counter, still plugged in from last night. As usual I had forgotten to put them away. I stand staring at them for several moments before snapping out of my trance to wonder why I'm so fixated on them.

Robotically, I turn and open the medicine cabinet and grab a bottle from the middle shelf. "Use peroxide," I say to Rain's back.

She jumps. "Oh! You scared me! Didn't even know you were there."

I hand her the bottle, and she accepts it without really looking at me. "Thanks."

The tension in the small bathroom is almost palpable. I feel it closing in on me, squeezing the breath from my lungs. I know Rain feels it too, but she doesn't let on. I lean back on the counter and try to rest my hand on it, but I jerk it away swiftly as the metal flat iron sears my palm. I gasp loudly and hold my wounded hand tightly. Rain doesn't even bother to turn around to determine the cause of my sudden outburst. *Bitch!*

I glare at the back of her head as I yank the cord out of the wall.

"This peroxide is doing the trick!" Rain sounds excited.

I turn on the faucet and run the hot flat iron under cold water to cool them quickly. "Yeah, the oxygen lifts the blood right out. Separates it from the fabric. One of the only things I ever learned from GiGi."

"Umm hmm."

I turn off the faucet and hold the head of the now cooled flat iron in my left hand and the cord in my right.

"I can't believe all of this is happening. I'm so worried about Danny."

"Yeah." I calmly rotate my wrist to wrap the cord tightly around my right hand.

"I'm sorry about all of this, Carmen. I really am." Rain keeps her back to me, intently focused on her assigned task.

"Don't worry about it. We'll work it out. Danny'll be okay." I step toward Rain with the flat iron secured in my left hand and the cord stretched in a straight, taut line in front of me.

"I hope so." I can hear the onset of tears emerging in Rain's voice.

I'm standing just a few inches from her back. My heart is beating rapidly as adrenaline courses through my blood.

You gotta take care of that bitch! Jay-Jay's words ring in my ears.

In one swift move, I bend down and loop the cord in front of Rain, quickly yanking it upward so it nearly constricts her throat. She grabs and claws at the cord, and her panic compels me to pull even tighter. Crisscrossing the cord behind Rain's neck, I stand erect and plant my knee firmly into her back. She flails her arms and knocks the bottle of bleach off the ledge of the tub. It spills and splashes on the floor, drenching my feet. I slip a little, but quickly regain my composure and maintain a firm and fatal grip on my weapon.

Still on her knees, Rain gags and coughs. Her head is yanked backward, but my knee keeps her body in place on the floor in front of the tub. She keeps one hand on the cord, fighting desperately to get her fingers between the cord and her neck. The other hand reaches back, grabbing for me. She clutches the hem of my shirt, tugging it with all the strength her awkward position will allow.

I try, but I can't pull the cord any tighter. The veins in my forearm are showing through my skin and I break into a sweat. My teeth are clenched, my lips pressed together in a tight snarl.

Rain continues to gag. I hold on.

Just … a little … longer …

She stops moving. Her mouth is slightly open and her eyes are rolled to the back of her head as her body falls limp.

Immediately, I relax a bit and lean in to see if I can hear her breathing—nothing. I inhale and exhale a long, loud sigh of relief at the realization that Rain is finally dead. Finally.

I've avenged Jay-Jay's death. Now, I can live in peace. I release my grip on the cord and drop the flat iron from my hands. Rain's body slumps to the floor. I rub my palms together to soothe the red, painful creases left by the cord and the burn from just a few minutes ago. Then I walk calmly out of the bathroom, leaving my sister's body to grow cold on the tiled floor.

24 *Rain* / *Saturday, May 7th*

"OH no, Rain! My baby, my baby!"
Was that GiGi? It sounded like her, but I wasn't
sure.

"I've got a pulse! It's low, but it's there." Kyle's baritone,
although muffled, was familiar to me.

"Is this Lorain Moran?" a woman asked.

"Yes, officer, this is Lorain. Tell me what's going on.
Why are the police interested in my granddaughter? Kyle, is
she gonna be okay?" My GiGi sounded worried, but why?

"She's alive, breathing, but we won't know anything for
sure until we get her to the hospital.

"Stand back, ma'am, we have to be careful until EMS
arrives." Another voice I didn't recognize.

"Oh, my God, my baby! What have you done?"

"There are ligature marks around her neck. Are you a nurse?" I heard a man ask. His deep voice echoed a heavy southern accent.

"Yes, an RN. I'm her caregiver." That was Kyle.

"Ma'am, we're gonna need some room here. Please step into the hall." That one was a woman. Her high-pitched and serious tone carried authority. Warm hands cradled my head. More hands were on my legs, chest, and neck.

"Miss Moran, please, I'll ask you again to clear the area. Please stand back."

"No, I'm not leaving her. I want to see what you're doing to her," GiGi replied.

Kyle interjected. "Come on, GiGi, let them do their job. They're gonna take care of her."

I heard several overlapping voices, so close, but unclear. There were people surrounding me, but it was if they were talking *about* me, not *to* me. I saw nothing but darkness around me. I felt cold and wet. Something was wrong, but my brain failed to process any comprehensible thoughts.

"We have to get her to the hospital, quick. I don't know how long her brain has been without oxygen. There could be some serious damage," Kyle said.

"EMS is on the way. Hopefully, she'll be fine."

I fought to open my eyes, to make some sense of the commotion that was going on around me. I wanted to say something. I wanted to shout, "I'm fine! Leave me alone!" But the only sound I could make was a soft hum that I'm certain no one in the room could interpret.

"She's coming back to us!" Kyle exclaimed. "Come on, Rain. Wake up, sweetie."

I didn't know what they were talking about. I was okay. "Kyle, I'm here, baby!" I tried to yell, but it came out as an inaudible moan. "I'm alright," I screamed in my head.

No one seemed to be paying attention to me. No one understood that I was fine and I didn't need all these people around. Where was GiGi? I know if she was still in the room, she'd stop them from messing with me. "GiGi!" I moaned again.

"Just relax, don't try to overexert yourself." I felt Kyle's soft hand on my wrist, his soothing voice attempting to stop me from speaking. Finally my eyelids seemed lighter and the darkness began to fade. My eyes fluttered open just a bit. My vision was blurred like I was looking through a foggy mirror after a hot shower. I blinked once, holding my eyelids together for a few seconds before reopening them, but still everything seemed to blend together. I blinked again. This time I was able to make some sense out of what was going on around me.

I was on the bathroom floor, lying on my back.

Kyle was kneeling beside me, leaning over my body. A pale redheaded woman stood at my feet. Her navy police uniform was a size too small, making her look stiff and mechanical. I immediately didn't trust her. A stout, black man stood beside her in a matching uniform. His attention was turned to another man, tall and slender. His black leather jacket, burgundy sweater, and jeans distinguished him from the uniformed officers, but the chrome badge that hung from his neck told me he was also one of them. He turned away from the officer speaking to him and began to look around the bathroom. Another woman, Hispanic, whom I guessed to be his partner, stood on the opposite side of the room scribbling notes onto a small notepad.

I turned my attention back to Kyle and the deep concern shown on his face. "Kyle?" Instinctively, my hands went to my neck. I wanted to massage it to soothe the aching sting.

"No, Rain. Don't touch it. I know it hurts."

"What … what happened to me?" I was confused. Why were there so many people in the house staring at me, bustling around like this was a crime scene investigation?

"Ms. Moran, EMS is on the way. Should be here in a minute. How are you feeling?"

I didn't answer the redhead. Instead, my eyes wandered to the tub, where a bloody t-shirt rested on the ledge. The overwhelming smell of bleach suddenly filled the room. The bottle lay near my feet, which explained the cold, wet feeling on the floor beneath me. My eyes grew wide as I took in the whole scene. I turned my head slowly to the right and then I saw it: Carmen's flat iron on the floor beside my head with its cord tangled into a loose coil. That's when it all came back to me.

"Oh, my God! Carmen! She tried to—"

Kyle quickly cut me off. "Shh. Rain don't say anything. Just relax."

"Ma'am, I'm Detective Hayes, this is my partner, Detective Lang." The plain-clothed officer in the leather jacket said, turning slightly toward the Hispanic woman to introduce her. "Do you know a James "Jay-Jay" Gardner?" He looked down and asked me in his slow southern drawl.

Suddenly, the swarm of police made sense. I gasped. "Danny!"

"Danny?" his partner repeated with a frown.

"She doesn't know anything. She needs to get to the hospital. Someone just tried to strangle her to death." Kyle, with a curt tone, tried to take control of the situation.

"We understand that. EMS is coming." Just as Detective Hayes repeated his statement, I heard the faint sound of sirens drifting in from outside. "But we found Jay-Jay Gardner murdered in his home this evening and we have reason to believe that Lorain knows something about it."

He eyed the bloody t-shirt.

GiGi burst back into the bathroom. "She don't know nothing about no murder! Can't you see somebody just tried to kill my baby? Why aren't you *looking* for them?" She rushed toward me, trying to push past the officers who grabbed her.

"It's okay. Let her go." Lang gave permission to the stout uniformed officer to let my GiGi come to me. She snatched her arms from the officers' grasp and kneeled down beside me, opposite Kyle. GiGi began fussing over me like I was a newborn baby.

"GiGi! I'm so glad you're here." The sight of her induced a storm of tears. "They're asking me about Jay-Jay. GiGi, he killed my mom. That's who I saw in the vision. Jay-Jay, Carmen's boyfriend."

"Jay-Jay ... Carmen's boyfriend?" GiGi's voice drifted off. Her mind seemed to travel to another place.

"Jay-Jay killed your mother?" Officer Lang never looked at me as she continued to scribble on her pad.

"He told me everything, GiGi. He told me what happened. He told me about ... the money." GiGi glared at me. "Why didn't you tell me, GiGi? You knew all along."

"No! I never knew who killed Corrine. I had an idea, but they never found the proof."

"And the money?"

"I never asked your mother where that money came from. I didn't want to know. I used it to make a better life for you. To take care of you. You needed it."

"Danny ... Danny went to Jay-Jay's house after I told—" My eyes darted over to the police officers as I contemplated whether to rat Danny out.

"Hush! Don't you say nothing about that." GiGi placed a finger over my lips. The detectives shot each other glances from the corners of their eyes.

"Who did this to you?" Kyle finally spoke up.

"Carmen! She ... where is she? She tried to kill me, GiGi!"

"Carmen?" Both GiGi and Kyle said in unison.

"Who is Carmen?" the redheaded uniform asked.

"And Danny?" Hayes joined in.

Kyle dropped his head, staring at the floor. GiGi ignored them both. "Rain, baby, what are you talking about?"

"Carmen, GiGi! She ..." Sobs took over my speech, making my voice shaky. "She tried to strangle me with the flat iron. I was right here." I tried to prop my body upward and I pointed to the tub. "She walked up behind me and wrapped that cord around my neck. Where is she?"

GiGi didn't answer. She stared at me with a look of sadness and frustration plastered across her face. Kyle's eyes were still on the floor.

"Who is Carmen?" Lang repeated.

GiGi shook her head slowly from side to side. She placed a caring hand on my arm and the other hand behind my back for support as I tried to sit up. "Rain, baby, you have to stop this. You can't do this anymore."

"Do what, GiGi? Did you hear what I said? Carmen tried to kill me! Kyle! Did you hear me?"

Kyle refused to look into my eyes. "Yes, Rain, we all heard you." It was almost a whisper.

I looked back over to my GiGi and saw tears streaming down her face. "Rain, baby, please! You have to stop. Look at what's happened because of this nonsense."

The sirens drew nearer until it sounded as if they were right outside the house.

"GiGi, you're not listening to me! I'm telling the truth. Danny ... then Carmen. I never wanted any of this to happen." My sobs grew thicker.

"Rain! No! Look at what you've done!" GiGi screamed. Kyle reached over me and rested his hand on her shoulder to calm her. "Why did you do this?"

"Me? I know I was the one who told Danny, but Carmen did it. I didn't do anything wrong. Listen to me!" I was beginning to get exasperated. Everything I said seemed to pass right through her.

"Rain, it's *you*! It's not Danny or Carmen; it's *you*! Can't you see that? Rain, please!" GiGi screeched.

Hayes jumped in, waving his hands. "Wait, wait, wait! what the hell is going on here?"

"My sister and brother. They—"

"GiGi forcefully grabbed me by my shoulders, shook me for emphasis. "You don't have any siblings, Rain! Carmen and Danny don't exist!" Her tears poured rapidly from her face, landing on her chest and thighs. "It's all in your head, baby!" She spoke slowly, pronouncing each syllable as if she was speaking to a foreigner.

I was confused. I heard what she was saying, but none of it made sense. No Carmen and Danny? How?

"I knew it was getting out of hand, but I never thought you'd try to kill yourself—or someone else." GiGi rose from her kneeling position on the floor. She covered her mouth with her hands, shaking her head again and again. "I … I can't take this." She abruptly turned and left the bathroom.

EMS banged on the lower level door. "Rodgers, get that will ya?" Hayes instructed the stout black uniformed officer. Rodgers scurried off to answer the door and let EMS in. "Now," Hayes turned his attention back to me and Kyle, "you wanna tell me what the hell is going on?"

Kyle spoke up first, not giving me a chance to explain my side of things. "Lorain suffers from dissociative identity disorder."

"What?" The redhead frowned.

"Multiple personalities," Detective Lang interjected.

Stunned into silence, I let Kyle continue. "She's been this way since she was seven. When Lorain was five years old, she witnessed her mother's murder. After the murder, she went mute for about two years. We believe she developed her two alter personalities—Carmen and Danny—during the time when she wasn't speaking." The officers listened intently, so did I. They wrote down as much as they could, trying to keep up with Kyle. "I believe she formed the personalities to cope with the trauma of her mother's murder.

"Kyle, what are you saying? You *know* Carmen and Danny. What are you talking about?" My confusion was morphing into panic. What in the hell was he talking about? Was this his way of trying to cover up Danny's crime?

"You believe in that multiple personalities crap?" Hayes asked his partner with a raised brow.

"It's very real," Kyle shot back. "Rain had blocked out the memory of her mother's murder completely, using Danny and Carmen to disassociate herself from it. We thought getting her to remember the murder would dissolve these alter personalities and bring her back down to one— her own. But instead …"

"It caused a disaster." Lang seemed to be in awe as she absorbed what Kyle was saying.

"Yeah. She suffers from delusions, aggressive behavior, acute amnesia, drug abuse, and bouts of depression. We were trying to cure her by making her remember."

Rodgers barged into the hallway with two EMS workers close on his heels. They stood on either side of a gurney, wheeling it to the bathroom doorway.

Hayes was still skeptical. "So, you're telling me that

she killed someone else and tried to kill herself, all while thinking she was somebody else?"

"Both alters have very distinct personalities. Danny, Danielle actually, is abusive. Danny has a lesbian girlfriend who knows about her condition. Carmen, well … she's promiscuous." Kyle looked at me with an apologetic expression. "Carmen is addicted to ecstasy and is pretty out of control."

The EMS workers, dressed head-to-toe in white, entered the bathroom. GiGi followed close behind. "We have a twenty-five year old female, suffering from self-inflicted strangulation. We found her unconscious. You'll need to check her vitals." Hayes spoke to the EMS workers in a matter-of-fact way. They moved toward me, reached down and helped me to my feet with Kyle's assistance. Stunned, I kept quiet as they ushered me out of the bathroom and into the hall.

"I'm so sorry, baby. I never knew any of this was going to happen." GiGi spoke through loud cries.

They tried to assist me onto the waiting gurney, but I resisted. "I'm fine to walk," I said.

"If she's so messed up in the head, why hasn't she been institutionalized?" Hayes shot the accusatory question to GiGi.

"She's my baby! I wasn't gonna let anybody lock her up. She'd already been through enough. She was just fine before … before all *this*."

Kyle interjected, "People that suffer from this disorder don't necessarily have to be institutionalized. She was very functional. Her grandmother set her up in this house to live with her 'siblings.'" He formed quotation marks with his fingers two emphasize the word "siblings." "I stayed downstairs in the lower flat to keep an eye on her as a caregiver."

"I see. Well we'll have a lot of questions for Miss Moran. We'll be following her to the hospital." Lang addressed both Kyle and GiGi.

"You leave her alone. She's sick!"

"Ma'am, a man has been murdered, and it's our job to get to the bottom of it. We found the murder weapon at the scene. CSI is at Mr. Gardner's home now," Hayes answered.

With the bathroom now empty, the redheaded officer carefully picked up Danny's t-shirt from the ledge of the bathtub with gloved hands and placed it into a plastic bag. She did the same with the flat iron.

"Maybe you should call a lawyer, GiGi," Kyle declared.

25 *Rain* / *Thursday, October 18th*

I sat in a hard, uncomfortable plastic chair facing the only window in the room, thinking about the visit from my mother the night before. I hadn't seen her in months. In fact, the last time was back in May when I'd relived the night of her murder. I was relieved that she'd left me alone after that, feeling as if she'd fulfilled her purpose by telling me who her murderer was. But when I saw her last night, I realized that I'd missed her and I was happy to see her face, even if it was for the last time in my life. I now had a memory of her that I could hold forever. I knew what she looked like, sounded like, how she smelled. I needed that in order to find peace in the storm of my life.

She'd appeared in my room as I lay in the bed staring at the brilliant white walls that GiGi had decorated with paintings by her favorite artists and pictures of her and me at various phases of our lives. Unlike the previous times when she'd come to me, I was calm last night. I smiled at my mother, the beautiful smile I'd inherited from her. When I sat up in my bed, she walked toward me, her arms outstretched, awaiting a hug. Her smile was beautiful, peaceful. I could feel the heat of her love radiating from her body as she drew nearer. When she was close, I dove into her arms and squeezed her until I exerted all of my strength. "I love you, Mommy," I said as I snuggled my face into her neck. "I'm sorry for everything that happened."

She pulled back and frowned, shaking her head as if to say there was no need for apologies. Still, I hadn't wanted things to end this way. I had never intended for anyone to get hurt. My mother caressed my face with her hand and gave me reassurance with her kind, piercing black eyes. With that gesture, I knew everything was okay. I also knew, when she began to back away from me, that I would never see her again. Something about her tranquil expression told me that things were settled and she could rest peacefully. I was happy to give her that solace. "Bye, Mommy," I'd called out to her vanishing image. She waved back at me and disappeared just as suddenly as she had come. I lowered myself back onto my narrow bed, resting on the thin, hard mattress and falling into a dreamless sleep. I was finally unafraid of what thoughts might haunt me.

I reveled in the memory of my vision as I stared out into the garden just outside my barred window. As the rain poured almost violently, pounding the flowers and vegetation beneath, I found comfort. The darkness of the night was soothing. If I didn't know it before, I sure as hell knew it then—I'm not crazy. How could a crazy person appreciate something as breathtakingly beautiful as night rain?

Insane. That's what they'd concluded during the trial for Jay-Jay's murder. My doctors tell me that Danny and Carmen don't really exist. They say I created them in my mind. I guess that means I'm really the one that killed Jay-Jay—or maybe I'm just the one that took the fall. The evidence? Fingerprints on the gun and throughout the house, Jay-Jay's blood on a shirt in the bathroom, and an eye witness that claims to have seen me running from his house—it all stacked up against me. I contemplated the possibility that Danny had framed me, but I quickly dismissed the idea. I know that he'd never do anything like that to me. He did what he thought was right to protect our family; he wouldn't turn on me after something like that. I know it. Then what *did* happen? What other excuse is there? I wasn't there; I didn't do it. I swear!

Dissociative Identity Disorder. I'd heard Kyle mention it to the cops the day of my arrest. GiGi has tossed the term around a couple of times too. That's the defense the attorney used in court to save me from a life sentence in prison. I don't understand, and I don't think I ever will. Carmen and Danny are my family. They're real just like GiGi and Kyle and all of the doctors and nurses that rush up and down the halls of this psychiatric hospital where I'll spend the next five years. Maybe I do have a condition. Could *everyone* be wrong?

Watching Kyle cradle a weeping GiGi in his arms the day of my sentencing was heartbreaking. I apologized over and over again for putting her through so much. She didn't deserve it, not after everything she'd done for me. GiGi visits me at least twice a week, and she always comes with care packages and little trinkets, snacks, or decorations for my room. Kyle comes with her sometimes. He said after spending the last five years with me, he can't help but to check on me every now and again. I knew it—he'd always love me. I smile to myself every time I think of him.

Even Maya came to visit once. I hadn't expected her to pop up at all, but about three weeks ago she walked in, looking all uncomfortable. I asked her about Danny, asked her whether she'd seen him at all. She never gave me a straight answer; she just cried and pleaded for Danny to come back. I wished I could have helped her or eased her pain. I missed Danny too. Maya left a message for me to give to Danny. She said Tone had been taken care of, that she had seen to it personally. I had no clue what the hell she meant by that, but I promised I would pass the message along. That seemed to satisfy her.

I hadn't seen Carmen or Danny since the day of the murder—the day Carmen tried to kill me. They've kept me so doped up in here, I wouldn't be surprised if they'd come to visit and I was just to stoned to notice. Kyle and GiGi kept telling me they don't exist, so I never asked them about my sister and brother. I don't know what happened to them; they just disappeared. At least the staff here is cool. I mean, they don't beat us or starve us like any of the horror stories I'd heard about places like this. But they do overmedicate. I saw them everyday, turning the patients into zombies in the name of mental health. Pills in the morning, injections at night. That's why I stopped. I wasn't going to take anything else they gave me. The last dose, served this morning, was still hidden under my mattress. That's where I'd placed it after pretending to swallow it in front of the nurse. I would still constantly daydream about going home to be with my family. It may seem unreasonable after all that has happened, but I still loved them—even Carmen—and I prayed every day that they came to visit. I was lonely here. I had no one to talk to, no one to share my life with. I was alone, with nothing more than my thoughts and this cold, empty room. I hated to be alone. I hated it …

"What the fuck is wrong with you?" I knew that voice without turning around: Carmen!

I whipped around toward the door, and my mouth dropped open at the sight of Carmen and Danny, both standing in the doorway. Carmen had her arms folded across her chest, and Danny stood slouched, with his hands in his pockets. I blinked three times to make sure they were really in the room with me. I couldn't help but smile broadly when they didn't disappear.

"Yeah, you over there looking like you done lost yo' best friend or somethin'." Danny started walking around, examining the small room.

I shot out of my seat. "How did you guys … Oh my God! I'm so happy to see you … well … Danny, anyway." I dropped my head to avoid eye contact with Carmen, unsure of how to interact with her.

Carmen flipped her long, straight hair over her shoulder. "Girl, quit trippin'. I'm over it, and you should be too. Ain't no nigga worth all that drama. I still can't stand yo' uppity ass though. That'll never change." She quipped at me with her head cocked to the side. A playful smirk crept across her face.

I looked at her sideways. "Carmen, what you did …"

"Okay, okay, I promise I'll never try to kill you again!" She laughed and plopped down onto the bed.

"You better not do shit to Rain or I'll kill you first. You know I'm capable." Danny punched Carmen in the arm playfully before sitting down next to her.

"Ow!"

"How did you guys get in here?" I asked, dumbfounded by their presence. "Visiting hours are over." I walked over to the bed and sat with them. Carmen and I were positioned on either side of Danny.

Danny replied, "Look, don't worry about all that. Just call us Bonnie and Clyde. It was easy as hell slipping past those white-coat stiffs."

"Enough talking, we need to get you the fuck up outta here." Carmen was on a mission.

"What? You can't. They gave me five years!"

"If you think you gonna spend five years in this shit hole, you really *are* crazy!" Carmen rolled her eyes and scrunched her face in disgust as she looked around.

"So … what are you saying?"

"We're *saying*," Danny began, "wait until one of the orderlies comes in to give you your medication." I leaned in close to Danny so I could hear his hushed whispers. "We'll hide and distract her right after she fills the syringe."

Carmen jumped in. "When she turns her back, I'll swipe it and stick her ass." Carmen giggled at their diabolical plan.

My eyes grew wide with disbelief and excitement. They were actually talking about busting me out of here! I knew they really cared about me. They must have been missing me as much as I missed them.

"The rest is easy. Slip on her white coat and badge and walk up outta here. Just. Like. That!" Danny snapped his fingers for emphasis.

"Then what? What about you two? How will *you* get out?" I asked.

"This is the criminal ward, so she'll have cuffs on her. Just, slap 'em on us and walk us up outta here like we're patients." Carmen made it sound so easy, like it was nothing.

"You think it'll work?"

"Hell yeah!" They answered in unison.

"Shh!" Danny placed a firm hand over my mouth. "I

hear the door. It's show time!"

The thin, pale nurse swiped the bar code on her badge against the sliding glass door to enter my room. She stepped lightly, pushing a silver cart stocked with pills and syringes. "Good evening, Miss Moran." She greeted me with no inflection in her voice. She didn't even look up at me, too busy examining the contents of her tray and preparing the syringe. She didn't notice that there were three of us in the room; I was still sitting on the bed while Carmen and Danny stood behind her.

We waited. Nerves made my palms sweaty and produced a lump in my throat. After a few moments of preparation, the medication was finally ready. The nurse held the syringe steady in her right hand, pointing it upward. She looked at me for the first time since she had entered the room. I eyed Danny and Carmen. It was time. I stood slowly and walked in a half circle until I was standing next to the nurse, right beside Danny. Carmen kept her place on the opposite wall.

"Hey, where are you going? You know what time it is." The nurse's voice hosted no emotion as she addressed me, walking casually in my direction.

With no cue or warning, Danny leaped out at her, knocking her backward.

Then … everything went black.

I don't remember what happened next.

INSIDE RAIN

Reading Group Guide

D*ISCUSSION QUESTIONS*

1. Why do you think Rain developed alters with such strong personalities? What purpose did Danny and Carmen serve to Rain's psyche?

2. Every time Rain was confronted with remembering her mother's murder, one of her alters took over (usually Carmen). Why do you think this happened? And why Carmen?

3. Discuss the results of burying your burdens instead of facing them head-on and dealing with your demons. How does this affect you and the people in your life?

4. Do you have an alter personality? If so, what is it, and does it help or hinder you in your daily life and interactions?

5. Discuss Danny's narcissistic and violent behavior. Why do you think he developed such traits?

6. Discuss Carmen's brashness and callous demeanor. Why do you think she developed such traits?

7. Carmen had a strong disdain for Rain because she thought that their mother loved Rain more than she did Carmen

and Danny. Have you experienced or witnessed this sort of sibling rivalry and/or jealousy in your own life?

8. The theory of dissociative identity disorder or multiple personalities is widely disputed by psychology professionals. Do you believe it's a real disorder? Why or why not?

9. GiGi loved her granddaughter dearly, and she was desperate to help her heal. Discuss her role in Rain's mental break down. Do you think she hurt Rain more than she actually helped her?

10. People who suffer from dissociative identity disorder can be functional and sometimes do not need to be institutionalized. GiGi didn't want to let anyone lock her baby up after the pain she'd already been through. Do you think it was a mistake for GiGi to allow Rain to live freely in society instead of having her committed to a psychiatric hospital? Why, or why not?

11. Danny was abusive to his girlfriend, Maya, but when Gigi made him realize that he was taking out his anger from his mother's murder on his girlfriend, he vowed to never hit Maya again. If more abusive men and women face the source of their anger and aggression, do you think they would be capable of changing?

12. Rape is difficult for any victim to cope with, but it drove Danny to self-hate and attempted suicide. Why do you think rape was particularly hard for Danny to deal with?

13. Discuss Carmen's low self-esteem and how she masked it

with being overly sexy and promiscuous. Look deep within yourself; how do you mask some of your insecurities?

14. What did you think of Jay Jay's character? Do you know a Jay Jay that preys on the insecurities of women?

15. Rain's mother haunted Rain until she finally faced the memory of her mother's murder. Why do you think this was the case? What lesson can be learned from the story and how can you or someone you know apply it?

16. People with dissociative identity disorder can have hundreds of alter personalities, who may all communicate with each other at any given time. What was the pivotal moment in the book when you figured out that Rain, Danny, and Carmen were all the same person? If you figured it out before the end, how did you guess?

17. Go back and read the poem that opens "Chapter One," "The Rapture of Rain" by Nakia R. Laushaul. Now that you've read the book, discuss the meaning of the poem and its relevance to the story.

18. Discuss the ending of *Inside Rain*. Do you think Rain escaped from the mental institution? Did you want her to escape?

19. What do you think should happen to Rain from this point forward.

20. Who was your favorite character and why? Use examples from the story to aid your answers.

WHO IS HE TO YOU

Excerpt by: Monique D. Mensah

Chapter 1

Simone

HE was coming! Simone knew he was coming. She could feel it in the air. It was colder, thinner. The atmosphere was pitch black, darker than dark. Everything was always more extreme, more heightened when he was coming. The tree branches scratched at the windows from outside. The wind whistled a chilling tune, and fat raindrops plopped on the windowsill. It was the soundtrack of her trepidation.

She was alone, surrounded by nothing but the dark shadows that engulfed her as she floated in the darkness of the starless, midnight air. But she knew that she would not be alone much longer because he was on his way. She knew it because she could feel the fear breaking through from inside of her. She could feel her heart pounding, fighting relentlessly as if struggling for freedom from the imprisonment of her chest. The pounding was getting louder, so loud that she knew he too would hear it soon. If the lights were on, she was certain she would have been able to see her heart throbbing in and out, back and forth, trying to escape, faster and louder. Her heart was about to explode!

Oh my God, am I dying? Am I having a heart attack? Yeah, that's it I'm dying of a heart attack. Oh God, please take me before he gets here. He's coming! Lord, please take me now! I want to die.

She wanted to escape that place and become a beautiful angel bearing brilliant, white wings and long, flowing hair. She would have wings so massive, fluffy and white, that she would be God's favorite angel. She would dance in the clouds and slide down the rainbows, laughing and playing with angelic benevolence. It would be just like a fairytale. She was certain the Lord would finally answer her prayer that night. He would not let her down. He couldn't, not again.

She could still feel her heart pounding, but she refused to move or make a sound. She just closed her eyes tightly, squeezing them shut as hard as she could.

I know that in a minute I'll be gone. Any minute now, I'll be up in Heaven, smiling and dancing with the angels. The pounding will stop and he won't be there. He will never come again.

She allowed a flush of serene calm and happiness to overcome her. Any minute now…

"Hey, baby girl."

He's here! Why is he here? Why am I still here? Lord, I asked you to take me up to Heaven. I asked you to take me from this place. Why won't you save me from him? Why would you leave me here to suffer? Don't you love me? Don't you want me to be happy? I've been good. I do my homework everyday after school. I do everything my mother tells me to do. I make sure my clothes are neat and clean. I get straight A's. I brush my teeth every morning and night before I go to bed. I pray every night and go to Sunday School every Sunday. I do everything I

*am supposed to do and you just left me here. I've asked you every night
to save me, to take me to Heaven. Why won't you answer my prayers?*

"Are you sleeping?"

Simone refused to move or open her eyes. But her heart
was still pounding. She was certain he could hear it. He
knew she was awake, petrified with dread. She could hear his
breathing; it was louder than the pounding of her hammering
heart. His breathing was heavy, as if derived from exhaustion.
With every inhalation, she could imagine him sucking the
breath right out of her lungs, leaving her to die a slow death
of suffocation. He was staring at her. His eyes were piercing
her through the night. He could see her through the darkness,
right through her purple fleece blanket. The blanket kept her
covered and did the best it could to shield her from his eyes,
but she knew it wasn't working. She suddenly flinched as his
cold presence snapped her back to a brutal reality. She was
no longer floating in the midnight sky. She was at home, in
bed, eyes still shut tight, heart still pounding uncontrollably
and wishing she were dead. He knew she wasn't sleeping. He
knew she had been up all night, fearing that he would come,
and praying that he didn't.

He knew that she hated him and he hated himself. He
told her the night before last. He hated himself for loving her
and craving her the way that he did. He wanted to take her
every night and he tried to fight it, but his desire was just too
strong to control. The nights that he did not come were the
times that he was able to win the battle with himself. Those
nights were becoming sparse.

He would often talk to her about when she was a baby.
He remembered holding her when she was just a few months
old and looking down at her wiggling in his arms. She was so
tiny, chubby, and pink, the prettiest baby he had ever seen. He
would put his finger out for her to hold and she would grab it

with the strong grip of a grown man. He would always laugh about that. He used to talk to her about what she would be when she grew up. He imagined her being a famous actress, singer or model. With a face like hers, she was destined to be on somebody's stage. Simone had an undeniable beauty. With the kind of face that one would only come across once in a lifetime, she was too pretty to be called pretty. She was extraordinary. Her skin was the color of roasted almonds. Her jet-black hair, thick and curly, grazed the small of her back. Her huge, green, emerald-like eyes were hypnotic. She had a perfectly symmetrical face with striking features that hit you with the impact of an explosion if you were lucky enough to catch sight of her. She was phenomenal and he was mesmerized from the day she was born.

He promised her, from the beginning, that he would be the best father possible, and he kept his promise throughout the years. He made sure that he played with her everyday, just the two of them. He bought her anything she wanted, before she would have to ask. She always had the best of everything and he made sure that she attended the best schools. Even on his busiest day, he took the time to help her with her homework. Her hair and clothes were always impeccable. Her poise and grace were flawless. Most of her peers hated her for her beauty and even more so for her perfection. He never let her forget how much he loved her.

He sat on the left side of her bed. Still, she wouldn't open her eyes, but she knew he was still looking at her, longing to touch her. He pulled back the purple blanket and exposed her shivering, petite frame. He tenderly touched her face and wiped the salty tears from her cheeks. She was lying there frozen with her hands glued to her sides as if prepared for burial. She tried her best not to make a sound, but eventually a sniffle crept through against her will.

Come on-- Come on, just do it! What is taking him so long? Why is he making me go through this?

Another sniffle interrupted the silence, but it was not her own. She finally opened her eyes to see her father, his back turned to her, crying. The cry was a soft one at first, then with uncontrollable sobs. His broad shoulders shook as his face rested in his large hands. Simone was confused and did not know how to react. Dumbfounded, she fought the urge to comfort him. This man had ruined her life. This man caused her infinite pain and self-loathing, yet she could not help but to feel sorry for her father.

"I'll pray for you, Daddy." She looked up at him and softly said this just above a whisper.

He turned to face her with tears streaming down his face. He was overwhelmed with love for her – this time the kind of love a father is supposed to have for his daughter. He wanted to hold her, but resisted the urge to act. How could he continue to destroy the one thing that he adored more than life itself? How could he be so monstrous and self-serving? He was killing his beloved baby and he knew it. He despised himself.

"I love you, Simone. You know that don't you? You know that I love you more than I can begin to express to you. Don't you ever forget that I love you, baby. I do this because of how I love you. No matter how hard you try, you just can't control who you love. You'll understand that when you get older. I know you think I'm horrible and that I want to cause you pain, but that's not true. You have to believe that. I don't want to hurt you, baby girl. I want to love you and I want you to feel the same way. You are everything to me and I'm just too weak to fight it when I know that I should."

Simone remained silent. Tears ran rapidly from her eyes. She knew that he loved her. She read it in his eyes every time he looked at her. She heard it in his voice and felt it in his touch. There was no doubt that he loved her. He was *in* love with her. She listened as he continued his attempt to justify the sick actions and irrational feelings he had for his 14-year old daughter with the word "love." Love. What was love anyway? She thought she knew at one time, but if this was love, she wanted no part of it. Love was pain. Her father was in love with her because she was the most beautiful creature he had ever laid eyes on. Her body had developed into that of a beautiful young woman, sparking a lust in his eyes. He constantly told her how gorgeous she was and she hated it.

She hated the image that stared back at her while looking in the mirror. She hated it so much, that she tried to avoid her reflection at all times. She kept her head down when passing mirrors. It felt natural to avoid pictures and to hide her face whenever possible. God had cursed her with her looks. He damned her to a life of misery and pain -- at the hands of her own father.

"I know you love me, Daddy. I just wish that you didn't."

He stood slowly, letting the tears fall freely down his face and forced himself to walk out of the room with slow, measured strides. He had won the battle for that night. But the following night he was defeated yet again.

About the Author

MONIQUE D. MENSAH is a native Detroiter with an innate love for the written word. Declaring her dream to become a published author at the young age of eight, she always knew this to be her purpose. She received high praise for her writing talents during grade school and college. After graduating from the University of Michigan with a bachelor's degree in business management, she went on to pen her first novel, *WHO IS HE TO YOU*. Shortly after, she founded Kisa Publishing and published her debut novel, launching a fulfilling career as a critically acclaimed author. She resides in Southfield, MI, with her daughter, Alana, where she works full-time as a student representative for a private university. She is also the principal and founder of Make Your Mark Editing Services. *INSIDE RAIN* is her second novel.

To learn more about Monique D. Mensah and her work, please visit her website:
www.MoniqueDMensah.com